BROKEN BAYOU

RHONDA R. DENNIS

DEDICATION

To my angels above, and to the special souls who are my angels on earth. I love you more than you could ever imagine.

ACKNOWLEDGMENTS

Big thanks to Donette Freeman for being such a fabulous editor! Yummy by Design, I'm in awe of your cover making prowess. To the most amazing PA I could ever hope for, I can't offer enough thanks for all of your hard work. I'm so glad you let me pay you in food and lip gloss, Jenny, even though I owe you so much more.

PROLOGUE

The light of the full moon offers no help as the driver of the battered blue van violently slams into yet another furrow in the darkened road. The sudden stop propels a severely sleep deprived and high-as-a-kite Earl against the dash. He reaches out and plants his palm squarely against the back of the driver's head.

"Damn it, Jinx! How about you just follow the damn levee instead of trashing an axle on this god-forsaken piece of shit cane road?"

"Hey, I can't control it! You're the genius who said we need to stay off the main roads. Me, I think it don't matter if we take the main road or not. We ain't never been caught yet, and we ain't never gonna get caught." He takes a quick swig from a bottle of whiskey then lets out a loud howl.

"Yeah, well, you're not exactly the thinker of the group, Jinx. Just shut up and drive." He swipes the bottle from Jinx and quickly finishes the last of the alcoholic contraband they'd procured from the convenience store heist three days and two states prior. "Hey Shoe, you and Bones ready to go?"

"Yeah, Earl. We're ready." Shoe, still riding

high on the group's week long binge, unsteadily rocks in the back of the van while tapping one of the large black bags.

"Well, don't just sit there! One more bump then start handing them out," Earl demands. Shoe takes his hit before passing the remaining drug stash to his accomplices then unzips the bag closest to him to pull out the first sawed-off shot gun. He tries to hand it off to a jumpy, bug-eyed Bones.

"Y'all said I get the MAC-10 this time." The thin, wiry-haired man quickly stands to pout, but Jinx runs through another rut just as Bones is crossing his arms over his chest. The momentum sends him flying between the front seats.

"You can't even keep your ass upright! Like we're going to give you the MAC? Get up and shut up! Move to the back and take two of the sawed-offs before I give you something to really pout about," Earl says with a snarl.

Bones rubs the knot forming on the back of his head. "Fine. But I get the Berettas, too, this time." Once he's up, he greedily shoves the pistols into the waistband of his acid-washed jeans before Shoe can stop him. Earl shakes his head with disgust and is about to say something when Jinx starts a profanity-laced tirade. It earns him another back-of-the-head smack.

"What the hell is your problem?" Earl demands.

"That!" Jinx asserts while pointing to the line of cars in the circular drive of the isolated antebellum plantation home.

"Son of a bitch," Earl mumbles under his breath.

"I guess we gotta call it off," Shoe offers.

Earl takes one more snort from the stash, and a sneer that sends chills down Shoe's spine emerges across his lips. "Why call it off? The more the merrier, right?"

Jinx gives him a sideways glance once he stops the van. "You are one sick mother fu…"

"I sure am! And don't you ever forget it," Earl interrupts as he takes one of the MAC-10s from Shoe. "Let's do this."

RHONDA R. DENNIS

ONE

Thirty years later.

One of the key differences between Oklahoma and Louisiana is the color of the dirt. An obvious statement no doubt, but as I roll down a particularly lonely stretch of I-49, I reflect on it. If I'd have known that rich ebony soil would bring me comfort, I'd have left the rusty red stuff behind long ago. No more hills. No more tumbling rocks. No more widespread cowboy hats and massive belt buckles at every turn. Running away from issues isn't supposed to be a good thing, but right now, as I finish the final leg of my journey from the farmlands to the swamplands, I can't find a damn thing wrong with escaping.

Teaching English at Oklahoma State was once fulfilling. I'm a great professor, admired and adored by my students. At least I was. I was the cool teacher; the one everyone wanted—the one who had to inevitably turn away students because my classes were already past capacity. It didn't stop them from begging though. I truly felt sorry for them, their cute little puppy-dog eyes pleading for a coveted spot that I couldn't give. However, about a year and a half ago that all changed.

The depression that came after my parents died in a house fire left me wallowing in a pit of darkness and despair. No matter how hard I tried, escape seemed impossible. Even now, after months of intensive therapy sessions, progress remains slow because everything in Oklahoma reminds me of them. Cows, horses, expansive farms, red dirt: all reminders of what was stolen from me. A large part of my soul died when they did because my parents were my everything.

Seeing the miles and miles of freshly plowed sugar cane fields has lifted a chest-crushing weight, and for the first time in months, I don't feel asphyxiated. My sabbatical had come to an end, and truly, I had zero desire to reenter the classroom. However, things changed after hearing from a staff recruiter for Shadow Oaks University. This small college nestled deep in the Louisiana bayous found itself in need of a head for their English department, and since an article I'd researched about healing from depression suggested tossing my resume around cyberspace, I was contacted to interview. What started as a simple exercise to prove self-worth ended up being the breakthrough I'd paid thousands of dollars to multiple therapists for, but could never find.

I wasn't completely sold on the move at first; however, while visiting SOU's campus for the final interview, I began to notice a trend. With each passing day, the constant grief and thoughts of loss began to subside. The landscape, the accents, the demeanor of the residents, the atmosphere in general, they were all refreshing and desperately needed. With hardly a second thought, I accepted the position as soon as it was officially offered to me.

Following the oak-lined roadway as it snakes around the curves of a bayou, I feel a rush of excitement when I notice a huge painted sign welcoming me to Cane, Louisiana. Boxes fill my trunk and backseat, but they aren't stuffed with mementos or household items, just books. I want a fresh start in every sense of the word—new furniture, new clothes, new household items. My past has to be jettisoned so I can secure a better future; one that won't include constant crying jags, gut-wrenching reminders, and an overwhelming sense of despair. I vow to be done with that.

George Thibodeaux, my new landlord, is trimming the hedges outside of the large blue Victorian he owns. Khaki shorts, a tank style undershirt, black socks, and sandals go quite well with his slicked-back salt-and-pepper hair and half-inch thick bifocals. Sweat copiously drips from his forehead, collecting to form neat little drops that fall from his matted chest hair. My stomach churns when he swipes it with his palm just before reaching out to shake my hand.

"Miss Douglas, I've been expecting you. How was your trip?" he asks with a voice more feeble than I expect.

"Please, call me Cheyenne. The trip was fine, thank you." Swallowing hard, I lightly grip his outstretched hand then run it down the back of my pants once he turns away from me.

"I have the keys to the apartment right here on the front porch. I trust that you'll be okay with settling in yourself? I got a bad back."

"Oh, yes. Absolutely. I didn't bring much with me so there's not much to unload."

He casts an uncertain over-the-shoulder squint in my direction. "You know the place is unfurnished, right?"

"Yes, sir." I give a slight smile. "I'll go furniture shopping soon. Is there a place in town, or must I go elsewhere?"

"Hold up," he says, shuffling into his house without another word. I'm left to admire the architecture of the structure which I estimate to be at least a hundred years old. My eyes follow the length of the white columns that contrast with the blue clapboard siding and continue all the way up to the turret on the right side of the home. Lace curtains in the highest window are pushed aside to reveal an elderly woman who appears to be scowling down at me. Fraught with discomfort, I offer her a scant wave which is not returned. Instead, she turns away from the window, and the curtains snap back to their original position.

"Okay," I draw out as I turn away from the house to admire the scenic bayou across the street.

"Here." Mr. Thibodeaux hands me a note with some scribble scratch on it. I'm able to make out a phone number, address, and despite my best efforts, the bottom line evades translation.

"I'm sorry, Mr. Thibodeaux, but what's this say right here?" I point out the offending text.

"Don't dick with her, Richie."

"Excuse me," I say in a near whisper.

"Richie. My sister's greedy ass son owns the local furniture store. I'm telling him he shouldn't take advantage of you."

My eyes widen. "Oh, okay. Thank you very much for that."

"No problem," he says, once again wielding the hedge clippers. "Is there anything else you need?"

"Keys."

"Oh, yeah. Keys." He fishes around in his pocket and produces a neon green *We're #1* keychain with two ancient-looking keys that dangle from the rusted ring. "Pull around back. That entire area back there is yours. I keep my car in the side garage over yonder, so the garage under the apartment is yours. The clicker is inside the apartment. The courtyard is yours to enjoy, but don't steal the roses. The roses are for Agnes; don't cut them. No late night parties, no men, or women if you swing that way, in and out all hours of the night, no repairs unless I authorize them. If you need anything, try to make it known between the hours of seven A.M. and seven P.M., with the exception of two to three. That's nap time."

"Yes, sir. You don't have to worry about any of that. I assure you, I'm quite boring."

He huffs slightly before continuing the onslaught of the holly bush he's standing near. Fairly certain the conversation is over, I return to my car and park it in front of the specified garage. The bright sunlight glints off of a huge sugar kettle koi pond in the center of the courtyard, while a melodious welcome calls from wind chimes scattered throughout the flowering crape myrtles. I wander the red brick path and anticipate spending lots of free time reclined on one of the wooden benches with my novel du jour.

Peeping up through the branches of a giant oak tree, I catch who I presume to be Agnes snatching shut the lace curtains covering the upper story window.

"Ah, poor Agnes. You're going to be so bored snooping on me," I mutter under my breath as I leave the courtyard to climb the white wooden stairs leading to the apartment. Pushing the key into the lock, I'm excited to see what old-world charm the residence will afford me.

With no time to spare in getting prepared for my new position, I'd only seen the apartment in pictures sent by the recruiter. While I was wrapping up final details in Oklahoma, she was working diligently to make my transition as smooth as possible; hence, one of the things I was least looking forward to, finding a place to live, was handled for me before I drove down.

I'm instantly in love. Two huge picture windows flank a white brick fireplace, and the view overlooks the courtyard below. There is a door against the far wall that leads into the master bedroom. Glass paneled French doors open to a balcony with a cast iron bistro set and a selection of potted plants. The view is of the rose garden Mr. Thibodeaux spoke about. Gobs of brilliantly colored blossoms beg to be plucked, and I'm disappointed because he's already warned me about doing such a thing. A small but functional kitchen, a huge bathroom with a claw foot tub, and a second bedroom that I plan to use as an office complete the tour.

"This is good. This is just what I need," I affirm, actually feeling somewhat positive when I say it this time. Eager to furnish the place, I don't bother unloading the car. I plug the furniture store's address into the GPS device, and I'm there within five minutes. The brightly painted building is smack dab in the middle of Cane, a town whose older wrought iron balconied buildings are reminiscent of the French Quarter in New Orleans. Near the furniture store are two cafés, a police station, a bookstore, gift shop, and jewelry store. On the opposite side of the wide street are a law office, a feed and seed shop, a trendy clothing store, and a seafood market. I look forward to venturing further into Cane to see what other surprises the quaint town holds.

An obnoxious cow bell announces my arrival at the furniture store, and two older ladies, one in a wrinkled pant suit, the other in a cardigan and polyester skirt, diligently work to rise from the sofa they are seated on. The first lady up, the one in the pant suit, extends her hand to the other woman who is still rocking back and forth to build momentum.

"Please, no need to get up. Really." I wave my hands in the sit down fashion.

"It's no problem, darling. What can we help you with?"

A tall man I guess to be around my age of thirty-five suddenly bursts through a set of double doors in the back. Black dress slacks, a patent leather belt with matching shoes, and a ruby red dress shirt unbuttoned to mid-chest all look about a size and half too small for his build. His thick hair sticks straight up in a flat top, and the extra thick mustache adorning his lip reminds me of something seen in '70s B movies. "Aunt Ruth, stay where you are. Mom, I got this one. Y'all just continue to chat while wearing holes in the fine furniture I stock my store with. I'll take care of anything this beautiful lady might need."

His mustache tickles the back of my hand when he goes for a kiss instead of a handshake. "It's so hard to find good help these days, but me, I'm so soft-hearted and compassionate. How many sons would employ their decrepit mother, as well as their aged aunt? Not many I assure you." He bows his head in a fashion that's meant to show humility.

"If you employed us, we'd be getting paid to be in this shop, Richie," wrinkled pant suit says.

His head snaps upright and his eyes are wide. "How many times do I have to tell you?" he asks through clenched teeth. She rolls her eyes and begins a fresh conversation with her sister. He ushers me away from them, then propping his elbow against the top rail of a bunk bed he whispers, "I'm sorry you had to hear that. They really are sweethearts. A little senile, but gosh I love them." He gaze turns lustful. "So, what can I do you for?"

"I just moved to town, and I'm looking to furnish my apartment."

"That's a lovely accent you got. I'm really good at this. Let me guess—Georgia, right?"

"Oklahoma."

"Damn!" He snaps his fingers. "So close."

I offer a fake smile. "Your uncle sent me, and he said I should give this to you."
He scowls at the paper then crumples it as he shoves it into his pocket. "Yeah, well, so you must be the professor lady moving into the side apartment."

"I'm a little thrown off by his comment. "How did you…"

"Small town. Word travels fast, ya know?"

I squint. "Hmmm. Interesting. Perhaps we could start with a sofa?"

"I never got your name."

"Cheyenne."

"Awww, Cheyenne. Now that's a real nice name. Are ya Indian?"

"Yes, my father was part Native American," I answer matter-of-factly.

"I can see it. You kinda got that Indian look about ya."

"Thanks? Could we discuss furniture, please? I need a sofa."

"Sofa? Sure. As you can see, we have a great selection. It usually takes you ladies a while to pick out furniture, so why don't you come get me when you finish and I'll write up your ticket? Or maybe you'd like me to give you a VIP tour of the store?" He suggestively runs his finger across a vase that sits atop a sofa table.

What a jerk! "No need; my mind's made up. I'll take this sofa, that recliner, these two arm chairs, this coffee table, and those matching end tables. I'll need these two lamps, as well. Shall we move on to dinette sets?"

He smirks while tugging his pants upwards. "I like a woman who knows what she wants." He lets out some sort of purr-growl.

"Down, boy. Moving on. I'll take this dining set." I point as I move to the bedroom furnishings. "This bedroom ensemble with that mattress, this rug, that rug, and that mirror. Done. Did you get all of that?"

He stumbles over his words. "Uh, yeah. I think so."

"Good. Now please run the numbers, and I expect to get the best possible deal."

"You sure are a take charge kinda woman. I like that, too." He giggles excitedly as he starts towards his office at the back of the store. He stops briefly, turning back to call, "Now don't you go wandering off on me. I'll be right back lickety split."

"I'll be around," I hesitantly assure while perusing a set of paintings. He does a running hop to show his excitement, and the only witness to my eye roll is the jazz player in the painting before me. Richie returns with an invoice that is within my budget, so I fish my credit card from my wallet. "When can I expect delivery?"

"I'll get Jimmy and Barry on it right now. They can be there within the hour. Too soon?"

"Not at all. Thank you for the prompt service."

The lustful smile returns. "I pride myself on my prompt service." I give him a questioning look. "No! I didn't mean it like that. I don't do everything prompt. I meant to say that I can take my time, but I deliver to you promptly." This time my eyes widen. "No. I didn't mean it that way, either. I mean..."

I cross my arms over my chest. "Richie, your sexual innuendos are wasted on me. All I want is to get settled into my new place so my time can be devoted to preparing for my job and maybe finding the spare time to read the new novels I picked up on the way down here. That's it."

He sucks his teeth in a self-assured manner. "Sounds super boring. You know what they say about all work and no play, right?"

"Richie..."

"It's Rich," he interrupts.

"Rich, may we please finish this transaction?"

He licks his lips, and I thrust an index finger into the air before he can speak. "No." His mouth opens again. "No," I repeat, my finger giving a warning wave. He turns on his heel to run my credit card, and thankfully he remains silent when he hands it back to me. "I'll be waiting at the apartment," I say, immediately wishing I could reclaim my words.

"For me?" he asks.

"For the furniture," I say with a sigh.

He softens his voice, "Surely you'll need someone to show you around town."

"I'm sure there are many women who would appreciate your attention, and perhaps even eagerly welcome your advances, but I'm not one of them. I don't mean to sound harsh, but I'm very capable of doing things on my own, and frankly, I prefer it that way. I wish you lots of luck with your future endeavors. Have a nice day." The two women still situated on the sofa giggle in response, while a deflated Rich retreats to his office. "I didn't mean to hurt his feelings," I offer as a sort of apology.

"He deserved every bit of it, and a hell of a lot more. Never met such a spoiled, nasty, inconsiderate…"

"Hey, that's my boy you're talking about," Ms. Wrinkled Pant Suit proclaims.

"Yes, and he's my nephew. Don't make him any less repugnant," Cardigan returns.

I leave the shop before the serious arguing begins, and I would have slipped out completely undetected if it hadn't been for the stupid cow bell. They stop tormenting each other long enough to wish me a good afternoon before continuing on with Granny Brawl-Furniture Store Edition.

Thankfully, the furniture delivery goes much smoother than the acquisition, and as soon as the men leave, I'm off to stock my new place. I offer up a quick wave to Agnes who has been peering through the window since the delivery truck arrived. Far from shocking news, it's not returned. Instead, the lace curtains snap shut in what is becoming an all too familiar greeting.

Later that night, as I slide into the freshly washed silky sheets, I cry. This jag is different than the others. Normally, my body is wracked with uncontrollable grief-filled sobs that go on for hours at a time. This time, a few lonely tears streak down my face as I think about how proud my parents would be of me for starting over. The pain is finally subsiding, and I'm so grateful I can finally function in the world of the living again that I believe some of those tears are ones of relief. My hurdle has been jumped. The mountain has been climbed. The new day has begun. Life is going to be just fine.

TWO

Smiling, I rest the back of my head against the heavy wooden door once it's closed. My office is double the size of my last one and much more suited to my position. The last one was basically a glorified cubicle farm. This office has huge paned glass windows that are trimmed in brilliant white and offer a pristine view of the oak filled quad below. Rows of cherry wood bookshelves beg for my collection to be placed upon them. I'm trying to decide what should go where when a soft rap on the door startles me.

Upon opening it, I find a handsome man standing in the waiting area. He's mid to late thirties with light brown hair, a neatly trimmed beard, and is smartly dressed in khakis, a lavender shirt, and yellow tie. His pale green eyes sparkle with excitement and perhaps a hint of mischief? He eagerly thrusts a hand in my direction.

"Hi, Callahan Gage, head of the history department. Being that we're going to be neighbors, I'd thought I'd pop in and say hello."

"Neighbors?" I ask with confusion.

"Office neighbors. I'm right there." He drops my hand to awkwardly point to his left.

"Oh, office neighbors. Right. It's nice to meet

you, Callahan. I'm Cheyenne. Your name is pretty interesting. I don't believe I've ever heard Callahan used as a first name."

He quickly runs his fingers through his hair. "What can I say? Dad's a huge *Dirty Harry* fan. Harry…"

"Callahan," I interrupt, and he nods.

"The one and only. Most people call me Cal, though."

"Nice," I say, and the room is awkwardly silent for a few long seconds.

"The introductory announcement that was sent out to welcome you said you're from Oklahoma. It's really nice there. In fact, I spent some time at a conference in Oklahoma City, and I considered moving there."

"Really? What stopped you?" I return to my spot behind the desk while he remains propped in the doorway.

"Too many cowboys to compete with for dates. I'd be lonely," he teases with a wink. "Nah, just kidding. Not about the lonely part, just the cowboy part." I cast him a smile. "Okay, I wasn't kidding at all. It's all true." When he sheepishly hangs his head, I can't hold back the laugh.

"So, you're from this area?" I ask, offering him a seat which he readily bounces into.

"Yep, born and raised. I did move around a little for school, but I ended up coming back to town once my dad took a turn for the worse. He doesn't need me to live with him or anything, but I do try to check in a couple of times a week to do some of the things that have grown difficult for him. You know, yard work and such. And, why am I telling you all of this?" he asks with a playful tone.

A pain shoots through my heart, and despite attempting to hide my discomfort, Cal is all over it. "I'm sorry. Obviously, I've said something that upset you."

I shake my head. "No, it's nothing. It's just… Nothing."

He leans forward in his seat to rest his elbows on my desk. "Do you have a sick parent?"

I inhale deeply while trying to decide how to answer. Instinct tells me to snap at him with the hopes of making him leave. Basic decorum says just answer the man's question. Decorum wins. "My parents are deceased." Deceased feels better than passed on, dead, gone, or the myriad of other synonyms that float around my brain.

"I'm sorry to hear that," he answers. I anxiously await a barrage of questions that never comes, and I find myself really starting to like this guy. Funny, friendly, and cordial, yet respects boundaries.

"Thank you," I finally answer, shuffling a pile of books and papers. "Any helpful hints or words of advice before I head off to my first class?"

"Advice?" He ponders the question for a minute. "Be confident. They prey on fear," he answers ominously.

"Are you telling me the murky swamps bear unusually aggressive english students?"

He playfully tugs at his tie. "No, but it sounds good, right?"

I laugh. "Indeed."

"You'll be fine. Everyone here is super friendly. If you have any issues, you know where to find me, neighbor."

"Thanks. Oh, wait. Aren't history heads supposed to be gray haired bearded men who smoke pipes and wear tweed jackets with elbow patches?" Might as well show him that I have a sense of humor, too.

Cal smiles broadly. "About as much as english heads are supposed to be matronly women who refuse to wear makeup, pull their hair back in tight buns, and carry huge wooden pointers to smack against their desks." With a wink and a quick tap on the door jamb, he takes off down the hall. With renewed vigor, I gather the books and papers into my arms then make my way to the classroom assigned for the technical writing course I'll be teaching.

The typical hustle and bustle of students coming and going, finding seats, and scoping out the new teacher occurs, and though expected, it's somewhat intimidating. For a split second, I debate my life choices, but reality is, I made my decision and now I have to deal with it.

Though I start the class with some uncertainty and nervousness, I leave the class period pleased that I managed to develop the beginnings of good rapport with most of the students. However, like nearly every other class I've ever taught, there is one silent loner who draws my attention. His name is Billy Thibodeaux, and I silently wonder if he's any relation to George and Agnes. His long black hair is greasy and unkempt, while his clothes are tattered and unwashed. He appeared disinterested the entire class period, yet he wasn't disruptive or distracting. The one time I tried to sway him into participating in the class discussion, I was given a confused stare followed by a menacing grimace. I let it go at the time, but I will certainly be keeping a close eye on the young Mr. Thibodeaux.

I'm exhausted, but taking some time to reflect on the past week, I realize how much I've missed having a steady routine, and I sincerely appreciate having the normalcy that has evaded me for so long. Mornings are spent preparing paperwork and teaching, lunch is for grading papers, afternoons include student conferences and administrative duties, while evenings find me curled up with a book before drifting off for a much appreciated good night's rest.

Only this night is different. As I'm getting out of the bathtub, a knock at the front door startles me. I quickly slide on a robe and peep through a hole I've made in the blinds. Nothing. I open the blinds further to get a better look, and a red blur streaking through the dimly lit courtyard catches my attention. I move to get a better view, but whatever is out there is long gone now. Shrugging it off as nothing, I close the blinds, but not before catching a glimpse of Agnes staring out of the upper story window. I shake off the unsettled feeling as best as I can before climbing into bed and opening my book.

This disruptive pattern continues for a solid month, but it's not enough to run me out of the apartment. I notice strange things in the courtyard, but never get an unobstructed view to make out what it is. I once thought it was a child, but quickly brushed that thought aside. What would a child be doing in the courtyard in the middle of the night?

There were scratches at my window, but I assure myself that they are simply the rose bushes rubbing in the breeze. The knocks at the door, especially the ones that seem to come from inside the apartment scare the daylights out of me, but I realize it is likely the place settling. Certain it's the move to Louisiana that has my imagination running wild, it gets easy to dismiss the things that go bump in the night.

One day the charismatic Professor Cal surprises me as I'm at my desk grading papers during lunch. He lightly raps on the partially opened door while carrying two take out trays.

"I know I've asked you to lunch several times before, and you've politely declined each time, but I sure would hate for this second plate to go to waste. Any chance you'd like to join me in the quad?"

I offer him a slight smile. "That's really nice of you, but I brought my lunch."

"Hmmm. What did you bring?"

"An apple."

He shakes his head while pointing to the top box. "An apple? I happen to have piping hot shrimp stew, potato salad, buttery green peas, a nice hunk of French bread, AND there's dessert—strawberry cake."

"That all sounds really delicious, but…"

"But what? Come on. It's far too beautiful a day to be trapped in here grading papers. Wait a minute…" He gives a look of extreme contemplation. "Is it the food you're turning down, or is it the company?"

I playfully roll my eyes. "It's not the food because it smells wonderful."

"Ouch!" he says, clutching his chest with his

free hand. "So it's the company. That dagger went right through the heart, darlin'."

"Are you certain you're not the drama professor?" I ask, putting my ink pen down.

"Aren't all teachers actors to a certain extent?"

"Good point. So, shrimp stew, huh?"

"Louisiana's finest. Okay, that's a massive exaggeration, but I can guarantee that it's at least edible… I think." He waves the plates under his nose and breathes in deeply. "Yep, edible at the very least."

I laugh as I come from behind my desk. "I suppose edible is good."

"Yeah, it's pretty hit or miss with our cafeteria."

"That's good to know. All right, I'll join you. Lead the way," I say while grabbing a light jacket.

Once downstairs he picks a spot away from the students sunning in the unusually brisk fall air then sets down the trays on a picnic table nestled under one of the ancient oaks. He points to me. "Coke, Sprite, Diet Coke, water…pick your poison."

"Water, please." With that, he jogs to a nearby vending machine and returns quickly with two bottles of water.

"Dig in," he insists, producing two sets of plastic wrapped utensils from his pocket and holding them in the air. I snag the set closest to me and pop the top of the tray. I stare down in disbelief. "What's wrong?" he asks through the slice of French bread in his mouth.

"There's no way I'm going to be able to eat all of that, and I'm not sure what I was expecting when you said shrimp stew, but this isn't what I pictured."

"No?" he asks, putting the bread down. "Should I get you something else?"

"No! I'm not a picky eater, but I'm not used to eating like this. It smells really good." After one forkful, I'm madly in love with all things Cajun and Creole. I may have moaned while eating, and Cal confirms it.

He points to the food with his fork. "This isn't even the good stuff. This is mediocre at best. I often forget just how different our cuisine is from the rest of the nation."

"My brain can't comprehend anything tasting better than this," I remark while greedily shoveling stew into my mouth. Cal chuckles.

"Sorry," I say as I wipe my mouth with a napkin. "Not very lady like, I know."

"What? Are you kidding? I'm glad I finally found someone who appreciates it. Eat up!"

"Where else can this be found? Is it available at most local places?" I query.

"Pretty much, but I have a great idea. Let me take you out and show you around," he insists. I freeze. Noticing my deer in the headlights look, he clarifies. "Just to be sure we're on the same page here, this will in no way be a date of any kind. Consider it Southern hospitality—merely someone local doing the right thing by showing a new resident the area. In fact, I insist that you pay your own way; however, we'll take my car. Depending on how far out of town we go, I'll probably cover the gas, but I can't guarantee it. I might make you chip in for fuel." His playful tone sets me at ease.

"If you're sure it won't be an inconvenience, I'd like that. I've wanted to explore, but I wasn't sure where to start."

"I wouldn't have asked if it were inconvenient," he says with a playful smirk. "Saturday? Nine o'clock?"

"Sounds great. Should I meet you somewhere?"

"Absolutely not. I'll pick you up from your place, which is…"

"Are you familiar with the big blue Victorian on…"

"George and Agnes' place? Oh yeah. Everyone knows that place. You're in the garage apartment?"

I give a questioning look. "It seems that my apartment is famous around these parts, or perhaps infamous? Oh, please don't let it be infamous. Did something terrible happen there? No! Don't tell me! I don't want to know. There are these things happening that I can't really explain, but I have used rationale to help them make sense if you know what I mean?"

Cal laughs heartily. "Okay, I won't tell you."

"Something did happen there?" My voice goes up an octave when I ask the question.

"It's nothing to be concerned about. I have a better story for you—a tragedy that happened right here on this very campus." His voice is low and soft, like someone telling a ghost story. I'm already intrigued, so I make a "go on" gesture. "John Davidson was the president of the university back in the forties, and June Bastille was his secretary. John was married to Shirley, but June was, how should I put this?" He's quiet for a moment.

"Oh! So, he wasn't exactly faithful to

Shirley?" I answer when it suddenly occurs to me what he's implying.

"Exactly." Cal returns his attention to his plate.

"What's their story?" I greedily inquire. I'm almost embarrassed to ask, but attributing it to basic human nature makes me feel less guilty about pleading for gossip.

He tosses down his fork, and that sparkle returns to his eyes. "I thought you'd never ask." He quickly glances around, and once he's sure we're out of earshot from any passersby, he lowers his voice. "John had already retired by the time I got here, so I don't know any of this first hand. Supposedly, John and June had been seeing each other for quite a while before his wife found out about it. She ran the local bakery, and John would pop in every morning for two reasons: one, to get coffee and a pastry, and two, to inquire about Shirley's schedule for the day. I guess that it wasn't out of the ordinary for a husband to ask about his wife's day, but one day she got an unexpected cancellation for a major order, so she was able to leave early. She shows up at his office, and June isn't at her post to announce Shirley's arrival. Shirley cracks the door and finds them going at it hard and heavy. What does she do? Does she throw the door open and raise hell? Nope, not Shirley. She quietly shuts the door and leaves to come up with a plan."

"This sounds like a movie plot," I interrupt.

"You haven't heard anything yet. After a few weeks, Shirley comes up with a plan. She puts enough sedative in John's coffee to take down an elephant, and she gives him a special pastry with ground glass baked into it, but here's the deal. John never ate or drank the stuff he picked up from Shirley in the mornings. He brought them as gifts for June. Shirley closes the bakery and follows him to the campus where she hides behind a cluster of trees and bushes. You see that balcony over there?" He points to the building farthest from us across the quad. I nod. "That was John's office, and Shirley hid right over there somewhere." He points again to a densely landscaped area. I'm so enthralled with the story that I'm barely breathing.

"Go on," I encourage.

"June downed the coffee, and when she takes a bite out of the pastry, blood pours from her mouth. She freaks out, running into John's office, but the combination of the drugs and panic caused her to misjudge her step. She stumbled out of the opened doors onto the balcony and went right over the railing."

I gasp.

"John runs downstairs, all the while calling for help. He takes June into his arms, and that's when Shirley comes out of the bushes with a gun. She curses him for ruining her life and for making her the joke of the town. She aims the gun at his head, all the while June lies in his arms barely clinging to life. Just as she's about to squeeze the trigger, she suddenly turns the gun on herself and ends her life. Chaos filled the quad as students and staff poured out of the halls to surround the sobbing John, grossly injured June, and deceased Shirley. June survived for a while, but never left the hospital. John stayed by her side. He stepped down from his position, and after her death, he moved away. Rumor has it that Shirley never got over it though. Her tortured spirit supposedly roams the quad at night, especially when there's a full moon out. Some have even seen her inside the buildings. Have you met Odell yet? He's the janitor with the bright white streaks in his hair. They say the streaks happened after a run in with Shirley's ghost."

My heart thuds in my chest. The way Cal tells the story with such passion and intensity has my nerves on end. "You don't believe that, do you?" I cautiously ask.

"Me? Nah."

"Good, although I have to admit that it will be creepy spending late nights on campus now." A shiver runs through me.

"I'm happy to stay behind to escort you anytime you need, but you shouldn't worry about it."

"Why? Because I can call campus police to walk me to my car? Because Shirley's ghost is only after men?"

"Because it's made up." The mischief shines brightly in his eyes, and I don't know whether to furiously sock him one, or to laugh because he caught me hook, line, and sinker. "Please don't be angry. It was all in fun. Kids have been telling that story forever. The shooting and such happened, but it was far less dramatic. And the ghost stuff, well, you know how that goes."

I give him a sideways glance. "You got me good with that one," I say, shaking my head. "How am I supposed to believe anything you tell me from here on out?"

"I'll always tell you if it's not true…" He pauses briefly. "But only AFTER I finish the story."

His grin is contagious.

"I see. So, I shouldn't be worried about ghosts?"

"I've never had a run in with one, but Odell might tell you otherwise. That part's true, too. He swears he was visited by Shirley."

"What happened at my place? Was it very tragic?"

"Aw, I wouldn't even bother with it. I'd let it go if I were you."

"So George isn't an ax murderer and Agnes his love slave?" I ask jokingly.

"Nah, I don't think you have to worry about that. George and my dad used to be acquaintances. I would go with him to visit every once in a while when I was a kid. Do they still have that rose garden?"

"They sure do. I'm not allowed to touch the roses, but I get to enjoy them from my bedroom balcony."

"Yeah, leave the roses alone for sure," Cal warns.

My gaze goes to a dark blob moving in the distance, and I realize it's Billy Thibodeaux slowly making his way into the English building. A repulsed sneer crosses his lips when he notices me looking his way. I sigh heavily. "I just don't get that kid," I mumble under my breath. Cal turns to see to whom I'm referring.

"Wow. Looks like he carries a mighty large chip on his shoulder."

"I guess," I answer. "I've tried different tactics to break through to him, but nothing has worked. Frankly, he gives me the creeps." I quickly draw my hands to cover my mouth. Cal offers a reassuring smile.

"Anything you say stays between us."

I let out a pent up breath. "Thanks. I don't normally talk about students, especially when the connotation is negative."

"Well, I do. Let me tell you about this dumbass I had last period…"

I burst out laughing. "Thank you for helping to make this transition easier for me, Cal. You have no idea how much it means to me."

"Well, you can show me just how much on Saturday." I sit in silence, stunned by his blatant forwardness. "When I let you buy me my favorite dessert, bread pudding with rum sauce. What were you thinking?" He feigns shock. "Did you think I meant? Oh, shame. Shame, shame, shame." He rises from the table and tosses his plate lunch box into a nearby trashcan. "Well, we know whose mind lives in the gutter now, don't we?"

I toss my plate on top of his. "You're terrible."

"I agree." His tone becomes serious. "Let me know if that kid doesn't straighten up his act."

"I will. Thanks for lunch."

"Can we do it again?" Cal calls as I walk away. I turn to face him.

"Absolutely, but I'm buying next time." "Damn right you are," he teases. I'm still shaking my head when I enter the building.

THREE

     I sit in the courtyard doing my best to pay attention to the story I'm reading, but fail miserably. The same paragraph rolls through my brain about four different times, yet its message is never comprehended. George is butchering the hedges, while Agnes pretends not to watch me from the sanctity of the upper floor. The only reason I know she's there is the gentle sway of the curtain when she adjusts to get a better view.

     I'm nervous about this trip with Cal. I'm not a prude by any means, nor do I think this is anything more than a simple outing. However, the fact is, I haven't been in the company of a man in quite some time. The few moments that I've spent with Cal here and there on campus have helped me realize that male companionship is another one of those things I've missed.

     As expected, there have been some good and some bad relationships throughout the course of my life. The bad were mostly the result of my stupid rebellious streak. Mom and Dad were strict on me as

I grew up, and the older I got, the more I fought it. I was frequently accused by my mother of being hotheaded like my dad, yet I never witnessed this temper myself. Dad was always gentle and mild-mannered around me. His discipline often involved sitting me down and discussing problems instead of reaching for a switch like some other kids' parents.

He was the type of man who commanded attention simply by walking in a room. His super tall frame and broad shoulders were complimented by hard muscle that came from tending to the farm. His skin was dark and leathery and his hair jet black, much like mine. I inherited a good bit of his Native American features, but my eyes are clearly from my mother's side of the family. They're an odd shade to be seen on someone with my features, kind of a mix between emerald and amber, and they're generally the topic of conversation when meeting someone new.

My parents demanded I maintain excellent grades, and I did. They insisted I act like a proper lady, attend church faithfully, and help out on the farm, and I did—until my first year of college. I'd been kept on such a tight leash that my first taste of freedom sent me on a rollercoaster ride of bad decisions and promiscuity, but that rebellion started and stopped with Luke White. He was the epitome of masculinity wrapped up in a tight, muscular package. I was smitten the second I saw him, and he knew it, too. He was a total bad boy, constantly in trouble with the law, but never anything more than a misdemeanor or warning from the local authorities. He'd get booked and released, never once showing fear or remorse for his actions.

He asked me to marry him, and being young,

dumb, and stupid, I accepted his proposal. My parents weren't happy about their eighteen-year-old marrying, but I played the religion card knowing it would get me what I wanted. I confessed that I'd "caved to my carnal desires and allowed Luke to deflower me" even though it was a complete lie. My "flower" had been plucked long before Luke came around. They gave their blessing for our marriage but stipulated that I should continue with college and that they would cover the expense. Other than that, I was on my own in every sense of the word. I truly enjoyed my classes, and surprisingly, Luke provided well for me, so that was an easy compromise.

About two months into married life I discovered how Luke provided for us so well on a farm hand's salary. It wasn't unusual for him to drop me off on campus then take the truck to his job site and pick me up later in the day. This one day, instead of going to the ranch, he detoured to a local convenience store and robbed them of every cent in the register. He was responsible for a rash of robberies in the county, and I had had no clue. What Luke didn't know was there was a police cruiser in the back parking lot of the store and an officer in the restroom. The officer came out just as Luke was forcing the terrified cashier to the ground. Luke aimed his gun at the officer and pulled the trigger, clipping him in the shoulder.

I was gotten out of class by a uniformed officer and led to a car where my father stood, arms crossed over his broad chest. His eyes cut through me, and though I had no idea what was wrong, I instantly felt guilt and remorse. After hours of interrogation, I was released into my parents' custody.

Though the detective didn't look altogether convinced, he couldn't prove that I had any knowledge of Luke's sinister pastime. He's still in prison, convicted of attempted murder of a police officer, and he'll continue to reside there until the day he dies.

Finding out your husband is secretly a felon makes one grow up pretty damned fast, and before I knew it, I was graduating with full honors. Continuing the quest for excellence, I barreled my way through graduate school. The day I became Dr. Cheyenne Douglas was the only time I ever saw my father cry. It's a memory I still hold tightly in my heart.

I'm not sure why I never married again. Maybe the experience traumatized me? Maybe I realized I didn't need marriage? With all the therapy I've undergone, perhaps I should have broached the marriage issue? I was content taking care of my parents. Mom had a stroke not long after I started teaching, and Dad suffered a broken hip and femur after falling from his horse. Neither of them was in any shape to care for themselves, much less each other, so I did it. Until the day they weren't there anymore and I was left with no one for whom to care.

The sound of Cal's car pulling into the driveway breaks my train of thought. I slam my book shut and rush up the stairs to deposit it on the nearest end table. Cal's standing in the open doorway when I turn around. *Knock. Knock.*

"Hi. Come on in," I say, searching for my keys.

"Nice place," Cal comments.

"Thanks. I enjoy it."

He does a quick jig. "I just got the *frissons*."

"Excuse me?" I ask with a slight chuckle.

"A cold chill. The goose bumps." He slowly turns around, and his gaze fixes on the upper story window.

"Agnes," we say in unison.

"Does she do that often?" he asks.

"Yes! Let's get out of here," I offer, turning off the lights before closing the door and locking it.

Once we're situated in our seats, belted in, and the car is running, Cal looks in my direction. "What would you like to do today?"

"I thought you were going to show me all the important stuff."

"Do you know where the grocery store is?" he asks.

"Yes."

"The bank?"

"Yes."

"The hospital?"

"Yes."

"Sounds to me you know all of the important stuff. Want to go have fun in New Orleans?"

I shake my head. "You are so terrible."

"Have you ever been?"

"No, I haven't but..."

"But nothing. A visit to New Orleans is important for visitors, but essential for citizens. I think there's some requirement or law that states newbies have to visit the city within three months of assuming residence."

"A law, eh?"

"Well, maybe not so much a law. A strong suggestion?"

"I certainly wouldn't want to violate any laws or ignore a strong suggestion. New Orleans sounds wonderful."

"I was hoping you'd say that," Cal says, grinning broadly. He lowers his window long enough to wish George well and to offer a quick wave goodbye as he pulls onto the street. "I have you trapped in a car for the next hour or so. That's plenty of time for you to tell me all about you. Who is Cheyenne Douglas?" he asks in a commentator voice.

"There's really not much to know. How about you go first?"

"Aw, come on. Everyone has a story, Cheyenne."

"True. But still, you go first."

"Okay. I told you that I was born and raised in the area. I never knew my mom, and for the most part, I raised myself. My dad worked as a police detective, so I saw him on occasion, but most often, he was pulling extra shifts. It wasn't until I was much older that I overheard some stories about him. Supposedly, he was reclusive because he didn't deal well with my mom's disappearance, and he tried to bury his pain in the bottom of liquor bottles. Times were different then, and his behavior was overlooked by the department because he was good at solving cases. Anyway, about ten years ago, he sobered up, straightened up, and had a heart attack—not necessarily in that order. That's when I came back to town to help him."

"Did you move around a lot before moving back?"

"Just for school, and I have taken lots of trips. I've always been passionate about history, so I traveled around hoping to suck as much knowledge into my brain as possible. Telling the stories of our ancestors is important to me. To accurately relay those stories is something I love doing, because unfortunately, some of the versions floating around out there aren't as accurate as they should be."

"So you're the truth seeker, roaming from town to town, searching for historical inaccuracies everywhere?"

"I was, but dissecting the past is exhausting. I'm not as zealous about it as I used to be. I'm happy to be in the classroom, hopefully sparking some interest for the hundreds who roll in out and every semester."

"I understand that. You must be doing something right. I hear your classes fill up quickly."

He slows the car to barely a crawl, and he stops it in front of a run-down convenience store. "I try to make it fun for them. We've all had the antiquated professor who never moved from behind the podium while reading notes in monotone, right? I'm the anti-him."

I look at the shabby store. "What's in there?"

"Culinary bliss," Cal replies.

"In there?" I ask, warily looking around. A huge oyster shell parking lot reaches from one end of the store to the other. Just behind it is a boat launch; one of the slips holds a small bass boat while the owner backs his trailer into the water. To the left of the launch site are more slips, most of which are occupied by medium-sized boats with shrimp nets that jut high in the air.

"Absolutely. Have you ever had a crawfish stuffed pistolette? What about boudin?" he asks.

I shake my head. "I don't even know what that is."

"Prepare to be enlightened." He holds the door open for me, and entering the store only serves to increase my anxiety. Preserved gator heads of varying sizes, their mouths permanently agape to showcase their impressive teeth, line one entire shelf at the far end of the store. There are gator claw back scratchers, gator tooth jewelry, and even gator meat for purchase.

Mostly unoccupied wooden picnic tables fill up the right side of the store, whereas the left has a cashier and a glass case filled with piping hot foods. Cal encourages me to that side of the store, and I stand in front of the glass case utterly clueless as to what's inside.

"Are you about to feed me alligator?" I sort of whisper.

Cal laughs. "No. I'm going to break you in slowly. Two crawfish pistolettes and a link of boudin, please," Cal requests from the lady behind the counter. The older woman dons a clear plastic glove before assembling his order. She tosses the fried bread rolls into a paper tray then slides them across the counter to Cal. Next, she opens the lid of a steamer pot and pulls out a link of sausage unlike anything I'd ever seen. She wraps it in foil and pushes it next to the pistolettes.

"Need a bag for those?" she asks in a voice far raspier than I expected.

"Nah, we'll have them here, and two drinks, as well." She passes over two Styrofoam cups, and he suggests I fill the fountain drinks in the self-serve area while he pays. Once finished, he sits across from me at one of the picnic tables.

"Okay, tell me what I'm eating," I demand now that I have his undivided attention. "This looks frightening."

Cal laughs. "It might look frightening, but it tastes amazing." He slices a good sized chunk off of the stuffed sausage link, and I thoroughly inspect the inside before I'll take a bite. "It's just rice, meat, and seasonings. Try it."

"I will, but tell me what this is first." I point to the paper tray with the deep fried bread roll.

"That is crawfish cooked in a sauce, stuffed into a pistolette and deep fried."

I eye the two unique dishes, unsure of which I want to try first. Reaching for a piece of boudin, Cal laughs when I close my eyes to take a scant nibble.

"Really?" he teases.

"I know I said I'm not picky before, but I guess I'm really not all that adventurous when it comes to trying new foods."

"I see that. So what do you think of the boudin?"

"It's okay."

"You don't like it do you?" he asks. Offering a coy smile, I shake my head. "What about the pistolette?"

With an apprehensive sigh, I lift the fried dough to my lips and hold it there to procrastinate before finally sinking my teeth into the rich filling. "Wow," I cover my mouth with my hand. "I've found my new favorite food."

"Good, huh?" Cal asks, obviously relaxing as he reaches for his roll.

"Do they offer these in Cane?"

"They sure do," he says with a smile. "You'll find little convenience stores with food like this all over the place. This is only the beginning. Wait until we get to New Orleans."

"More good food?" I question.

"The best." As soon as we finish up, Cal says, "Come on. Let's get back on the road. It's your turn to tell your story."

Once we're back in the car, I considerably condense my life story. I tell him about my childhood growing up on the ranch, about my strict parents, and about how I married at a young age, but it ended in disaster. He doesn't push for additional details, so I thankfully move on to graduating, teaching, and almost as a side note, I mention the death of my parents. Again, there aren't any of the follow up questions I've been bracing for. I am very much at ease.

Cal easily manipulates the conversation away from our pasts and starts fresh with comparing our favorite things. We laugh nearly the entire ride to New Orleans, and I have to admit I haven't felt this comfortable around a man in a very long time.

The French Quarter is charged with energies collected over centuries; energies that are virtually indescribable—they're something a person has to experience to understand. My spirit is renewed, and my mind is refreshed. The trip to New Orleans is more cathartic than anything I've experienced in years, yet I'm reluctant to share this information with Cal. I don't want him to know how bad off I was not all that long ago, and secondly, I don't want him to get the wrong idea and think I'm interested in anything other than friendship. A little voice in my head that sounds very much like my therapist nags at me to quit over thinking things. I semi-ignore it.

Cal points out historical buildings and sites and tells stories of days of yore that leave me mesmerized and excited for more. It's while we're sitting in the crowded beignet shop having café au lait and fried doughnuts that I finally let my guard down and confess my enjoyment and gratitude.

"No thanks necessary. I'm just glad you're having fun," Cal says over the cacophony of voices that surround us. My response is a smile. A yellow-orange glow coming from the setting sun adds to the ambiance of the historical city, and I take out my phone to snap a few pictures of a jazz band playing nearby. I turn the camera on Cal, and he quickly stops me. "You're doing that wrong. Here, like this." He takes the phone from me, slides in close, and adjusts it so we both fit in the frame. The goofy face he's making causes me to laugh, and he starts snapping off a series of pictures. "There. One of those should be a keeper," he insists while sliding back to his previous seat.

I smile as I flip through the photos then tuck my phone back into my pocket. Cal tells me that he'd like to take me around Jackson's Square before driving back to Cane, so after leaving the beignet shop, I allow him to usher me across the street. Essentially, the Square is a gigantic courtyard with a black wrought iron fence around it. Wide sidewalks border the Square, and are littered with tourist, artists, and street performers. The artists hang their work from the posts, street performers put on unique and entertaining acts, and rolling food carts offer refreshments to anyone craving a snack. The yellow-orange sky fades, and a soft glow from the shops surrounding the Square light our way once the darkness sets in.

Cal excuses himself to find a restroom, so I meander to the far end of the Square where several women, each seated at individual card tables, offer to read palms and tell fortunes. Basically ignoring them because I'm more interested in the architecture of the Cabildo, I'm shocked when one of the women grasps my wrist.

She wears a long patchwork skirt and a wispy white blouse. Her hair is covered by a long red scarf, and her eyes desperately search mine for something. I'm extremely uncomfortable and try to break the hold she has on me, but her grip is as tight as a vice.

"Let go!" I demand.

"You poor child," she begins. "You poor, poor child."

"I don't know what you're talking about. Please, let me go."

"The pain. The agony. The horror. You've been through so much."

"You're scaring me. I'll scream if you don't release me now."

"I'm supposed to warn you. The compulsion is strong, so I must do it. If you choose not to heed it, that's up to you, but I have to give you this message."

"You're crazy!" I exclaim, searching for Cal to help; my stomach turns when I can't find him.

"Don't fear me. Please, just listen. You've survived it once, you'll survive again, but only if you live without sin. The boy in black, the girl in red, the lady in white, the man who prays—beware, beware, beware. Don't go their way. Don't run from the past,

just let it go. Hold onto it and you'll welcome a foe."
She releases the grip on my wrist, and I snatch it to
my chest while rubbing it briskly.

"What's going on?" Cal asks, startling the hell
out of me.

My breathing is still somewhat erratic as I try
to find the words to explain, so the woman takes over.
"Nothing, dear. I offered her a reading, but she
declined. Not very accepting of the sixth sense, I
suppose."

"It'll be fun," Cal prompts. "You should do
it."

"No, I'd like to go home, please. Now." Only
one thing she's said makes any sense, and there's no
way she could possibly know about the little girl in
red who may or may not haunt my place. I feel like
I'm losing my mind. Thoughts race in and out like a
roaring hurricane. I can't concentrate on anything but
getting away.

"Did something happen? What did I miss?"
Cal asks, confused.

"Nothing. I'm just ready to go," I anxiously
assert.

"Take care, little owl," the fortune teller says.
That sends me over the edge. Bursting into a full run,
I scurry through the crowds and don't stop until I
reach Cal's car even though he repeatedly calls after
me to stop. A mix of panting and crying hunches me
over as I try to catch my breath.

"Cheyenne! Cheyenne, stop!" Cal calls
before finally catching up with me. His stance is
protective, and his voice laden with concern. "What's
wrong? I don't understand what happened."

"It's nothing," I gasp.

"Nothing? Cheyenne, you just ran six blocks to get away from a kooky fortune teller. *Nothing* is not a valid answer."

Slowly, I slink to the ground while putting my face in my palms. Sobs that had been kept at bay since the move return, and I'm embarrassed that I can't control my emotions in front of this man. Cal sits next to me on the warm asphalt of the parking lot. "Should I call someone?" he softly questions.

I shake my head. "There's no one to call. I'm sorry. I'm a grown woman, and I'm crying like a toddler. You probably think I'm nuts, and you know what? You'd be right to assume as much."

"I don't think you're nuts. I think you're hurt. That woman said something that brought back some bad memories, didn't she?"

I swipe away some of the tears from my cheeks. "Good and bad memories." Cal patiently waits for me to elaborate. "I've told you that my parents are gone, but what I haven't confided in anyone except my therapist is how much their deaths have affected me. I went into such a deep depression that I couldn't teach anymore. I completely shut off myself from the outside world. I'm embarrassed to say that I couldn't handle it. There I was, a fully grown woman, and I couldn't handle something that everyone is forced to deal with eventually."

"Were their deaths sudden and unexpected?"

I nod. "Mom's mind was a jumbled mess after her stroke, and Dad could barely get around because of some old injuries. I lived with them and took care of them. A sitter came in to help them during the day when I worked, but other than that, it was all on me. Some may have grown resentful being so tied down, but I truly loved every second of it. My parents were my world, and I was thankful that I was well enough to care for them myself." I fall silent for a moment.

"You're doing great. Just take your time," Cal encourages while lightly patting my knee with his palm.

"The pharmacist called to say their scripts were ready, so I went to town to pick them up. It wasn't something out of the ordinary. I often left them alone when I ran short errands like shopping or paying bills. The fire trucks barreling down Main Street, sirens wailing and air horns blaring left me feeling uneasy, yet I went inside the pharmacy and picked up their medications anyway. When I left, smoke wisping high in the sky told me that my uneasiness was warranted. I don't even remember driving back to the ranch, but I remember the sight of the trucks surrounding the shell of the only place I'd ever truly called home. Running through the crowd of emergency workers, I desperately searched for my parents. Once I started shouting for them, a paramedic came to me and asked if I'd follow him to the ambulance. Guessing my parents were being treated, I ran to the ambulance and threw open the back doors. It was empty."

Silence hangs heavily for a while. There are a few times that Cal looks like he wants to say something, but the words don't come.

"The rest is pretty much a blur: finding a new place to live, making their final arrangements, the funeral, the succession. I was on autopilot through all of it. I tried to go back to life as usual, but couldn't. Every single thought was commandeered by guilt and loss. The nightmares were horrid. Nothing mattered to me anymore. My students were fed bullshit babble, and that was only when I bothered to show up or actually speak to them. I'd just give them some random writing assignment and send them on their way.

"Complaints poured in, but the school was very understanding. I was given a sabbatical and encouraged to seek treatment. Once I finished treatment, I was welcomed back with open arms, but there were just too many reminders. I was better, but I couldn't get back into the groove of things. In my search on the internet for helpful tips, one site mentioned that I should send resumes out to prove my importance to myself. Shadow Oaks responded, and when I came down to interview, I realized the pain wasn't so bad here. There weren't constant reminders, and I felt functional again. I accepted the job, and now I'm here. In New Orleans, crying my butt off in a parking lot with a man who assuredly thinks I'm insane. Anyway, that's my story. I'd really appreciate it if it stayed between us, but I understand if you feel the need to report this."

"Why would I do that? I'm sorry you had to endure such pain and tragedy, and I most definitely do not think you're insane. I think you're incredibly brave and that you have a very kind heart. Recovery doesn't happen overnight, especially when it comes to such a traumatic experience."

"Thank you for understanding. I'm not really a weak person…"

"I never thought you were," Cal interrupts.

"I did. I still do sometimes. Look at me." I wave my hands in a *ta-da* fashion.

"So, what did she say that upset you?"

"She rambled some nonsense, but it was the way she said it that creeped me out. She wouldn't let go of me."

"No, it was something she said at the end. The color drained from your face, and you bolted."

"Little owl," I murmur.

"Little owl?"

"Yes, it's what my dad used to call me. Cal, how could she know that?" I ask getting upset again.

"Take a deep breath and try to relax. There's a very logical explanation for it, I'm sure."

"Really? Like what?" I prompt.

Cal points to my throat, and instinctively I run my hands up to my neck and feel the cool metal against my fingers. I roll my eyes.

"My necklace," I say with a sigh. "Of course! I just made a fool out of myself because she made a lucky guess based upon her powers of observation. I'm so embarrassed."

Cal pulls me in for a hug. "Don't be embarrassed and don't feel foolish. It's how she makes a living."

"I can't even begin to imagine what you must think of me."

"Still? Haven't we been through this? I think you're a beautiful and charming woman."

"Nope, just say it. Insane."

"How did you get insane out of beautiful and charming?" he asks with a huff.

"How could you not after what I've told you and what you've witnessed?"

"Because you're human, Cheyenne."

I look in his direction. "Thank you."

"Anytime," he says with a smile. "Can we get

up now? This asphalt is really burning my ass."

A hearty laugh escapes as I nod my head. I decide against confiding in him about the woman mentioning the little girl in red. I'm still not convinced of what I've been seeing, plus she probably just pulled some random gibberish from the air. The woman in white? The man who prays? I know no people matching those descriptions, and the only boy in black I know is Billy Thibodeaux. Don't most boys wear black? Feeling rationale once again win over the panic; I am much calmer and more focused.

Cal stands while holding out a hand to hoist me upright, and I dust off my shorts before getting into the car. Reflecting on his words makes me smile. *Beautiful and charming.* Maybe it would be okay to let him in? Whoa, way too soon to be thinking about this stuff. I was a babbling mess not thirty seconds ago. Louisiana has turned out to be a great move for me, but she sure can keep her hoodoo and voodoo. I'm over the ghost stories. Unfortunately, I sense there will be more to come.

FOUR

The beam from Cal's headlights slices through the darkness as he pulls into my driveway. The fluttering of the upper story curtains in the blue house lets me know that Agnes has noticed our arrival.

"You have zero privacy; you know that, right?" Cal asks, peeping upwards.

I smile. "It's okay. I've got nothing to hide, plus I'm pretty boring. If the old lady wants to watch me read in the courtyard, so be it."

"You're a better person than I am. I believe I'd have to have a conversation about boundaries with ol' Agnes."

"I'm sure she's harmless. Besides, how do we know it isn't George? Maybe they're both peepers?"

"Because George is right there," he says, opening the car door. Donning a semi-opened terrycloth bathrobe, black socks, slippers, and a frown, George stands squinting in the driveway.

"How ya doin', George?" Cal calls.

"Who's there?" George grumpily asks.

Cal kills the headlights before walking over to George with an extended hand. "Callahan Gage. Felton's son. How have you been, George?"

"Oh, Cal. Right. Look, I've been sent down to tell you that late night arrivals disrupt Agnes' sleep."

"It's nine o'clock, George," Cal says with a laugh.

"And Agnes goes to bed at eight," George fusses.

"So you're saying Cheyenne isn't allowed to come home if she's going to be out past eight?" Cal asks.

"No, I'm saying that the pain in my ass sent me down here to fuss about it, so I'm doing it. Enjoy your evening, kids. Kill the damned lights the next time you pull in after dark." He turns on his heel and shuffles up the steps to the house.

Cal and I chuckle once the door is shut. "I'll walk you upstairs. It's pretty spooky out here at night."

"It is, isn't it? That's why I try to stay inside after dark," I say, nervously looking around and praying there's no child in red. Branches reach out from the darkness like sinister hands searching for something to grasp onto, while dark shadows play tricks on the eyes. The dim porch light coming from my upstairs apartment does little to illuminate anything past the stairs. I feel like eyes are watching us, separate from the obvious stare from Agnes. I peer out into the darkness while Cal fumbles for the doorknob, but I only see shadows and darker shadows.

Cal hands over my keys once the door is open, but he stays towards the banister. I'm not even afforded the opportunity to play out the whole should-I-let-him-in argument because he wishes me a good night and waves upward once he hits the bottom step. "See you Monday, unless…"

"Unless what?" I ask.

"Unless we see each other sooner. Would you'd like to go with me to tour a historical site tomorrow? Purely educational. Definitely not a date."

"What would this non-date entail?" I question.

"Touring an antebellum house, perhaps picnicking on the grounds. Ham and cheese sandwiches only. Nothing sexy like wine and cheese."

"You had me at ham and cheese," I tease. "What time should I be ready?"

"Ten thirty. Hoop skirt is optional."

"Good to know," I say with a smile. "Thank you for today."

"It was my pleasure. Good night, good night. Parting is such sweet sorrow that I'll say good night till it be morrow."

"Shakespeare. You just earned bonus points, good sir."

"Don't be too impressed. I flunked Shakespeare."

I giggle while shaking my head. "Good night, Romeo."

"Sweet dreams, Juliet." He offers one final wave before leaving, and I'm overwhelmed with everything that has happened.

A glass of wine, a long soak in the tub, and soft music help me to relax as I replay the events of the day. Did I have a set back today while in the

French Quarter? I don't think I did. In fact, I'd almost be willing to classify it as a breakthrough. The one thing that plagues my thoughts even more so than my growing attraction to Cal is the fortune teller's warning. Cal's right; she was probably trying to pique my curiosity so I'd pay for a reading, yet the phrase she spoke continues to haunt me.

As soon as I'm dried off and in my oversized t-shirt, I pick up a notebook and pen from the end table in the living room and sit down to write. *You've survived it once; you'll survive again, but only if you live without sin. The boy in black, the girl in red, the lady in white, the man who prays—beware, beware, beware. Don't go their way. Don't run from the past, just let it go. Hold onto it, and you'll welcome a foe.*

I stare down at the paper for about five minutes before I fold it and tuck it away in the book closest to me. Peeking out into the courtyard wasn't the smartest thing to do before going to bed. As soon as I turn off the dim porch light, the eerie branches are softly lit by beams of moonlight. Lacy curtains moving in the next house catch my eye, and I'm quick to close the blinds. Cal is right, privacy means nothing to Agnes Thibodeaux, plus I dread seeing the little girl in red anymore. I'm happy living in ignorant bliss if she does happen to roam the night. She stays in the courtyard, and I stay in my apartment. Still a little spooked when I curl into bed, I reach for my ear buds and let the soothing voice of the person narrating my audio book lull me to sleep.

Upbeat music plays in the background as I search my bedroom for something to wear. It's not until I open my closet that I realize I'm not only dancing, but I've been singing along, too. Is it the move? The new job? Cal? A smile crosses my lips. Of course it's Cal. Whether we remain friends, or we get brave enough to take the plunge into something more in the future, he's a good person to have in my life. I trust him implicitly; my gut tells me to do so.

I pull my long black hair into a simple braid that falls across my shoulder. Though it's fall, the weather is crazy. One day it's freezing, the next is hot as sin. Today is one of the warm ones, so I choose to wear a long flowing skirt along with a simple off the shoulder top and sandals. It's exactly ten thirty when Cal raps at the door.

"Hi, wow you look nice," he says so quickly that it almost sounds like one word.

"Thank you. Is this going to be okay for our trip? I can change if…"

"No. It's perfect."

Smiling, I nod. He opens the car door for me, and as usual, our audience supervises. He offers a quick wave upwards as we leave the property. Not surprisingly, it isn't returned.

It takes about half an hour to get to the plantation home, and the ride is spent with Cal showing me some of the highlights of the area. I learn that there are loads of seafood restaurants, and though many of them look like shabby holes in the wall, Cal insists that they have delicious food. He also points out some more familiar places, basically franchises that are available everywhere. There's something comforting about knowing they're around.

My jaw drops when we travel down the windy gravel drive to get to the main house. Plantation homes in pictures are fabulous, but to see one in person is absolutely breathtaking! An older woman rises from one of the many rocking chairs on the massive front porch, and eagerly waves as we approach. As soon as Cal stops the car, she races down the steps with open arms and a huge smile.

"Cal! How I've missed you, my sweet boy!"

"Mrs. Milly, how are you, sweetheart? You look just as lovely as ever." He gives her a gentle kiss on the cheek which causes her to flush.

"Oh, you're such a darling. I've been doing quite well. With whom do I have the pleasure of meeting?"

"This beautiful lady is Miss Cheyenne Douglas of the Oklahoma Douglas'. She's recently come to her senses and has joined us as a resident of this great state."

"Better late than never, dear," Milly says, giving me an approving nod. Listening to the banter between the two makes me feel like I'm trapped in an episode of *The North and the South.* It's odd, yet fascinating. "Welcome to Belle Aline, Cheyenne. This house has been in my family for over one hundred and fifty years, with the namesake, Aline, being my great grandmother. Will you join me in the parlor for some coffee?"

I look to Cal and he nods. "We'd love to, thank you," I answer.

The outside of the house is amazing, but the inside is spectacular. It's as if time stood still inside of Belle Aline. Huge and elaborate chandeliers decorate the grand foyer, along with intricate wood work that graces the twelve foot high ceilings. She leads us to a room on the right, and before we're seated, a woman, slightly younger than Mrs. Milly, sets a silver tray before us. Ever the gracious hostess,

Mrs. Milly asks how I take my coffee first, then Cal, and finally takes a cup for herself.

"Cheyenne, Cal tells me that you teach with him at the university. I think that's lovely. Are you enjoying your new position?" She daintily sips from her china cup.

"I love it. I'm very glad I accepted the position."

"That's wonderful to hear. And Cal, have you finished that book you're writing?"

I raise a questioning eyebrow in his direction. "Book?"

Cal wriggles in his seat. "Not yet, Mrs. Milly, but I'm still working on it. It's just something that tells the history of the area. No big deal."

"It absolutely is a big deal, Callahan Gage. If you don't immortalize the history of our area, who will?"

"I understand, Mrs. Milly, but some aren't as willing to share their stories as you are."

She begins to mumble under her breath. "Fiddlesticks. You have some who want to pretend that they are holier than thou, that their families never did anything dishonest, deceitful, or treacherous. Please, every last one of these families has skeletons in the closet, and they best quit worrying about unleashing them and just do it! People already know the stories for goodness sake. It happened, it's over, it's in the past, and most of the participants are dead and gone. Let it rip, I say. Spilling the family secrets is fun. Everyone should do it."

I look on stunned, while Cal wears a full grin. "That's why I adore you, Mrs. Milly. If only everyone shared your opinion."

The older woman puts her cup on a saucer. "I won't profess to know it all, but if Mr. Lee from Azalea Downs won't fess up, come see me. I have a lot of dirt on that family from the days before the most recent tragedy. Everyone knows about that one. I'm talking about the other terrible things that occurred there." She makes a *tisking* sound with her teeth.

"Tragedies?" I ask.

"Oh, yes," she proclaims, as she picks up her cup once again. "Lots of people have died in that house. Some from illness, some were killed in awful accidents, and some were murdered. One of the murders happened just a few decades ago. It's the one I was referring to as the most recent tragedy."

"That's horrible."

"Indeed, it was extremely horrific. We were all very fearful for a long time after those murders. Surely you've heard of them; they were quite infamous and newsworthy at the time. Some criminologists still study the case to this day. Have you heard of the Nuit Rouge murders?"

"I've heard them mentioned, and I know it was in Louisiana. That happened in this area?" I ask.

"Yes, unfortunately they did," Mrs. Milly is silent for a moment then quickly makes the sign of the cross before continuing. "Nuit Rouge, Red Night, is what they called it because of all the blood that was spilled during the massacre. People who have done work in the house report that some floor boards are still saturated with the blood of the victims. There was no way for them to remove them all. They'd have to tear the house down and start again."

My breath catches. "How many people were killed?" I ask.

"Eighteen."

My gasp is louder than I intend, and Cal picks up the story where Mrs. Milly left off. "They were having a dinner party when a group of robbers came in and slaughtered them. The police caught up with the assailants as they were leaving town. It was a group of drugged up misfits who were making their way across the country by busting into peoples' homes, holding them at gunpoint, and robbing them blind. No one knows why they chose that house, or why it escalated to murder that particular time. I guess no one ever will."

"What do you mean? Surely one of them confessed once they were caught? What about the evidence?"

Mrs. Milly speaks up. "Times were different, dear. The police apprehended them, but they all died of mysterious circumstances once in custody." She shoots air quotes around mysterious circumstances.

"They were murdered before standing trial?" I ask.

"No dear, they died mysteriously," Mrs. Milly gives me an exaggerated wink. "I believe one hanged himself, one had a seizure and never recovered, one asphyxiated because he choked on his food, and it seems to me the last one fell out of his bunk and hemorrhaged internally."

I shake my head. "I'm shocked."

"Imagine how we all felt. Cal, you were knee high to a grasshopper during that time. Do you remember the adults being on edge, or were you too young to remember all that mess?"

"Yes, ma'am. I remember some of it. Dad didn't really share much with me directly, but I overheard others talking about it."

"Shame your daddy had to work so much," Mrs. Milly remarks.

"Yes, ma'am," Cal answers.

"Enough of this morbidity. Let's move onto a more cheerful topic. Would you like to see the rest of the house, dear? I assure you that no tragedies have befallen this bountiful estate, and any deaths that occurred here were the result of purely natural causes."

"That's reassuring," I say with a slight smile. "I'd love a tour."

"Wonderful!" she exclaims. "Cal, would you mind doing the honors? You're familiar enough with the estate. Be sure to show her the children's room and the old kitchen, too."

"Yes, ma'am. I'll do that."

"Very well, I'm off to the hairdresser. Make yourselves at home, and if you need anything, Judith is in her quarters. Very lovely to meet you, Cheyenne. Please promise that you'll visit again."

"It was nice to meet you, too. I look forward to visiting again."

"Excellent," Mrs. Milly says as she wraps a scarf around her stiff hair. Cal gives her parting kiss on the cheek, and while giggling like a school girl, she disappears through a door at the opposite side of the parlor. I'm amused that Cal has such an effect on the geriatric woman.

"Ready?" Cal asks, leading the way through the same door from where we entered. "Forgive me for sounding like a tour guide, but here it goes. The house was built by Mr. Lionel Doucet for his bride, Aline. He came from a family of wealthy sugar cane farmers, whereas she was the daughter of a very wealthy judge. They had six children; sadly, all but two died before the age of seven because they were a sickly bunch. The house has remained in the family, and now Mrs. Milly is the second to last heir of the Doucet family."

"Who is the last?" I inquire.

"You're looking at him," Cal replies.

"What?" I ask with surprise.

"Nah, just kidding, but it would be cool, right? Who wouldn't want to live in a place like this? Mrs. Milly has a daughter who lives in Dallas. She'll likely sell the place once Mrs. Milly's gone, so I'm doing my best to document the history before it falls in the hands of someone else. She's helped me a lot with information gathering for my book. Now, we're good friends."

"That's really nice," I say. "It's obvious she enjoys talking with you and sharing the knowledge she has."

"It's a symbiotic relationship. She gives me info; I give her an ear to fill." He assumes the tour guide tone again. "Now, if you follow me upstairs, you'll see that the banisters are hand carved with intricate scrollwork that was done by the very gentleman who did the ceilings. It took him four years to finish all the decorative woodwork in the house."

Each new room he shows holds an intriguing story, and I'm basically awestruck during the entire tour. After we finish up with the inside, he leads me out a screen door and onto a massive gallery. Beyond it are row after row of gigantic Magnolia trees and past that, oak trees dripping with Spanish moss.

Separate smaller standalone buildings dot the grounds, and I'm curious to find the purpose of each. Cal catches me eyeing one of the closer structures.

"The kitchen used to be separate from the house. It helped keep the heat out the main house, plus if a fire broke out, it was easier to contain, and there was less risk of the whole place going up in flames."

I nod as I peek into the mostly brick interior. "What are the other buildings?"

"The overseer's cabin is still standing; it's over there. The carriage house was torn down many years ago, but a greenhouse was put in its place." He points to a glassed-in building at the far right of the property. "Obviously, it's very much neglected," he mentions, referencing the thick layers of dirt that make it impossible to see inside.

"This is unbelievable. I love it here. Thank you so much for bringing me."

"Wait, I promised you a picnic. Are you still game?"

"Here? Of course!"

"I'll be right back," he says, slowly jogging towards the front of the house. "Take a load off," he yells just before rounding the corner and disappearing from sight.

I take a seat on one of the many forest green rocking chairs that line the gallery, and breathe in deeply the fresh air that's perfumed with a myriad of fall scents. Despite the telling of the harrowing story from earlier, I'm completely at peace.

"Come with me," Cal calls as he returns with a wicker basket.

"Kind of fancy for a couple of ham and cheese

sandwiches," I quip when I catch up to him.

"Nothing but the best, baby," he teases while lightly patting the basket. I follow him past the run-down greenhouse to a trail that whittles through the oak trees. It suddenly opens into a clearing with a beautiful white and green gazebo that flanks a large pond. As we get closer, I notice a table with several wooden chairs inside the gazebo. Cal whips out a checkered tablecloth, and after dusting off a few leaves from the flat surface, he drapes the table. He shakes off a chair, and offers it to me before taking a seat himself.

The first thing he pulls from the basket is a bottle of wine and two wine glasses. I give him a questioning look. "I ran out of juice boxes," he explains. I playfully shake my head. Next comes a fruit and cheese tray, and again I give him a look. "It's just a few leftovers I need to get rid of." Finally, he pulls out a dessert tray with chocolate covered strawberries, mini brownies, and dainty petit fours. This time I smirk, and he shrugs while taking out plates and silverware. "I have no clue how those got in there."

"It looks like the only thing you DON'T have in there are ham and cheese sandwiches," I remark.

"Are you disappointed?" he asks. "Cause I can run down to the store and get you a sandwich."

I laugh. "No, thank you. This is perfect."

The smile on his face is broad when he pours a glass of wine and passes it to me. "I'm glad you came with me today."

"I'm glad you invited me. The history is fascinating, and the way you tell it... I'm almost jealous that I can't be in your classes. Your students are lucky to have you."

"As are yours. I've been hearing lots of good things. News of good teachers and bad teachers travels very quickly around campus."

"That's reassuring to hear. I often wonder if I'm getting through to them, especially with the difficulties I had after..."

He places his hand on top of mine. "Hey, you're doing excellently. No need to worry about that."

"Thank you, but there are a few students who are still struggling. For the most part, they are receptive to my suggestions about extra help, but there's still that one I can't seem to get through to."

"The strange one? What's his name?"

"Billy Thibodeaux. Yes, him. I have no idea what I've done to warrant the malicious looks and disgruntled behavior."

"Still? That's really odd. Should I have a talk with him?"

"No, he's not threatened me. He hasn't even held a full conversation with me. Usually he communicates with looks and grunts. I'll give it some more time before I pursue it. Maybe he'll stop if I simply ignore the behavior."

"Please let me know if you ever feel threatened or in danger."

"I will. Thanks. Other than Billy, teaching here is a dream come true. I love everything about the area: the sights, the weather..."

"You won't be saying that come summer," Cal interjects.

"We've been known to have some scorchers in Oklahoma," I say, popping a grape into my mouth.

"Dry heat is nothing like sub-tropic heat. All I can say is thank God we have air conditioning. I can't even imagine how sweltering it was for our forefathers… and the mosquitoes. Pure misery. Let me shut up before I say something to run you off. Okay, go on with the things you like about the area, please."

"No worries. I'm pretty sure I'm here to stay. Things I like… Let's see, I enjoy the sights, the weather, the food, the people…"

"Let me stop you right there so we can discuss that further, if you don't mind."

"Discuss what?"

"Your fondness for the populace. Would there happen to be one particular person in this generalization whom you find yourself more fond of than the others?" He takes a swig from his wine glass, yet his eyes never leave mine.

"Perhaps," I tease though I'm starting to get a little apprehensive as to where this is going. I want this, but then again, I don't.

He slides a little closer to me and refills my wine glass. "Are you willing to share with me who this special person is?"

"Absolutely." Not missing a beat, I reply, "Odell the janitor."

Cal chuckles. "Odell with the one eye and hunchback? The same Odell with the stringy, greasy hair, and six teeth?"

"That's the one. He's so kind to me." I playfully flutter my lashes.

Cal roars with laughter. "I hope you two will be very happy together."

"I'll make sure you get an invitation to the

wedding."

"I look forward to it. I'm sure your children will be handsome little boogers."

"You know it," I tease.

"I want to kiss you so badly," flies from his mouth and time completely stops for me as an internal struggle ensues. If I let him kiss me it will complicate things tremendously. Ignoring the list of warnings my inner voice is giving me, I greedily reach for him and pull him close, but he stops me. I'm a cross between confused and disappointed until he lovingly strokes my cheeks while peering deeply into my eyes. His Adam's apple nervously bobs up and down as his thumb gently grazes across my lips. "I want to remember every second of this," he says softly. "Give me a little time to take it all in."

I'm done. No more pretending that I'm happy being a loner. No more pretending that I don't crave companionship. He's won me over, and even if things don't work out between us in the long run, I know with all my heart that I want to give this a try. I long to feel his lips against and I'm fearful I'll start trembling if it doesn't happen soon.

He moves his face so that his nose is near my neck, and he breathes in deeply the scent of my shampoo and perfume. His cheek tenderly moves across mine until we finally connect. With a kiss more precious than anything I've ever experienced, his lips meld with mine.

He smiles as he pulls away. "You have no idea how many times I fought the urge to do that."

"Well, that's a lot of pressure. I hope it was worth the wait," I say, a little embarrassed.

"I can't be sure. We should try it again." I'm

still smiling as he leans forward in his chair to offer me a more playful and relaxed kiss. I completely lose track of time, but by the time we pack up the picnic basket, my lips are puffy and I'm elated. It feels so good being held in someone's arms. It's an intimacy I didn't think was necessary, but I now can't seem to get enough of Cal touching me, holding me, and my favorite, kissing me.

Far as I know, Mrs. Milly is still running the roads when we leave, so we pack up the car and head back to my place. George, in his usual attire, is blowing leaves off the main walkway, while Agnes observes from the window above. He doesn't acknowledge us when we walk past him, so either he doesn't hear us over the sound of the blower, or he's simply ignoring us. Either scenario is fine by me.

I ask Cal if he'd like to stay for a pizza, but he politely declines the offer because he's swamped with tests to grade, and I, above anyone, understand that predicament. Once he leaves, I still order a pizza. While waiting for the delivery person, I change into some lounge clothes, pour a glass of red wine, and pop in a movie.

A knock at the door startles me, and realizing it's the just the pizza guy, I grab a twenty from my purse before answering the door. Imagine my astonishment to find Billy Thibodeaux, scowl and all, on my doorstep. He's holding a pizza box and a red rose. "Looks like someone left this for you," he says with a growing sneer. The way he says it sends shivers down my spine. Figures he'd be the delivery guy.

"Hi, Billy. Listen, did I miss something? I'm not exactly sure what I've done to warrant the hostility..."

"Hostility? You think this is hostile? I'm bringing you a freaking pizza that YOU ordered."

"I didn't mean with the pizza, I mean in general. In class, it seems..."

"It seems that you are trying to make an issue where there is none. Do you have something against me? Is it because I don't dress like the others? Is it because I don't kiss your ass?"

"No, not at all. Billy, I just..."

"Just do your job. Teach, grade my shit, and leave me the hell alone. That's it. Unless you're hitting on me?"

"No! No, I have never and will never seek a romantic relationship with a student. In fact, the rose is nice, but it's obvious it came from over there and the owners are very strict about..."

He gives me a disgusted look before snatching the twenty out of my hand. "Like I'd give you a rose. Enjoy your pizza." He jogs down the stairs and is gone before I can get the door closed. After locking it as an extra precaution, I can't seem to bring myself to eat the pizza. I toss it into the garbage and heat up a TV dinner instead. The rose joins the pizza box. Thinking twice about it, I put the rose INSIDE the pizza box. I wouldn't put it past George to dig through the garbage, and I'm not keen on finding out the consequences behind plucking a rose from the sacred garden.

Pushing the food around with my fork, I'm more perplexed than ever as to what Billy's problem with me could be, but I'm determined to not let it ruin my day. My thoughts drift to Cal, and my smile slowly returns. I can't wait to be in his company again. Maybe he left the rose? No, it was a mature, fully bloomed rose from the garden, and he knows better. I chalk it up as yet another unsolved mystery before heading off to bed.

RHONDA R. DENNIS

FIVE

Work is somewhat strange the next day. I've never really classified myself as distinguished, but I AM a department head. However, inside I feel like a love-sick kid instead of a professional adult. I smile whenever I think of Cal. Every time someone passes in front of my office or classroom door, I'm secretly hoping it's him. I check my phone constantly to see if he's messaged me. Oh, I've got it so bad!

As the day goes on, I get apprehensive because there hasn't been one Cal sighting, nor a text, call, or message. I eat lunch alone in my office, and insecurities and self-doubt begin to surface. Refusing to kowtow to the negativity, I grab my things and make my way to my technical writing class. I sigh. Billy will be there, but damn it! He's not going to intimidate me.

I walk in the room with my head held high, and with a no nonsense tone, I start barking out the requirements for the next assignment. Just as suspected, Billy's there, but his face holds less malice. In fact, I believe he might be smiling. Ah, the pizza. There's my confirmation that he did something grotesque to it. Jokes on you, buddy! I didn't eat it. A broad grin crosses my face, too, and I'm back to answering questions and demonstrating proper formatting techniques.

Once class is over, back to my office I go, and I'm stunned when the door closes by itself behind me. Turning around as quickly as I can, Cal pulls me tightly into his arms. "I've been trying to get to you all day long,"

"So you've resorted to breaking and entering?"

"I didn't break, I just entered." He kisses me lightly on the lips. "How's your day been?"

"Good, but it's better now."

"Because of me?" He correctly assumes.

"No, because today's my early day, and I'm going home," I tease.

"You love tormenting me, don't you?"

"It is kind of fun."

"I'll show you fun," he growls, hugging me tightly once again. "Question," he says as I push him away to take a seat behind my desk.

"Okay."

"The Bayouland Waterway Museum is having a gala to celebrate a new exhibit that will showcase the history and importance of the logging industry in this area. It's one of those fancy things where everyone dresses up and eats finger foods while getting smashed. Interested in going with me?"

"You make it sound so spectacular, how can I possibly decline?" I say sarcastically.

"I can't promise the event will be fun, but I'll do my best to assure good company."

"Sold. When is this supposed to take place?"

"Tomorrow night."

I practically choke on the water I'm drinking. "Tomorrow?"

"Is that going to be a problem?" he questions.

"No, not at all. What time should I be ready?" I ask in as calm a voice as possible even though I'm freaking out inside. I have to find a dress, shoes, someone to do my hair. I don't know any hairdressers! Surely there has to be someone around here…

"It starts at seven, so six thirty?"

"I'll be ready. I need to get going," I say, opening my desk drawer to pull out my purse. I make quick work of packing up the things I need to bring home with me.

"What's going on? Why the hurry?" Cal asks.

"I'm going dress shopping," I say with a smile.

"You'll probably need someone to keep you company."

"Nope. I think I can handle this one solo. Besides, you have a Louisiana history class to get to. Don't want to keep your students waiting," I taunt, as I glide past him.

He snatches my wrist and pulls me close. "I can cancel. Students love when the professors cancel class."

"They do, and no. Go to class."

"Fine," he grumbles. "Have fun dress shopping." He kisses me lightly on the lips before opening the door. We walk down the hall together, and I leave him at his classroom with a wink and a quick wave before pushing through the double doors at the end of the hall. I pull my phone from my purse and search for local dress shops. There's one on the main stretch, right next to Rich's furniture store. Ugh.

Oh well, at least I'll be able to find it easily enough.

To my pleasant surprise, I pass two hair salons, but one is closer to the dress shop than the other, so that's the one I wander into first. A lone young woman sits in the shop, twirling around in the salon chair, but she stops rotating as soon as I enter the door.

"Well hi there!" she excitedly exclaims before sulking back into the chair. "Wait, you're not looking for the real estate agency, are you? Cause they moved about three months ago."

"No," I answer, shifting my plastic covered dress onto my other arm. "I'm new in town, and I have a gala to attend tomorrow…"

"I'll do it!" she exclaims jumping from the chair.

"But…"

"Is that your dress? Lemme see so I can figure out what style will look best with it. I just love fixing people up for parties. Oh! It's so gorgeous! Simple, yet elegant! I know exactly what to do! We have to start today. You need highlights to frame your face, and they'll make your eyes pop more, too. I need to shape it up a little. Are you okay with layers?"

"But I…"

"Trust me, long layers will make a world of difference. You can hang the dress on the coat rack then have a seat in the chair." Somewhat reluctantly, I hang the dress up, and once I turn to face her, she squeals. "Oh, my gosh! I'm so rude! Please don't think less of me. I forgot to introduce myself! Tiffany Everett, and you are?"

"Cheyenne Douglas."

She gasps. "Ooooo, Cheyenne! I love that

name! You said you just moved here. Where did you move from?" she asks as she snaps a drape over my shoulders and gently runs her fingers through my hair. She studies it intently while waiting for an answer.

"Oklahoma."

"Oh, I love cowboys. You have lots of cowboys in Oklahoma, don't you?" Before I can answer, she's moves to another topic. "So what made you move down this way? I've lived here all my life, so I really don't know what it's like to live elsewhere. I guess it's exciting? Maybe scary? Are you married? Have kids? I was engaged once, but it didn't work out, but it doesn't stop me from dating around. Are you settled in yet? Where are you staying?"

She takes a breath long enough for me to answer. "The apartment behind the big blue Victorian house on…"

"Oh, my God! You couldn't pay me enough money to stay in that place! You are so brave. Look, I get the chills just thinking about it!" She holds up her forearm so I can see the bumps that have arisen.

"I'm not sure what you're talking about…"

"The little girl's ghost. Have you seen her? I'd absolutely die. Instant heart attack."

I shake my head. "I've seen something, but I don't think…"

"You know the story about George and Agnes, right?"

"No, and I'm not exactly sure I want…"

"Girl, let me tell you!" she exclaims as she starts smearing blue goo on portions of my hair then wraps them in little sheets of foil. "I know all of this because my momma's cousin's friend worked for the coroner's office back in the day. You ever see

Agnes? Probably not because she never leaves that house. Well, you know she's all crippled up, right? Do you know how it happened? No, how could you know? You just said you hadn't heard the story. So, George was supposed to be some sought after bachelor in town, and Agnes caught his eye. They fell in love and had a kid, a girl named Lucille. You know that back in the day they used to not have seatbelts in cars and kids just kinda sat wherever, right? Well, one night they're coming home late, and George swerves to miss something in the road making them plow right into some trees! Agnes is all crushed up, George is banged up pretty badly, too, but five year old Lucille—poor baby doesn't make it. I think she flew through the windshield or something like that. "

I gasp. "That's terrible."

"Wait, you haven't heard the terrible part yet. Hold onto your underpants. So, George and Agnes were in the hospital for months, and the funeral home couldn't wait that long to bury Lucille, so they had to do it without George and Agnes. Agnes never got over the loss of her daughter, much less never having the closure that comes from that final goodbye, you know? So she basically turns into this psycho zombie. She won't sleep, she won't eat, she won't do anything but stare out the window to the courtyard below, calling for her Lucille."

"I do notice her looking out of the window a lot."

"Girl, I still ain't got to the worst part! She made that man dig her up and bring her home, oh yes she did! He snuck into the graveyard with a shovel and reburied the child in the rose garden! Of course the police found out and arrested him, but it was a while before they figured out where the body was so they could put her back at the cemetery. They cemented the grave and did some other stuff so George could never do it again."

A shiver runs through me when I think back to the oddities I've been shrugging off nothing. I don't believe in ghosts. It's just another one of those spooky stories that the people from the area obviously love to tell. Cal has a ghost story, Mrs. Milly has a ghost story, there were multiple ghost stories told while we were in New Orleans. It must be a Louisiana thing. That's what I keep telling myself in an effort to remain calm.

"I find it odd that George and Agnes didn't face more severe consequences for their actions," I say with a tone meant to show my disbelief.

"Oh, they were pretty severe! George served time, and Agnes was sent to a psychiatric hospital out of town. She got those electroshock treatments and everything. George brought her home three years later, and no one's seen her out and about since. She hides behind the curtain, desperately searching for her long lost daughter. George feeds her, dresses her, takes care of the house. He's a nice man, really. Kinda talks gruff, but has a good heart, ya know? He only did what he thought would help his wife stop grieving so hard. Can't say that I blame the man, but ewwww... Digging up a corpse is beyond my boundaries, I don't care how much I love a person."

I'm set to freak out at any moment, but thankfully, the rest of Tiffany's conversation is geared towards much lighter topics. However, I still can't get the image of the little girl out of my mind. It's all a crazy coincidence, and I refuse to ponder it any longer. I turn my attention to tracking Tiffany's progress with my transformation.

Satisfied with the end results of my cut and highlights, I agree to meet Tiffany the following day so she can style my hair for the event. I give her a generous tip then leave for my apartment, but not before running into Richie from the furniture store.

"Well, hello there," he says, his eyes brimming with lust.

"Hi, Richie. Bye Richie," I say, trying to push past him. He reaches for me, but I'm able to move back before he can touch me. He holds up his hands in a surrender position. "I come on too strong sometimes, I get that. No problem. Look, my hands are up here. I just want to talk for a minute, if that's okay."

I sigh. "I suppose. What is it?" I shift the dress so it drapes over my arm instead of holding it over my shoulder.

"Dinner—you still opposed?"

"Richie, it's not that I'm opposed; it's that I'm sort of seeing someone…"

He sets his jaw. "I see. Well, maybe you can keep me in mind if things don't work out for you and your guy?"

"I'll do that," I say, opening my car door. "Take care, Richie. Enjoy the rest of your day."

"Oh, I will," he says, tugging on his belt to adjust his pants before going into the store. I fight the urge to gag but give in to the urge to get the hell out of there, so I put the car into reverse and head away from town.

As I pull into the driveway, the story I'd been told runs through my head. I'll never see the place in the same light again, especially knowing that a child had once been buried underneath my bedroom window. Again, I give myself a quick pep talk about not necessarily believing the story yet because there honestly was no proof it actually happened. It's a story told to me by a hairdresser who heard it from some distant source. Common sense wins out even though there's still a slight pang of fear in the pit of my stomach. I march up the stairs and settle in for the night. Thankfully, no one scratches at my window, no knocks come from the door, no little girls play in the courtyard, but Agnes does remain in that window, just like she does every other night. At least that's where she is when I go to bed that night.

SIX

I barely recognize myself while I gaze at my reflection. Since I usually prefer a natural look, Tiffany insisted on doing my makeup, in addition to my hair. I was hesitant, but now I'm grateful I let her do it. My dress is very simple, a black number with lace cap sleeves, a boat neck, and plunging V back. A black satin ribbon serves as a sash for the slim-fitting dress, while the floor-length skirt puffs slightly in the back around the knee area.

The only jewelry I wear is a pair of diamond drop earrings that were a graduation present from my parents. My hair is up in a loose, curly chignon, and my makeup is sultry and seductive. The black kohl smudged around my eyes makes them look the color of tiger's eye quartz. If only I could figure out how to do this stuff for myself!

Cal knocks at precisely six thirty. I reach for my small black clutch and smile as soon as I see him. He looks so handsome in his black tuxedo, and his normally wild wavy hair is contained in a neat style thanks to gobs of hair gel. He smells amazing, too. His scent drives me insane, and I have to fight the urge to pull him inside instead of leaving to attend the gala.

He's speechless for the longest time before I break the silence. "Cal?"

"Cheyenne. Wow. I guess it's apparent that I'm at a loss for words. You look amazing. I don't deserve to have you on my arm."

"Oh, stop," I say, starting to blush. "I was thinking the same about you. You look incredibly debonair. Thank you for inviting me to be your date."

"Thank you for accepting. Wow."

With a huge grin on my face, I accept his extended elbow, which I happen to be very thankful for because of the extremely high heels I'm wearing. Once we're in the car, he spends more time staring at me than at the road, and I'm embarrassed by the attention. It's something I discover I should grow accustomed to pretty quickly because once we arrive, I feel like the belle of the ball. Men come out of their way to introduce themselves to me, while old women quickly whisk their husbands away as the introductions happen. I'm not offended; I'm shocked. It's the first time I've ever been the center of attention at such a gathering.

When we aren't mingling, snacking, or having a drink, Cal finds excuses to lure me to dark areas of the museum for stolen kisses and whispers of sweet nothings in my ear. His lips just leave mine when the sound of a male loudly clearing his throat draws our attention in that direction.

"Father Donnelly, how are you?" Cal asks.

"I've been well, Callahan. How's your father?" the rotund priest with thick gray hair and even thicker eyebrows asks.

"He's doing fine, Father. Some days are tougher than others, but overall, he's okay."

"Seems that's the way it is for most of us this age. It's a lot harder to spring back than it used to be. Heck, it's harder to do everything now, even getting out of bed is difficult!"

"Sorry to hear that, sir," Cal offers.

"Ah, don't be. It just is what it is. So, who is this lovely young lady?"

"Father Donnelly, this is Cheyenne Douglas. She moved here from Oklahoma and is now a co-worker of mine. She's in charge of the English department at the college."

"Well, very nice to have you here. I hope you're enjoying the move?"

"I am. Thank you."

"Have you found a church yet?"

"Well, to be honest, I'm not all that religious anymore…"

"Ah, there's a story. I'll not pry tonight, but I will leave you with one of my cards if you should ever choose to discuss it. Every once in a while we lose a lamb, but with a little help, that lamb generally returns to the flock. No pressure, dear. It's only if you feel compelled."

I drop the card into my clutch and thank him. He offers parting pleasantries to Cal and me before making a beeline towards a woman he calls Sophia.

"Are you ready to get out of here?" Cal asks. "Cause I've been ready to leave since we arrived. These things are so boring."

"Maybe. I need to ask you something before we go back to my place. Why didn't you tell me the Agnes and George story?" I fuss.

"What? Who?"

"Tiffany the hairdresser filled me in. Did it

really happen?"

"I don't know. What did you hear?"

"That George dug up their daughter and buried her in the rose garden," I excitedly whisper.

"She's not there anymore," Cal offers. My eyes widen.

"You did know!" I loudly whisper.

"Listen, you understand grief, probably more than most, right? They were grief-stricken parents who made a really bad decision. George served time, and poor Agnes,... well, I hear that the things they did to her in the institution were downright barbaric. I feel sorry for them."

"I'm not saying I don't feel sorry for them, but Cal. Come on. The girl was buried under my bedroom window."

"Is this a ploy to get me to stay the night, because you can just ask, sweetheart. No need feign fright."

"I'm not feigning fright. I've slept there by myself every other night, haven't I? It's just that sometimes strange things happen, and they're somewhat unexplained and maybe borderline paranormal, even though I know there isn't such a thing. Oh, never mind. Even I think I sound crazy. Forget I mentioned anything."

"Wait. What do you mean strange things?"

"Roses keep popping up at my doorstep, and these aren't store bought roses. They're from Agnes' garden. I hide them in the trash so George won't have a fit."

"Sounds like you have a secret admirer. I need to up my game."

I roll my eyes. "Strange knocking sounds,

scratching at my window, and the little…" I pause.

"Go on," he prompts.

"You're really going to think I'm a lunatic."

"I haven't yet, have I?"

"I sometimes see what appears to be a little girl in red playing in the courtyard at night."

"You what? No. Really?"

"It's usually pretty quick, and I can't be one hundred percent certain because of the poor lighting, but something is definitely out there."

Cal gets serious. "Do you feel in danger? Do you think someone's watching you? Like maybe a stalker or something with the roses and such?"

"I don't know. I don't think so."

"Promise me that you'll keep your door locked at all times, even if it's during the day."

"I promise."

"Promise that when you arrive home after dark you'll call me so I can be on the line with you until you're safely inside okay?"

I smile. "I promise. Anything else?"

"Not right now, but that might change later."

"Noted."

"I wonder if the little girl in red will show herself if I stay over."

"I don't recall extending an invitation."

He gives me a playfully pleading pair of eyes before mentioning, "Speaking of invitations, I wanted to ask you to come with me to Azalea Downs this weekend. I need to take a few pictures to wrap up my section on local tragedies, mysteries, and such."

"Who lives there now?" I question.

"The Beauregards own it, but they use it as a bed and breakfast. During the Halloween season, it's nearly impossible to get in there because of all the thrill seekers searching for a taste of the supernatural. There are also visitors who stop by for the macabre aspect of it and tour simply because of the infamy." He shrugs his shoulders. "I don't get it, but apparently, it's a pretty popular thing, especially with older teens and young adults."

"Wow, that's pretty morbid. Sure, I'll go with you, but not because of the macabre aspect. It's because I enjoy visiting plantation houses."

"With you?"

"Excuse me."

"I enjoy visiting plantation houses with you. You forgot the *with you* part."

I move in close enough to hook one of the stray wavy chunks of hair with my finger and gently tuck it behind his ear. "That should be a given." He kisses me, but not for long. After some quick goodbyes to those in the immediate vicinity, he's whisking me out the door and into the car.

Careful not to disturb George and Agnes with the headlight beams, Cal turns them off well before we get into the driveway. We pull in just in time to see someone tall, bulky, and dressed in black from head to toe foregoing the stairs and catapulting over my balcony.

"Hey! Stop!" Cal calls, sprinting after the person. He catches up with him at the fence, and just as Cal reaches out to grab him, the guy makes it up and over. "Call the police," Cal instructs as he moves one of the benches so he can peer over into the next yard. "It's too freaking dark. I can't see anything."

George stumbles out of the back door. "What's all the ruckus? You'd think two grown ass professors would be better behaved."

"Someone was trying to get into my apartment, Mr. Thibodeaux. Surely Mrs. Agnes saw it all? Maybe she can help give a description when the police get here?"

Mr. Thibodeaux looks miffed. "What are you talking about? You trying to be funny?"

"No, sir. I just meant that because Mrs. Agnes looks out of the window a lot…"

"You obviously don't know," George says, his tone changing to something more somber. "Agnes don't talk anymore. Hasn't in years. She just jibber jabbers about nonsense or gestures what she wants. The lights are on, honey, but ain't no one been home for a very long time."

"What?" I question. "She seems to be very observant by always looking out of the window."

"What the hell else she got to do? She don't watch TV, can't follow a book, don't ever leave the house. Window watchin' is it."

"I'm sorry. I had no idea," I say, suddenly feeling guilty for the negative thoughts I had when I thought she was merely ignoring me or being nosy.

"How could you know? Ah, I've got so much to deal with. Keeping up with this house, the yard, the gardens, my meds, Agnes' meds…" He sighs. "I forgot to call her doctor. Her new obsession is with the color red. Red, red, red… it's all she mumbles these days." Cal and I curiously glance at each other. "Anyway, did you get a glimpse at this fellow who tried to break in?"

Shaking off what Cal would call the *frissons*, I direct my attention back to George. "We only saw him briefly. He's tall, sort of bulky, but not overly so, and wearing all black."

"Did he get inside?"

"No, sir. At least I don't think so."

"You can hold off on making that call to the police then. It's not gonna do ya any good. They'll show up, take your story, and leave. It's not like they're gonna comb the porch for DNA and footprints. It ain't all like TV, princess."

I slowly pull the phone away from my ear. "I suppose you're right, but would it be okay for me to have an alarm system installed, Mr. Thibodeaux? I'd feel much safer."

"Depends. Who's paying?"

"I'll pay for the installation."

"Do it. No half-assed work though. This property is a historic landmark, and you can't be having people coming in and destroying it. No cameras. No wires everywhere. Nothing that's going to call in the cavalry every time a gnat farts. Simple and understated. Understand?"

"Of course. I'll make sure it's very basic and does nothing to change the look of the place."

He retreats back to the house grunting and huffing. I'm disheartened to find another rose, a pink one this time, placed on the wrought iron table near the door. Sighing heavily, I take it inside with me, pluck off the petals, and shove it into an empty cereal box in the garbage can. Cal turns me so I face him.

"I'm worried about you."

I close my eyes and rest my forehead against his chest. "I don't know what to think of all this. Maybe it's just a kid having fun with me? In fact... Billy! He knows where I live because he delivered a pizza to me. He even handed me a rose with the pizza box and got miffed when I asked him about it. He said it didn't come from him, but who else can it be? He's obviously playing games with me—knocking and running, scratching on the windows. He really despises me."

"Maybe it's time for me to have a talk with Mr. Billy?"

"No, Cal. You shouldn't get involved. I'll talk to him. Plus, Mr. Thibodeaux said I can have a security system installed. Try not to worry. He's just a punk kid trying to get a cheap thrill out of harassing me. If he thinks I'm intimidated by him, he'll run with it. I'll set him straight."

"You're probably right, but I still don't like it."

"You don't have to like it," I tease as I run my fingers inside his jacket and across his shoulders so that it falls to the floor. His breath catches when I start to unbutton his shirt. My fingers follow the previous path and now his shirt rests on top of the jacket. He lightly grips my hand once it's upon his bare chest.

"Are you sure?" he softly whispers. I let a kiss serve as my answer before taking his hand and leading him to the bedroom. My back's turned to him so he can unzip my dress, and chills run up my spine when his lips touch my exposed shoulders. It's been so long since I've been touched intimately that every nerve ending feels energized and tingly. My skin puckers with anticipation when he softly blows on the damp trail his tongue has left along my neck. His arms encircle my waist, drawing me so close to him that his erection presses against my rear.

The cap sleeves of my dress fall to my elbows,

exposing my sensitive flesh to the air. Closing my eyes so I can fully enjoy the sensation, my breathing begins to quicken. His hands glide down my hips, and the dress falls into a black pool onto the floor. The only thing between his body and mine is the fabric of his pants. With the dress gone, he cups my bare breasts while my fingers reach behind to run through his wavy hair.

"Cheyenne. Beautiful Cheyenne. Where have you been all my life?" he whispers in my ear.

"Looking for you," I answer, as I turn in his arms. His lips lock with mine as he gently pushes me towards the bed.

Once he's poised above me, he stares into my eyes. "I don't want this night to end."

I shake my head. "Neither do I." His body fills the void in my soul, while his words fill the void in my heart. After a night of lovemaking beyond anything I'd ever dreamed of, I lie in Cal's arms convinced he's the man I'm meant to spend the rest of my life with. I should be scared to feel this way so soon after connecting with someone, but I know it's right. I wonder if he feels the same, and when I glance over at him, the look on his face tells me all I need to know. He's smitten.

SEVEN

The most difficult part of having an amazing sexual relationship with a coworker is keeping the silly grin off my face whenever I see him. There are lots of stolen kisses, coy and sometimes lustful glances, and quick touches whenever we can sneak them in.

The weekend arrives, and relief sets in because secrecy is no longer an issue. Friday night is basically a repeat of Tuesday night, except the lovemaking starts much earlier since we don't have the pesky obligation of attending a gala. Saturday morning, as we're going out the door to head to Azalea Downs, a white rose waits in the usual spot. I'm not as apprehensive about it since the security system has been installed, but it's still unsettling to know someone continues to broach my personal space. Frankly, I'm shocked that George hasn't complained to me about it. Surely he's noticed the blooms disappearing from the garden? I think to myself how strange it all is, but little do I know things are about to get a whole lot stranger.

When we arrive at Azalea Downs, my stomach instantly fills with dread. The house is gorgeous, a white and dark green stately manor with amazing architecture, but the feeling gets worse the closer we get. The only thing I can figure is perhaps its unfortunate history has influenced my opinion to the point that it's affecting me physically, or perhaps it's something less sinister, like the beginnings of a stomach bug.

I'm doing a good job of hiding my unease until we walk up the steps of the porch. Suddenly, I begin to feel very weak, and bizarre things start happening to my body. I grasp one of the columns as my vision narrows, and a series of graphic images flash in rapid succession in my mind. All my senses are rendered useless, and it's as though I'm strapped to a chair in a dark room while being forced to watch an old 8mm movie.

Bodies are everywhere; partially congealed blood as thick as molasses pools around most of the victims in the massive room. A man slumps over the keyboard of a grand piano, blood oozing from a wound at his temple. His lifeless eyes stare towards the door. It's like I'm viewing the carnage through someone else's eyes, and this person is now moving into another room. Through the kitchen, across a hall, into the parlor where more bodies litter the floor. A woman, her short hair fixed in large curls, very obviously gasps for breath. Just to her side is a large, unmoving man. I can't see his face, but his back is riddled with bloody holes. The focus goes back to the woman beside him. Blood continues to splay across her white dress until it reaches a sparkling rhinestone broach pinned to her chest.

My vision moves out the door and up the stairs, searching room by room for anyone breathing, but I find no one. The closet door opens in one of the bedrooms; inside I go, and suddenly everything goes black. I struggle to pull in a breath as I feel my body rushing back to reality.

"Cheyenne! What in the hell? Are you okay?" It's Cal calling for me. I can't move my body yet.

"Should I call for an ambulance?" a male voice I don't recognize asks.

"I don't know," Cal says, his voice laden with concern. "Cheyenne!"

I'm finally able to pull my eyes open, and I'm shocked to find myself kneeling on the porch. "What happened?" I manage to ask.

"We don't know. You were walking up the steps with me then all of a sudden you fell to your knees and starting rocking back and forth. I tried calling to you, but you wouldn't answer. It's like you were in some sort of trance or something." He moves close and wraps me in his arms. "Are you okay?"

"I think so. I've never had anything like that happen before." The images rush back to me and I'm suddenly very agitated. "I saw it. I saw the massacre. Could it be the power of persuasion that did it?" I rapidly wonder aloud. "No, it can't be especially if…"

"If what? You're not making sense, sweetheart," Cal says. The mystery man simply looks on with confusion.

"If what I was seeing was accurate. The house. I've never stepped foot in it, yet I saw it. I saw the inside. I saw the bodies. Oh, please be wrong. Please be wrong!" I say, barreling through the front doors without a thought of asking the owner for consent. "Oh, my God. The grand ballroom, it's here. The piano. It's still here." I run across the hall. "The kitchen is here, and a parlor," I say running to the next room. "Bathroom." I yank open the door, and indeed, it's the bathroom. "Upstairs to the right: bedroom, bedroom, bathroom. Middle: sitting area and balcony. Left: office, linen closet, bedroom," I say, pointing in the general direction of each room with my finger.

The mystery man, who is obviously the owner, looks stunned and confused when he nods.

"How do I know this, Cal? How is it even possible for me to know this!"

"Slow down, Cheyenne. There has to be a logical and simple explanation for this. Take a deep breath."

"This is used as a bed and breakfast. Did you visit with us before? Perhaps you've visited our website? Lots of pictures on there."

"No. I was born and raised in Oklahoma. I've never even been to Louisiana until I moved here not that long ago."

"Uh, why don't you come into the kitchen for a cold drink?" the owner suggests, looking even more confused than before.

"Thanks, Ben. That's a good idea." Cal takes my elbow and helps me to the kitchen. Ben opens a massive stainless steel refrigerator and starts to lay out an assortment of beverages onto the counter.

"May I have some of that?" I ask, nodding to a selection of bottles that line a shelf on one of the far walls. He pulls a rocks glass from the shelf below it, drops two cubes of ice inside, and pours it about two fingers full of bourbon. He looks at me, looks at the glass, and then adds about two more fingers' worth before passing me the glass. He then pours one for himself.

The fire starts in my mouth and quickly descends to my belly, and the sensation slowly spreads to every inch of my body. As the heat spreads, calm begins to replace the anxiety.

"Better?" Cal asks when he notices the transformation. I nod.

"Thank you," I eke out to Ben. He gives me a salute and simultaneous wink before pouring himself another. He holds the bottle up and waves it to ask if I'd like another. Shaking my head, I have to look twice because it suddenly occurs to me how much he resembles Boss Hogg from *The Dukes of Hazzard*.

Though I'm much calmer, I still have the same questions. "Cal, how can I know the layout of a house I've never been in?"

"You told Mrs. Milly that you were familiar with the murders. How are you familiar with them? Maybe you saw pictures in a book or a magazine? Because of the attention the case got, things continue to pop up here and there."

I try to remember, and I vaguely recall reading a few books that contained true crime stories. But why were the images in my mind so vivid. If it's something I simply read in passing, why do I remember details so well? I put my face in my hands. "Maybe so." I concede because frankly, it's the only feasible option I've got right now.

"Unless you've been possessed by one of the

murder victims," Ben chimes in. Cal and I give him simultaneous disparaging looks before I put my face in my hands.

"Hey, how many famous crime scenes have you actually visited?" Cal asks once he pulls my hand away from my eyes.

"None, until today."

"Then that has to be it. You're simply remembering what you saw. Being inside the house triggered a memory of the pages you've read."

"That has to be it, right?" I ask, sincerely trying to convince myself. I look towards Ben, and he offers me a shrug and a nod.

"That's it," Cal says, scrunching me in a super tight hug around the shoulders.

"Okay," I say, before taking a slow deep breath. "I'm sorry for all of the commotion."

"No need to apologize, little lady. I'm just glad you're alright," Ben says.

"Would it be okay with you if we reschedule due to the circumstances?" Cal asks Ben.

"No!" I interject. "Please don't reschedule on my account. I'm fine. Really."

"I don't know…," Cal starts.

"I promise I'll let you know if I start to feel bad," I insist.

"Okay," he says with a reassuring smile.

"Why don't we take this to the screened porch? I believe we can all use a little fresh air," Ben suggests.

"Perfect," Cal says, readying a notepad and pen once he's seated. Cal asks questions, and Ben patiently answers them; however, my mind drifts to earlier. I'm still scared. I've never blacked out or lost control like that before, and it makes me consider checking in with a family doctor or maybe even a therapist.

"You can if you'd like," Ben says.

"I'm sorry," I say when I realize he's speaking to me.

"You keep eyeing the place. You can look around if you'd like. Maybe before was just a lucky guess. You might go upstairs and nothing will look like it did during that spell you had. Should make you feel better."

"That's true. It might look nothing like...., well, whatever it was," I excitedly wave my hands. Ben has given me hope that I'm not going bonkers, and he's rewarded with a kiss on the cheek.

"Awww, thank you for that, darlin'. Now you take your time and just holler if you need anything."

Cal looks somewhat apprehensive, but ultimately gives me a reassuring smile. I start up the steps and end up back in the kitchen. No strange sensations or sightings happen in there. Moving into the main foyer, I make my way to the large ballroom. The grand piano has been moved to a different corner of the room, the furnishings replaced with new fabrics, and a long bar that once filled a large portion of one wall has been removed. "How did I know there was a bar there? Pictures," I explain to myself. As I walk through I *remember* every place a body once laid, and though I feel anxiety raring, I'm able to keep it at bay.

I slowly start up the stairs, hoping beyond all hope that it looks nothing like what I saw in my mind. The closer I get to the top landing, the more disappointed I become. It's just as I recall, and some of the rooms still have the same antiquated décor. I stand in front of the closet I saw in my mind trying to draw up the courage to open it. My heart thuds in my chest as I reach out to open it. Just as my hand touches the knob—

"Cheyenne?" It's Cal. He startles the hell out of me, and I nearly fall on my rear when I trip over a footstool.

"I'm sorry. I didn't mean to scare you. Are you okay?" he asks, helping me to regain steady footing.

"Yes, I'm fine. My heart might not agree right now, but I'm okay."

He smiles. "I'm sorry, sweetheart. I thought you'd hear me coming up the stairs."

"The only thing I heard was the sound of blood swooshing through my ears while I tried to muster the courage to open this door."

"What's in there?"

"A closet."

"And you know this…"

"From earlier."

He looks at me briefly before reaching out and opening the door. Sure enough, it's a large walk-in closet. "It used to be a bathroom before they converted it," I speak without even thinking. Drawing my hands to my mouth, I gasp when that information comes out. "How could I know that, Cal?"

He gently pushes me aside so he can shut the door. "In what other rooms did you have experiences?"

"The grand ball room, but I've already been there. Some of the furniture is different, a bar is missing, and the piano has been moved."

"Where else?" Cal asks.

"The parlor, but I haven't been in there, yet."

"Take me with you, and tell me everything, okay?"

I nod, leading the way to the room. As soon as I walk in, it's as though I'm seeing it through someone else's eyes. I don't go into the trance like before, but if I close my eyes, I can vividly imagine everything. "There were two people found in this room: a man and a woman. He was lying across her, face down, and had many bullet holes in his back. She had black hair that was cut short and styled with large curls. She wore a white dress with big gold and white buttons and a rhinestone pin shaped like a flower. I can see the blood make its way up her dress as she gasps for air, and that's all I remember. Do you honestly think I'd retain this much knowledge from a picture I may have possibly seen years ago? And how do I know about the positions of the people, their injuries, what they looked like…"

"I don't know, but there is someone who might be able to help us."

"Who's that?" I ask, desperate for a lifeline of any kind.

"My dad, Felton Gage. He worked the case, so he'd be familiar with those kinds of details. At the very least, he can refute or affirm whether what you're seeing is accurate."

"Your dad is going to think I'm nuts," I protest.

"He won't. Like he'd say, he knows a nut when he sees one, and baby, a nut you ain't," he says jokingly, and he moves in for a quick kiss on the forehead.

"Yeah, well I'm even having a hard time believing that right now."

"Come on. Let's get out of here. May I take you to lunch? I know a place guaranteed to take your mind off all this mess."

"I'm intrigued, yet slightly apprehensive."

"Rightfully so," he chides. "Now get in the car."

After a series of windy roads, a few small towns, and a pontoon bridge, we come to a place situated right on the water. Zydeco music pours from the long building nestled amongst a cluster of cypress trees. Quite like New Orleans, the air holds a distinctively different energy.

"Where are we?" I ask.

"My hometown, Frenchman's Cove. This restaurant is run by my old neighbors, so expect a lot of shouting, hugging, and kissing. It's the Cajun way."

"I'm scared," I say jokingly.

"I told you, you should be." With that he opens a large set of wooden doors to reveal an open room that is wood from floor to ceiling. The walls are decorated with Cajun themed paintings, shrimp nets, and a variety of animals indigenous to the region. As I slowly take in everything around the room, it becomes clear to me that these people must keep a taxidermist on standby.

"Oh, my word! Cal Gage, you carry your little butt on down here and give Miss Nelly a big ole hug. Right now, young man!" a very large woman with short gray hair and a wooden spoon in her hand screams from the doorway of the kitchen.

I expect the entire restaurant to quiet down and

stare with bewilderment, but it's as if no one even notices the squeals coming from Miss Nelly. She swallows Cal in a bone-crushing embrace, smashing his cheek tightly into her bosom. She slowly rocks side to side. "Lord have mercy, I miss me some Cal Gage. How you been? You still at the college up the road, yeah?" She finally turns him loose, and Cal works to smooth his hair back into place.

"Yes, Miss Nelly. I'm still down the road. I want you to meet a friend of mine. Cheyenne…," Cal calls, extending his arm and waving me over.

I reluctantly head in that direction because I'm scared Miss Nelly will snap me in two if she hugs me like she hugged Cal.

"Mmmm. Mmmm. Mmmmmmmm. Aren't you just gorgeous? *Mais*, you prolly the prettiest person to pass through them doors. Cal, how a stinker like you manage to land a woman like her?"

"I ask myself the same thing every day," he says, smiling in my direction. I blush from the extra attention.

"Joel! Carry yourself out here for a sec. Come see who done popped in. Joel!"

"I'm right here, woman. What you goin' yelling for. You know I'm right behind that door right there. Always so loud…" He stops grumbling for a second. "Cal! How you been, son?" He grips Cal's hand for a shake before pulling him in tightly for a quick hug.

"I've been great. Cheyenne here is having a rough day, though. I believe a bowl of Miss Nelly's gumbo might be the right medicine."

"Sure fixed you up when you was down, didn't it?"

"It surely did many times. Miss Nelly's gumbo can cure anything from depression to the flu," Cal responds, his Cajun accent growing thicker by the second. Miss Nelly beams with pride.

"You two go grab a seat outside. The weather's perfect, and some sunshine will do you some good. You let God's light warm your outside, and soon enough, my gumbo's gonna be warming you on the inside. Nobody can feel bad after ingesting all that goodness!" Miss Nelly exclaims.

Cal pats Joel on the shoulder before moving towards a set of wooden doors at the rear of the restaurant. We're stopped briefly on the way out by Father Donnelly who is making his way to the front to pay his bill.

"I just left your dad's," he mentions. "He's looking pretty spry for an old geezer."

"Yeah? I'm glad he's having a good day. I'm bringing Cheyenne over to meet him once we leave here."

"Ah, he'll enjoy that. Here's a warning to you, missy. He acts rough and gruff, but he's nothing but an old softy," Father Donnelly offers. I give him a slight smile. "Well, I should get going. You two have a blessed day." Almost as an aside he mentions, "I'm here if you ever need to talk. I see the worry in your eyes, child. No judgment. I'm just here to help."

"Thank you, Father." I'm embarrassed because I'm obviously not doing a very good job of hiding my emotions. Father Donnelly nods towards Cal as he puts on his black felt hat and makes his way to the cashier. We continue through the wooden doors onto a veranda that overlooks the water. The entire area is a maze of tables and chairs, and Cal picks one in the far corner that offers the best view of a boat chugging down the river.

"Got the entire place to ourselves," he says, stretching his legs to the chair across from him while putting his hands behind his head. He leaves his position long enough to push a chair right beside his then he pats the seat. "Come on. Let's relax together."

I move from the chair I was sitting in to the one beside him, and he reaches around my shoulder to cradle me. Following his lead, I kick my feet up on the chair opposite me and settle into his embrace. "What if your dad can't give me the answers, Cal?"

"I've learned that nothing good ever comes from what-ifs."

"I suppose, but I feel like I'm teeter tottering on the edge of insanity. Nothing makes sense."

"You're not insane. Maybe you can't explain what happened yet, but don't even entertain that thought because that's not it."

"Do you believe in the paranormal?"

"I don't know. Why? Do you believe Ben's theory that a ghost possessed you and put those memories in your head?" he quips.

"So many strange things have happened since moving here, and Louisiana is known for being a paranormal hotspot. I thought you might have the inside scoop being you're from here. Is that stuff real? I thought it was just stories told to add to the ambience."

Cal kisses the top of my head. "I have lived here most of my life. I've been to supposedly haunted sites, I've visited a voodoo priestess, and I've even hidden out in a graveyard all night as a kid. I never saw anything; never witnessed anything. The power of suggestion is a very real tool that is often used to guide a person into thinking a certain way. Remember that fortune teller?"

"How can I forget?"

"She took a few simple things she observed, strung them together with some stupid rhyme, and she had you convinced she'd channeled one of your parents."

"What about the girl in red? How could she know about me seeing her?"

"Did she say the little girl in red who dances around in the courtyard below your apartment?"

"No," I answer.

"How many little girls wear red? Go to the store or any other public place and I bet you run into at least ten. It was just random and generic guesses that she made."

"Thank you." I offer him my lips for a kiss.

"You're welcome," he says, accepting my offer. I gasp and his brows furrow.

"The man who prays!" I say excitedly. "Do you think she was talking about Father Donnelly?"

Cal laughs. "Once again, how many people run into priests? There were no specifics. Cheyenne, I promise you, there is nothing accurate or foreboding about what she said. She probably tells the same rhyme to every person she comes across."

I settle back into his arms. "You're right. Ah, I hate this."

"Look. See that island way out there?" He points, and I see a cluster of trees a good ways in the distance that appear to emerge from the middle of the river. I nod. "I used to pretend like I was Huck Finn and paddle out to the island to play. I had a club house and everything."

"You did?"

"Yep, until my dad found out I was playing over there and put an end to it. He said it was far too dangerous for me to be exploring on my own."

"I have to agree with him. Weren't you scared at all? What if you'd gotten hurt?"

"Yep, that's pretty much the lecture I got from him, too. I used to dream that one day I'd build a house there."

"Why'd you give up on that dream?" I ask.

"Do you know what a bitch it would be get to work every morning by boat?"

I laugh. "So no bridges or ferries to get you across"

"Nope. Boat only."

"Wow. You were an adventurous young man."

"Nah, not really, just bored. Most of it was because I had to come up with ways to keep myself entertained. Unfortunately, most of them ended with phone calls to my dad. That's why I liked playing at the deserted island. No tattlers."

"I'm sure he appreciated those phone calls," I say playfully.

"Oh yeah. My butt got torn up more than once."

I laugh. "Your dad was a spanker, huh?"

"Yep. One or two good solid swats to the butt. Hurt my pride more than my ass. What Father Donnelly said about him is true. He's often brusque, but all in all he's a good man. The one thing I fear the most is letting him down."

His sentiment is so heartfelt that my breath catches in my chest. "I'm sure he's very proud of you, and there's no chance you could ever let him down."

Cal shrugs it off. The wooden doors open and Joel sets two steaming bowls of seafood gumbo, two large saucers of potato salad, and a basket of French bread before us. "Y'all enjoy," he says before disappearing through the doors once again.

I place my hand on top of Cal's. "Thank you for bringing me here. I needed this—a breather."

Cal smiles. I draw my hand back to dig into the food before me, and I easily finish every last bit of it.

"I'm going to get fat living here," I say, tempted to unbutton my jeans.

"We can work those calories off later," Cal replies, and I blush at the suggestion. Once he pays the bill and bids his farewells to Miss Nelly and Joel, we drive deeper into Frenchman's Cove. It only takes a few minutes to get to Cal's dad's house, a very simple structure tucked in a clearing at the end of a windy shell road that cuts through masses of thick foliage.

"Wow, it's nice and isolated out here," I remark.

"Yeah, Dad likes it because he's pretty much off the grid. You know, spiteful criminals, deranged lunatics... He didn't really need to worry about them finding us way out here. I guess I liked it, too. For me it was like growing up at a wilderness retreat."

"Ah, Huck Finn." I playfully pinch his cheek.

He points towards the bank at the rear of the property. "That's the very dock I'd take off from. I had my own boat and everything."

"How old were you?"

"Nine? Ten?"

"Oh, my goodness! You had your own boat at ten years old?"

"Doesn't every kid?" he asks with a teasing smile. "Come on. Time to meet Dad." He takes my hand as we climb the steps leading to the front door. Cal pounds on it, and though it takes a while, it finally opens.

"Cal, I wasn't expecting you today. Come on in, son." The door widens and we're led inside. The living room is as understated as the exterior. A simple sofa, a severely worn recliner, and a newspaper covered coffee table are the main furnishings. Aside from that, a desk butts up against a wall. A small flat screen TV is perched atop it, as is an antiquated PC with a fat monitor. Between the two is an 8x10 photo of a much younger Mr. Gage proudly wearing a law enforcement uniform while posing in front of an American flag. School photos of Cal, which are set in older, tarnished metal frames, litter the walls.

Mr. Gage appears to be a no-nonsense, laid back kind of guy, as evidenced by the green sweat suit and white socks he dons. He chomps on a cigar stub, and rolls it to the opposite side of his mouth when he asks, "Who's this?"

"Dad, this is Cheyenne. Cheyenne, this is my dad, Felton Gage."

"It's a pleasure to meet you, Mr. Gage."

"Felton," he rumbles.

"Felton," I repeat.

"You've been spending a lot of time with my boy lately, haven't you?"

I'm not quite sure if it's a statement or a question, but I go with question. "Yes, sir. I suppose I have."

"Good. He ain't been coming around here bugging me as much."

Knowing that Cal has talked about me with his dad makes me smile; however, Cal shifts uncomfortably on the sofa. "Dad, I was wondering if you could help us with something. It's about one of the old cases you worked—the Nuit Rouge murders."

Felton's cigar stub shifts back to the other side of his mouth. "What about it?"

"Let me start with a hypothetical," Cal suggests. Felton shrugs. "Let's say someone who has never been inside Azalea Downs shows up there and instantly knows the floor plan and details about the murders. How do you suppose he or she would know such things?"

"I'd suppose it was one of those conspiracy theorists running around out there drudging up drama where none exists anymore. The case was solved, the guilty are gone, and even so, you have these fools running around trying to make something where there is nothing."

"But what if it wasn't someone who studied all of that?"

He thinks for a while. "Maybe the person saw a write up or something? I know there are some people out there who reported on it, wrote about it, studied it and such."

Cal looks in my direction, and I give him a shrug.

"What's going on here? Why are we bringing up something that happened over thirty years ago?"

Felton asks.

I speak up, "I'm from Oklahoma, born and raised. I've never been to Louisiana before I moved her; however, when we visited Azalea Downs, there was an incident."

"Incident? What kind of incident?" Felton asks. The expression on his face never changes.

"I'm not exactly sure how to explain what happened, other than it was like I was seeing a rapid progression of photographs or like watching a movie of the carnage. I saw where the bodies were positioned, the blood, and it ended with a dark closet upstairs. After that, I came to, or whatever."

Felton gives me a hard stare. "Weird. Do you normally have an overactive imagination?"

I'm stunned by his abruptness. "Uh, I, no."

"Tell me what you think you saw," he demands with a skeptical tone.

Somewhat reluctantly, I relay my visions of the grand ball room, the piano player who was shot in the head, as well as the slew of other victims. I tell him about the man and woman separated from the rest of the group in the parlor, going so far as to mention the dress and jewelry she wore. He sits back in his recliner and taps the cigar nub to his lower lip that is now stretched out by a scant smile.

"Well, little lady, I can put your mind at ease right this very second. You didn't see the crime scene," he grumbles.

"I didn't? But it was so vivid. And the floorplan…"

"All of the bodies were in one room, the ball room. I don't recall anyone wearing a white dress that night, either. Granted, I can't be sure unless I pore through the case file again, but the things you've described so far don't match anything I recall from the scene."

"Really?" I ask. Part of me is relieved, but a larger part is confused. "So where did those images come from?"

"You been watching a lot of movies or those criminal TV shows?" Felton asks.

"No sir. I rarely watch... well, I have, but I don't see how it would cause me to black out, experience those images, and such. Nightmares, I'd understand. This, I'm so confused," I sigh heavily.

"Has this ever happened before?" Felton prompts.

"No."

"Have you had anything like it happen since? Do you get any vibes or images sitting in my house?" he asked in a somewhat patronizing fashion.

I slowly look around, almost embarrassed by his tone. "No."

He sits back on the edge of his seat. "Then listen to me, and please take my advice. In the course of my life I've experienced so many mysterious occurrences that hearing just a few of them would make your head spin. Forget about it. Sometimes things just happen, and we don't know the logical explanation. If it was happening all of the time, I'd say you might have something that needs to be looked into further. Being that the information is inaccurate, and it never happened to you before, just let it go."

"But the floor plan? How could I know that?"

"Always with the questions and answers. You young people always gotta be in the know. Look, it's simple. Them old houses, they're all pretty much the same on the inside. Cal told me y'all went to visit with Milly not too long ago. Isn't her floor plan similar?"

"I suppose it's sort of similar," I concede.

"And there you go," he says, smacking the arm of his recliner to drive the point home. "Case solved! Damn, I'm good. Still got it after all these years. Plus, there are pictures of the damned house all over the place. I could poll twenty people right now and I guarantee you at least fifteen have seen photos of Azalea Downs."

I'm still uncertain, but I jump at the explanation because continuing to delve into the unexplained is making my head hurt, not to mention I'm scared to get on the old man's nerves. If this is his normal behavior, I'd hate to see him pissed off. "Thank you for your help, Felton. I feel better now."

"Good. Nine times out of ten, there's a logical explanation. That other time, there's something logical there, we just haven't figured out what it is yet. Just shrug it off or you'll run yourself mad. So, what you kids got planned for the rest of the day?"

"We haven't really discussed it," Cal says, looking my way. I shrug.

"How 'bout we take a ride to the riverfront to see JuJune. He just opened the seafood market back up, and I'll get some shrimp, oysters, and catfish to fry. He might even have some soft-shell crabs, too," Felton says.

"Dad, we'd like to, but we're still stuffed from Miss Nelly's. Rain check?"

Felton nods. "Just as well. The Padre was over earlier. Brought me a care package from Widow Eastland."

"You need anything before we go, Dad? Did you remember to take your meds?"

"Yes, I took my damn meds. I keep telling you I'm not an invalid. I'm fine. You two get on out of here, and come back next weekend with empty bellies, you hear?"

Cal nods his head. "Okay, we'll see you next weekend. Call me if you need anything before then."

"Yeah. Yeah. Yeah. Get going."

"It was nice to meet you, Felton. Thank you for the help and the advice."

"My pleasure, sweetheart. Glad you ain't a looney tune. I was kinda worried about that for a while. See you next weekend."

I'm taken aback once again, but I manage to eke out, "Should I bring anything?"

"Yes. An empty belly. I thought we'd been through this already," he says, waving us out the door. "Go! Go!"

Once we've been on the road a while, I prop my head against the car window and take in the sights all around me. Cal holds my hand, his thumb softly stroking the area between my thumb and forefinger. I decide to take Felton's advice and try to not give the incident anymore thought. It was a fluke, and the chances of something like that happening again are slim to none. It's time to move forward. The first thing that pops in my mind is how badly I want Cal to stay the night with me. A smile creeps across my face.

"Penny for your thoughts," Cal requests.

A devious smirk crosses my lips. "How about I show you what I'm thinking about?" I move my hand across the center console to rest on his thigh. He tenses immediately. As I slowly run it up his leg, he begins to push back against his seat.

"Okay, I got it. Stop before you cause a wreck," he warns. I laugh at his reaction, and take heed of his warning. I watch as the speedometer begins to creep upwards, and I'm happy to know that Cal has the same thought as me—let's get home as fast as we can.

RHONDA R. DENNIS

EIGHT

Trying to get back into the swing of things is harder than I thought it would be. The mysterious roses continue to appear, but the person leaving them has gotten more cautious about placing them. They are no longer around my apartment, but further away being placed on my car instead. One was tucked in a windshield wiper blade, one in a door handle, and another on the roof. Not sure what else to do, I penned a note asking to please be left alone.

Instead of deterring my creepy admirer, it must've served as inspiration because now along with the flowers, I'm left messages. Well, not necessarily letters, but unsigned greeting cards, magazine cut outs, and most recently, a huge heart-shaped Mylar balloon tied to my side view mirror. My arms are loaded with papers and books when I notice it gently swaying in the breeze. Chucking my bundle onto the hood of the car, I use my house key to pop it before throwing it into the trash. Agnes' silhouette darkens one of the upper windows, and a chill runs through my spine. I shake it off and start the commute to the SOU campus.

The car behind me didn't raise any red flags originally. It's not until it parks a few spots away from mine when I stop for a cup of coffee that I take notice. While waiting for the cashier to ring up my purchase, I anxiously shift back and forth trying to remember how long the car has been following me, but then I shake it off. *I'm being paranoid. No one is following me. No one is trying to get me. I have a secret admirer who is most likely a love-sick student. It's not the first time that's happened. Stay calm. Relax. You're fine.*

The car is behind me again once I resume the commute. Now I'm starting to get very anxious. I suddenly take a right into a residential neighborhood that takes me away from the campus. The car follows. Huge knots form simultaneously in my throat and stomach. Reaching for my phone, I dial Cal.

"Good morning, beautiful," he says in a sultry voice.

"Cal, someone is following me," I blurt out with panic.

"What? Go straight to the police station. Now." His commands are laced with urgency.

"I will if I can find my way back to one of the main roads. I tried to get rid of him by going into a residential neighborhood, but now I'm lost."

"What street are you on? What does this car look like? What does the person driving it look like?"

"I'm on Greenbrush Street—the five hundred block. I'm going north. The car is dark blue with tinted windows, and I don't know who's driving it. Cal, I'm scared."

"Listen to me. Greenbush is going to intersect with Cypress Street. Take a right on Cypress, and it'll put you back on the main highway."

"Okay," I say, trying to hold as much of the panic as possible at bay. I find Cypress Street and take the right as Cal suggests. Fighting the urge to floor it, I glance in my rearview mirror. He's still there, a few car lengths back. "Cal, I found a cop. He's loading gear into his car. I'm going to pull into his driveway."

"Okay. Please be careful. Call me to let me know what's going on."

"I will. I'll call you back." I hit the disconnect button as I swing into the officer's driveway. He gives me a questioning look, but I don't notice it for long. My eyes are on my rearview mirror and the dark blue car that cruises by slowly. Damn the tinted windows!

I'm startled further by a rap at my window. The tall, lean officer has an on-guard stance while waiting for me to put down my window. He wears a dark brown uniform, his auburn hair is in a flat-top, and he has a self-assured air about him. "I'm sorry. I don't mean to intrude, but that car—the blue one—I think the driver was following me."

He looks down the street and has to squint to see the car because it's so far away. Suddenly, I begin to doubt myself. Maybe the car wasn't following me. Was it all coincidence?

"Did the driver of the vehicle do anything aggressive like try to veer you off the road, display signs of road rage, make threats, or something along those lines?"

"No, sir. The person simply followed me, staying a few car lengths back the majority of the time."

"What makes you believe the car was following you?"

"When I stopped for coffee, the person waited in the parking lot until I came out and then got behind me again. When I turned into this residential area, the person turned, too."

The police officer looks at me with uncertainty. "Has this happened before?"

"No, sir. This is the first time. Look, I didn't know what else to do. I teach at the university, and I was on my way to work when I noticed the car..."

"You did the right thing, but you won't always have a member of law enforcement available on the route you're taking. Call 911 next time so they can put someone on it immediately. I'm about to go on patrol, so I'll keep an eye out for this blue car. Can you give me any other description or identifying features of the vehicle? It was pretty far away when I saw it, so I couldn't place the make or model."

"No, sir. I'm not good at identifying car brands, makes, or models. I know that the windows were tinted, and it wasn't a brand new car. It was a larger sedan. Other than that, I'm sorry, I can't think of anything else to help identify it."

He rubs his jaw. "Yeah, that doesn't really give me much to go on. Look, here's my card." Velcro snaps as he pulls open the flap of his chest pocket. After fishing out a business card, he passes it through my window. "If you see it again, or if you feel you're being followed, try to get a better description and call it in. The department's emergency number is on the card, too."

"Thank you, officer," I say.

"Actually, it's Major Collins. And you are?"

"Cheyenne Douglas." No doubt he'll be running a background check later. I feel an overwhelming urge to ramble, but I work hard to contain it. He simply looks down at me with the same look he has had since the beginning—cautiously inquisitive.

"I'll tell you what, Cheyenne. I'll follow you to the campus just to be sure this blue car doesn't pop back up. If it's legit, the person could be waiting at the end of the street for you. If he follows, I'll pull him over. Do not stop. You keep going to work, and I'll call you with the details afterwards. What department are you in?"

"English," I answer.

He nods. "Let's get you to work. You lead the way, and I'll hang back a little. Even if you don't see me, I promise I'm on top of things."

I nod, feeling somewhat relieved. "Thank you, Major Collins."

"No problem," he says, backing away from my car so he can get into his cruiser. I leave first, and I don't see him again until he pulls up behind me once I'm in my parking spot on campus. The strong desire to profusely apologize overwhelms me when I get out of my car.

"I'm so sorry. I didn't see him, and maybe I'm losing my mind. I don't know. I'm so sorry I wasted your time, Major Collins..."

He holds up a hand. "Just because he wasn't there this time doesn't mean it didn't happen. Stay diligent, and call if you notice it again."

I nod. "Thank you for all your help."

"That's what we're here for, ma'am. Have a nice day, and stay safe."

"You, too." With that he's gone to serve and protect someone else. I'm much calmer when I finally make it to my office, but Cal is not. He's rapidly pacing back and forth when I enter the room.

"Are you okay? Did they catch him? Who was it?"

"I'm fine. No. We still don't know."

Cal lets out a heavy sigh. "This stuff is getting out of control. I know you think the secret admirer stuff is harmless and innocent, but I think it's getting creepy."

I put my load onto the desk then make my way to him. Taking his face in my palm, I say, "You're a good looking guy. I find it very hard to believe that you've never had a student admirer."

"Even old Hughley gets love notes every now and then. We all do. I guess it's an authority thing or something? None have gone this far for us. What has you so convinced it's a student?"

"Think about it. The roses are always from the garden. They're free, so the person probably doesn't have much money, and frankly, a lot of the stuff is juvenile. Kittens on cards, Mylar balloons…" Cal shoots me a questioning glance. "That was today—a gorilla that says he's bananas about me." Cal shakes his head. "It's a kid, Cal. Has to be."

"But the car?"

"I don't know. However, Major Collins has given me his card so I can call if it ever happens again, and he escorted me to campus with no incident. Maybe I imagined it all."

"I doubt that," Cal says.

"Well, I wrongfully witnessed the carnage of a famous murder scene too, recently. Remember?"

"You need to move past that," Cal encourages.

"Believe me, I'm trying." I say, shuffling some papers around in search of what I need for my upcoming class. "Now, I get to be scowled at by Billy, the sweet little ray of sunshine who makes my days even more delightful." My tone is facetious.

"Don't let him get to you," Cal suggests.

"I'll do my best," I return, giving him a quick peck before heading to the classroom.

Billy is extra snide and ornery, so much so that I send him away because of how disruptive he's being to the class. Before he parts, I slam him with a two thousand word essay on the importance of classroom decorum. He tosses up both middle fingers as he leaves the room, but I pretend not to notice. The students are restless for a little while after the disruption, but soon, class returns to normal.

I'm so backed up on paperwork that when Cal slides into my office doing a happy dance because the work day is done, I send him away, too. Well, I don't send him right out of the door. There is some exchange of affection before he finally leaves me to finish up my work. He asks that I call upon arriving home, and I promise to do so.

It's well after dark, and I suddenly realize how spooky the old building truly is, especially when I'm alone. The sounds of keys clanking and the squeaking of the janitor's cart are reassuring as Odell makes his way down the hall—I'm not entirely alone in the eerie place. Door creaks open, the cart squeaks, shuffling, door closes, repeat. The sound finally reaches outside my office.

"Hope ya not pullin' an all-nighter," Odell says with a nearly toothless grin.

"No, not an all-nighter. Those days are over for me."

"Good to know," he says, dumping the contents of my garbage can into a large plastic bag fastened to his cart. "How you likin' da area?" he asks with a thick Cajun accent.

"I'm really enjoying it. The area is beautiful, the people are friendly… It's nice."

"Been on any of them gator swamp tours? My cousin runs a boat out dat way if ya wanna go."

"No, no gator swamp tours. I've toured some plantations, though."

"Yeah, they got some right nice houses 'round here. My great grandpap worked as an overseer at Azalea Downs. Pity about all them tragedies dat place done had on them grounds. You couldn't pay me to go in dat place."

"Are you referring to the Nuit Rouge murders?" I ask, closing my laptop so I can give him my undivided attention. He uses this as an invitation to take a seat across from me. He pulls his chair as close to my desk as possible and leans in closely as if he's telling a secret.

"Oh no, honey. Da tragedy started long before them murders. Every family who ever owned that house had some major *gris gris* put upon them. Dat place is cursed, I tell you."

"*Gris gris*?" I ask.

"You know—bad ju ju?"

I nod. "Like what kinds of tragedies happened there?"

"Like the people who built the house. The wife caught her husband with one of the slaves. She slit her husband's throat while he slept then the very next day, she beat the slave girl to death with a cast iron skillet. They locked her away in the attic, and the owner's brother took over the estate from there. Things ain't worked out good for him, either. Murdered after getting caught cheating at cards. Died right in one of them fancy parlor rooms. The property was sold to the Jasper family, and the pregnant wife took a tumble down the steps. Snapped her neck clean. Both her and the baby died, and the husband was so grief-stricken they found him hanging inside the nursery."

I slowly shake my head. "That's so sad."

"That ain't all of it!"

"I'm sure it's not. Thank you for sharing the stories, but I think I've heard enough for tonight," I say, suddenly queasy.

"I hear ya, but if you ever get curious about the rest of the story, it's all in the library."

"The library here?"

"Sure 'nuff. I always save the library last for cleanin'. They got a lot of good stuff in there."

I smile. "Most libraries do."

"Yeah, but this one's extra special. Got them things with the tiny people and stuff in the glass cases and all. Yep, it's right nice in there. Almost like a museum. It's even two whole stories!"

"I'm embarrassed to say I haven't been yet."

"It's okay, Miss Douglas. You been busy settling in and such. You'll get to it when the time's right."

"Thank you for the information, Odell. Well, I suppose I should get going. It's getting late," I say, glancing at my watch. Nine fifteen.

"I'll get campus police to send someone over

to walk you to your car," he says, reaching for his portable radio.

"No need," I say, reaching for the sweater draped across the back of my chair. Looking out the window as I put it on, I notice Billy sitting on a bench in the quad thanks to the ambient light coming from one of the nearby lamp posts. As soon as he knows he's caught my eye, he bends down to pick up a poster board. Flashing it in my direction, I read "Decorum Sux Azz." I go to my supply closet and pull out a poster board of my own. In red marker I write, "Decorum Sucks Ass" before holding it up for him to see. "Yeah, you might as well get them coming this way," I say as Odell leaves the room.

"You got it Miss Douglas."

It's time for me to handle this situation with Billy Thibodeaux once and for all. I flip the sign and write, "8 AM. My office. BE HERE!" He indignantly takes off towards the men's dorms.

I meet up with the campus police officer as I'm locking my office door, and he is courteous and polite while escorting me to my car. Once I'm safely inside, he taps on my roof and yells through my window, "Be safe and have a good night."

I give him a wave once I've reversed from my spot and put the car into drive. The ride home is pretty uneventful. I continually peer into my rearview mirror, anxiously awaiting the glare of bright headlights, but none come. The roads are basically deserted, and I'm finally starting to relax when I make it up the stairs and into my apartment. I should have left well enough alone. Taking one last peek outside, I notice Agnes peering from her usual spot. When I look down into the courtyard, that's when I see it—the little red dress shimmying through the courtyard. Getting angry instead of scared, I decide to figure out once and for all what is going on, but first I need a light.

I fling the door open, but as soon as I do, the girl disappears. I race down the stairs then stop so I can listen for any clue as to in which direction she went. It's eerily quiet, and the only sound aside from my beating heart is my heavy breathing. Then I hear a click. My once wide open apartment door is now shut. That fear I'd evaded earlier grips me like a vice. Everything is inside. My purse, my keys, my PHONE, A STRANGER!

Swallowing hard, I slowly make my way up the stairs, listening acutely for any sounds from inside the apartment. I try to peek through the closed blinds, but see absolutely nothing. At that moment I'm thankful the blinds work so well, yet also disheartened because I have no clue if someone is inside. Taking a slow, deep breath, I carefully open the door. My phone is now within reach. Getting a dose of bravery, I slowly pull my body inside the apartment until I hear a massive *KA-THUNK*! I grab my phone and rush down the steps as I try to find Major Collins' number in my contact list.

"Hello, Major Collins?" I ask in a sort of a breathy whisper.

"Who is this?" he asks.

"Cheyenne Douglas from this morning. Remember? I pulled up at your house."

"Yeah, you tend to remember things like that, especially when they happened less than twenty four hours ago."

"I'm sorry, but it's really urgent."

"Is the car back?" he asks.

"No, but I think someone's inside my apartment," I whisper.

"Didn't I tell you to call 911 if it's an emergency?" he fusses.

"I'm sorry."

"Don't be sorry. I started heading your way as soon as you called. I'm almost there. Where exactly are you right now?"

"I'm near the stairs of my apartment. I'm hiding in the shadows. Wait, how do you know where I live?"

"You show up at my house and tell me you're being followed. Did you honestly think I wasn't going to check into the story?"

"Oh, okay. I guess that makes sense."

"I'm pulling up to the house now. You aren't armed are you?" he asks.

"No, why?"

"Some people have itchy trigger fingers. Can't be too careful. I'm coming around the corner."

He's so stealthy that I don't even see him until he's practically standing beside me. "Tell me exactly what's going on," he whispers.

"I thought I saw something or someone in the courtyard, so I ran to get a flashlight to check it out, but I couldn't find anything. While I was looking around out here, I heard the door close. Sure enough, when I went upstairs it was latched shut. I went up there…"

"You went up there after hearing it close?"

"What if it was the wind or something? Plus, I didn't have my phone." He points to the George and Agnes' house. I shake my head. "I'd rather take my chances with the burglar. Have you heard what those people did?"

Major Collins shakes his head. "So you saw someone while you were up there and ran out?"

"No, I heard something crash to the floor in the bedroom and then I grabbed my phone and ran out."

"Bedroom is where?" he asks. I give him a very brief rundown of the apartment's layout. "Stay here." Back in full stealth mode, he slowly makes his way up the stairs, hugging the wall as he goes. His gun is drawn, but he keeps it lowered as he ascends. Once he reaches the top landing, he extends his arm to the side and keeps his body low as he turns the knob and pushes the door open. Gun at the ready, he makes a sweeping motion as he enters the apartment. I lose sight of him not long afterwards. What seems like an eternity goes by before I hear, "SON OF A BITCH!" A wailing tan and white tabby cat rockets down the stairs, flies past me, and keeps going until it's no longer visible.

"Your demonic cat got out," he says, wiping at some bloody scratches on his forearm.

"That wasn't my cat. I have no pets."

"Well, that was your perpetrator. The apartment is clear—of humans, at least."

I let out a sigh of relief. "Thank you so much, Major Collins. Why don't you come inside, and I'll get something for those scratches?" He looks down at his injuries and starts upstairs. Taking a seat at the kitchen counter, he patiently waits while I retrieve the first aid kit.

I find some cotton balls, peroxide, antibacterial ointment, a roll of gauze, and some tape. Once everything is in place, I carefully dab at the injured arm. "Why do you think someone's stalking you?" he inquires abruptly.

"I wish I knew."

"Any jilted boyfriends? Angry relatives? Maybe an ex-husband hell bent on knowing where you are since you left town?"

I put down the cotton ball. "I take it you know about Luke?"

"I do."

I shake my head. "I don't think it's him. He's never tried to contact me, so why would he start now? And who would he get to come all the way to Louisiana to do it?"

"Just exploring the possibilities."

"Relatives?"

"I have none. My parents were pretty much my life until they died. Now I'm starting over again—alone."

Major Collins nods. "You've been here for a few months now. Anyone local come to mind?"

"As far as I know there is only one local person who has an issue with me—a student named Billy Thibodeaux. He's never actually threatened me, but he has a serious attitude problem and is incredibly disrespectful."

"What did you do to piss him off?" he asks.

"I wish I knew."

"Oh, and there is someone on the other end of the spectrum. I have a secret admirer who leaves roses, cards, and most recently balloons."

"And I suppose you have no clue who this admirer might be?" Major Collins inquires. I shake my head. "You know, that's quite a bit of drama for someone who's only been here for a few months."

Good thing I didn't tell him about the ghost girl in the courtyard. "Yes sir, I suppose it is. I've only dated one person since arriving, and we're still together. I'm thinking it could possibly be a student who is too shy to come forward."

"It's a good possibility." He looks at the bandaged arm. "Thank you for fixing me up. You have my number. Use it anytime you need, but if it's something that's possibly life threatening, PLEASE call the emergency number. I'm out in the boat a lot, or I could possibly be on another call… You just never know, and I don't want any delay in getting help to you, okay?"

I nod. "Thank you for coming."

"You're welcome. Have a good night, and lock up tight. Not later, now, as soon as I leave."

I smile. "I will."

"I'm serious. I want to hear that deadbolt latch."

This time I chuckle. "Got it. Good night, Major Collins."

"Brant. I think we've graduated to a first name basis."

"Agreed. Good night." I close the door and turn the latch into place as requested. I hear Brant trudge down the steps and then stop abruptly. My cell phone rings.

"What's up with the creepy lady in the window?" he asks once I answer.

"That's Agnes. She's always in the window."

"Maybe she's seen your admirer?"

"She's incoherent."

"Then what in the hell is she doing looking out

of the window?"

"I often wonder the same," I say with a smile.

"Fine. Night."

"Night." I disconnect from the call and run a bath. Not convinced that hot water and aromatherapy bubbles will be enough, I pour a glass of moscato to the brim. I sink into the heavenly liquid and wait for the relaxation to begin.

NINE

"Billy, this is Professor Gage, and he's going to sit in with us during this meeting," I say with as stern and authoritative a voice as I can muster.

"Yeah, cool. Whatever," he says, propping his combat booted foot on my desk. Cal knocks it off.

"Sit up straight," Cal warns. Billy shifts slightly in his seat.

"You realize you don't have to be here, right?" I ask.

"I don't? Well, see ya," he says, trying to jump from his seat. I push him back down.

"Not so fast. By here I mean on campus. In school. Particularly, my class. It's very evident that you have an issue so why don't you drop?"

He rolls his eyes. "Because my stupid advisor says I need technical writing for my degree. Believe me, if there was someone else, I'd be there, but you're it, lady."

"So what happens if I fail you?" I ask.

"I do my work. You have no grounds to fail me."

"Subpar."

"Enough."

"No, not really. Participation is a major part

of your grade."

"What does it matter if I participate if I'm getting the work done and I'm doing it well enough to pass?" Billy argues.

"Let's just get right to it. Do you have this issue with all of your teachers, or is it just with me?" I question.

"I have an issue with most authoritarians."

Sighing, I lean back against my chair. "We need to fix this problem because my next step is to remove you from my class—permanently."

"You can't do that. I won't get credit, and I won't graduate."

"Then I guess you'd better suck it up and play nice," I suggest.

"You wouldn't keep me from graduating," he says with a smirk.

"No, I won't, but your behavior might. I believe you owe me a paper on classroom etiquette."

He stares me down. Refusing to budge, I expectantly raise my brows. The room remains silent until he finally relents and pulls a stack of papers from his backpack and tosses them onto my desk. He pouts.

"Look Billy, I'm willing to give this another go. Lose the attitude, participate every once in a while, and keep up with the assignments. Do that, and you'll pass. There's not a whole lot of time left until the semester is over and then you can go on your merry way, and we'll never have to see each other again."

He glares again. My expression is steadfast. "I will fail you if need be. If you are checking to see what my limit is, you've already passed it. You're lucky I believe in second chances." Giving it some thought, he nods.

"This isn't a victory for you," he asserts.

"I never considered it to be. Believe it or not, I want you to pass."

"Whatever. Can I go?"

I nod towards the door, and he's gone in an instant.

"Wow, that kid's got some issues," Cal says, rubbing his beard.

"Do you think I handled the situation okay?" I query.

"I think so. You stood firm and made it known that you weren't going to tolerate his shit anymore."

"Think it sunk in?"

"Time will tell. So, how was your night?"

I push my chair away from my desk. "Crazy." I give him a brief rundown of the events, and he crosses his arms.

"Why didn't you call me?" he asks, and I'm not sure if he's angry or hurt.

"It was so late by the time Major Collins left that I decided to wait until today to fill you in. There's nothing you could have done at that point anyway."

"I could've come over."

"I suppose you could've, but for what? To protect me from the psychotic cat?"

He shuts the door before pushing his body close to mine. "Psychotic cats are no joking matter. Feral felines kill."

I laugh. "Do they now? I wasn't aware."

"Knowledge is a powerful thing."

"So how many deaths do you figure are attributed to these feral felines yearly?"

"Hundreds. Maybe thousands."

"Ah."

"Yes, they run a close second to baboon bites."

I wince. "Yes, I hear that's reached epidemic proportions."

"I wanna…"

I stop him before he can say it. "Just do it," I say, pushing myself into his arms. He kisses me passionately before smoothing his shirt, straightening his tie, and whistling a tune as he casually struts out of my office and down the hall. Gathering my things, I head for my class.

I'm in the grocery store making my way through the aisles like I'm on a game show. Quickly running through the list in my mind, I toss items into the buggy without so much as slowing down once I find them. Each makes a satisfying *clink* as it lands in the basket, like an audible score keeper. *Clink.* One point. *Clink, clink, clink.* Plus three! The crowd goes wild! Okay, it's nowhere near that exciting, but regardless, I'm hustling.

Clink, clink. Two cans of cream of mushroom soup. Then the basket goes *BAM!,* and I nearly hit the floor from the collision. Who would be at the other end of the offending basket? None other than Richie the sleezeball furniture salesman.

"Hey, if you want to knock me off my feet, never fear. Your beauty has already done so many times over," he says with an assured smile.

"We've seen each other twice, once when I

bought furniture from you. How could it happen repeatedly?" I ask with annoyance.

He leans in closely, "Cause you're in my dreams every night."

"Richie, what part of I'm not interested did you not understand?"

"I know you've been seeing people, so why not let me show you what a gentleman I can be?"

"Who I see is none of your business, and what does it matter to you anyway?"

"Small town. People talk. You shouldn't settle by dating only one man. You should play the field."

"I'm very uncomfortable with this conversation, Richie..."

"Maybe you should consider pluralizing so you have something to compare the professor to."

"I have no interest in 'pluralizing,' and do others seriously sit around talking about my relationship with Cal?"

"Pretty much. Been boring 'round here lately."

"Wow. Okay. Look, Richie. I'm flattered, but I assure you, I'm not the one for you. What about her?" I ask, pointing to the first woman I see.

"Married."

"Or her," I ask of the woman standing near the meat case.

"Been there. Done that. Couldn't handle my virility."

I shudder. "What about her?" I ask, pointing to a woman in leopard print pants and tiger striped shirt with an exposed shoulder.

"Oh, yeah," he says, biting his lower lip. "She

looks like someone who's looking for someone to tame her. Love them wild ones. I'll catch you later, Pocahontas."

I don't know if he's referring to my heritage or if he truly doesn't know my name, but regardless, I'm thrilled he's set his sights elsewhere. I get my stride back, and before I know it, I'm home unpacking the groceries. Cal knocks on the door, and when I open it he surprises me with a dozen roses. "Not picked from the bushes outside," he jokes.

"Thank you so much," I say, placing the vase on the counter before taking in the roses' delicate scent.

"It's been a hell of a day. I'm whooped." He stretches, yawns, and then plops onto the sofa with the TV remote. "What's for dinner?"

"Is this a fast forward into our future?" I joke.

He peeks over the arm of the sofa. "Do you mind? I kinda thought we were far enough along in our relationship that…"

"Stop. I'm picking. Besides, if it were the future, you'd be cooking for me."

"You'll be very disappointed and probably very thin if you're depending on my cooking to see us through."

"Isn't there a culinary school nearby?"

"Why go to culinary school if I have you?" I toss a dishtowel at his head. He catches it and still laughing at his quip, brings it into the kitchen, wraps it around my waist, and pulls me to him. "You're the only woman I'd go to culinary school for."

"That's a serious commitment. How does the old rhyme go? Cal and Cheyenne sittin' in a tree. K-I-S-S-I-N-G. First comes culinary school?"

"I think it's love."

"It is; I was just teasing."

"No, Cheyenne. I think it's love between us. I'm telling you that I love you." My breath catches. He always gets me when I least expect it! "Wait! Don't say anything." He scribbles on my scratchpad then turns it so I can see. *Do you love me? Circle one. Yes or No.* Smiling broadly I take the pen from him and circle *Yes.* "Yeah?" he asks. I nod, taking a sip from my wine glass. "Well, alright then. We're in love. Wanna get married?"

I choke on my drink and fight to keep wine from shooting through my nose. "Too soon for that joke?" he asks.

I nod as he pats my back. I fill a glass with water and after a few sips, homeostasis is restored.

"Hey, pretty lady. How about I take you out for dinner tonight?"

"I'd like that. Just give me a few minutes to change."

"Well, if you're going to be in there all naked and such," he says following towards the bedroom. I shut the door in his face.

"I thought you loved me," he whimpers.

I open the door a crack. "I do. I'll show you exactly how much later tonight. But as of right now, I'm starved, and if I let you in this room... well, we both know how that will end."

"Yeah, I'll be sated, and you'll be starving."

"We'll be sated, and I'll be starving. Nonetheless, go away."

"Kiss me?"

"Yes, but that's it. One quick kiss."

It wasn't a quick kiss, but I do manage to get

dressed and we get out the door for dinner at a reasonable hour. After a delicious meal with playful and fun banter, I'm completely relaxed when we return to my apartment. I fall asleep in Cal's arms, and all is right with the world—at least until the dream spoils my restful sleep.

The entire scene I saw inside Azalea Downs replays in my dream. The carnage, the blood, the bodies. The lady in white, the man whose face I can't see. It's different this time in that instead of gasping for air, it appears as though the woman in white is trying to tell me something. There is no sound, and as hard as I try, I can't read her lips. Growing frustrated, I take off up the stairs and take refuge in the dark closet. Just like the first time I had the vision, going into the closet pulls me from the nightmare. My eyes fly open and I'm a panting, shaky mess.

"What happened? Are you okay?" Cal asks, reaching out to hold me. "It's okay," he says soothingly as he lightly kisses the top of my head. "Was it a nightmare?"

I nod.

"You're safe, sweetheart. I'm here."

"I was in the house again, Cal. It's all so vivid. Why do I keep having these visions? It doesn't make sense. Your dad said it didn't correlate with the actual crime scene, so why do I keep seeing these things?"

"I don't know. I wish I did, because I'd do anything to make them stop. Just remember, it's not real."

I nod. "I know, but it's still frightening and disturbing."

"I'm sure it is. Here, lie back down," he says,

softly stroking my arm. Slowly, I feel the tension leave my body, and before long, I'm able to fall asleep once again.

The dream hinders my sleep for nearly a week straight. Each time, an extra detail emerges, none of which make any sense to me. A vase full of peacock feathers in the corner of the parlor appeared in one dream. A thick gold band with intricate scroll work appears on the hand of the faceless man in another. The black haired woman desperately tries to tell me something, but there is no sound to my dreams, much like watching a silent film. The newest addition is a white square of cloth with yarn fringes. Perhaps the woman in white's shawl or wrap? I need answers.

Cal and I arrive at Felton's for another seafood feast Felton insisted on having, and I'm relieved to have the opportunity to run the new details by him. If one of these things is accurate, then it will lend credence as to why I'm having these dreams. If not, then I'm stuck trying to figure out why my psyche insists on replaying a false crime scene over and over. Either way, I feel a therapy appointment is inevitable.

Cal's tending to the cooking device on the back porch, a propane fueled burner with an extra large frying pan on top, while I join Felton in the kitchen. He's battering the seafood assortment with a highly seasoned cornmeal based breading.

"Thanks for having us over again. I enjoyed the last dinner immensely," I say as an icebreaker once we're alone.

"Yeah, it's good for me, too. Usually it's a bowl of cereal or a sandwich—something quick and easy, ya know?"

"I do. Single life."

"It doesn't appear that you're so single anymore," he mentions, nodding his head towards the back porch.

I smile. "I guess not."

"He's a good boy."

"Yes, he is. I didn't come to Louisiana anticipating a relationship, just a change of scenery. Meeting Cal has turned out to be better therapy for me than the move."

"Therapy?" he asks.

"I had a hard time dealing with the death of my parents. I needed to get away from Oklahoma because there were too many reminders."

He nods. "Understandable."

"Felton, I have some more questions about the Nuit Rouge murders."

He stops what he's doing to look at me. "More?"

"Yes. I've started dreaming about it, and the dreams are so vivid that I'm remembering more details. I don't mean remembering, of course, but it's how it appears to me in the dreams."

"I'm confused. What is it with you and the murders? Are you sure you didn't overhear your parents discussing it when you were younger or something? Maybe they knew one of the victims?"

"No, our family has no ties to Louisiana whatsoever. I was relieved when you told me my visions weren't accurate, because I thought that would be the end of it, but..."

He stops what he's doing and pats off the cornmeal coating his hands. "Okay, what's new?

Let's see if we can put an end to this once and for all, or else we're going to have to get you down to New Orleans to get them spirits outta you."

"Possession? Ben at Azalea Downs mentioned something about that. You don't believe in that stuff, do you?" I ask, swallowing hard.

"I believe that anything's possible, but relax. I don't think you're possessed. An overactive imagination is still my guess. Lay the new details on me, and we'll try to get this sorted out." He gives me his undivided attention.

"Okay. Peacock feathers in a vase."

Felton looks deep in thought for a while. "I can't say that I recall a vase with peacock feathers, but remember, this was a long time ago, and that's not really the kind of thing you remember from a crime scene like that. What else?"

"A gold band on a guy's finger."

"I'm sure most of the guys had gold bands on their fingers. Most were married couples."

"This one had some kind of scrollwork. It was a unique pattern that made it different from most."

Felton shrugs. "I don't think I'd put too much stock in that one."

"The black haired woman keeps trying to tell me something, but I can't make out what it is, and there was this white fringed shawl or something. I saw that in my dream, too."

"Again, a shawl would be something expected at the scene. They were all dressed up for a party. Darling, I think you're worrying yourself for nothing. Maybe your subconscious is trying to tell you something, and you're not listening."

"Maybe so," I say, unsure of whether to feel

relieved or defeated. "The school janitor told me that the university library has some information about the murders. Maybe I can research it some, just to put my mind at ease."

"I'll do you one better. I'll go down the station and pull the old file. I'll flip through the pictures and search specifically for the new details you told me about."

"I hate for you to go through such trouble, but it would be a great relief to finally know for sure. Your theory about my subconscious trying to communicate with me seems plausible, and would actually be a lot easier to accept than my possible possession by an unsettled ghost," I say with a smile.

In a paternal way that nearly makes my heart melt, Felton kisses me on the forehead. "I'll take care of it. We'll get you all fixed up so you can get on with the important things in life, like getting that boy of mine to settle down."

I laugh. "I'm working on it. I'm just so glad you don't think I'm crazy."

"I told you before, I know crazy, and crazy you ain't. Now, if you don't mind, grab that bag of French fries out of the freezer and bring them out to Cal while I finish this up. Looks like he's done with the hushpuppies," he remarks, glancing onto the back porch.

"Sure," I say, doing exactly as he requested. Cal smiles when I join him.

"Hey, how are things going in there?" he asks.

"Great. I talked to your dad about the dreams, and he doesn't think I'm crazy. Hearing that makes me feel so much better. Plus, he promised he'd pull the old files and review the pictures to see if any of the new things I dreamed about show up."

"And if they do?"

"We've determined that I'm probably possessed by a restless soul."

Cal laughs. "And if it doesn't?"

"Your dad seems to think that perhaps my subconscious is trying to tell me something."

"Hmmm. Good theory, I suppose—as long as it's not trying to warn you away from me."

"I wouldn't listen," I say, encircling my arms around his waist.

"Good." He gives me a light kiss before going back to frying the food. Felton joins us outside, and we have one of the nicest, most relaxing afternoons I've had since moving to Louisiana. After dinner, we fish from the dock, take a sunset boat ride, and end the night with a cocktail on the porch. However, as usual, things don't stay tranquil for long.

RHONDA R. DENNIS

TEN

I'm dragging tail this morning because of all the tossing and turning that went on during the night. It was as if the dream was set on replay, and continually looped over and over until I finally woke up. Coffee is a must, and thankfully, the café on Main Street offers a spectacularly potent blend. I'm propped on the counter while waiting for the waitress to bring me my to-go order when someone takes the stool next to me. I smell him before I see him.

"Richie, how are things?" I ask in monotone.

"Rich. Remember? Not Richie. Rich."

"Sorry," I say though my apology is not all that sincere.

"You look really good this morning. Downright scrumptious," he says, awkwardly and blatantly sniffing me. I reel backwards.

"Please don't do that again," I demand, sitting down, but making sure there is an empty stool between us. "It's creepy."

"It's supposed to be a compliment."

"'Nice shoes' is a compliment. Sniffing someone the way you just did is not."

"That's not what the video says."

"Video?"

"*Jungle John's Primal Style Passion.* Men

and woman have these primal urges that we try to hide, but if they're tapped into…"

"No," I say.

"*No* what?" Rich asks.

"Just no. No to all of it. Please don't take dating advice from videos."

"No?"

I shake my head emphatically. "Look, Richie. You're trying too hard. Be subtle, be relaxed, be yourself. Women like confidence but not arrogance. There's a difference."

"That's nothing like the video says."

I sigh. "How many women have you actually won over based upon the advice from your video?"

He rolls his eyes upwards as he counts mentally. "None."

I nod. "Take it from me—a woman. Ditch the video and give my advice a try."

"So, if I walk up to you and tell you that your hair looks nice up like that?"

I smile. "I'd thank you for the compliment."

"It does, you know. It looks really pretty."

"Thank you." I relax my guard some.

"And that dress. Very nice." He bites his lower lip.

"Okay, we're going back into creepy territory."

"Gotcha," he says. "Guess that now's not the right time to tell you I have fresh sheets on my bed?"

"Ewww, no Richie."

"Can I get a do over?"

"No."

"Please?"

"No." The waitress hands me my coffee and

my bagged breakfast sandwich. "Have a good day, Richie," I say, passing the waitress a bill and leaving the café as quickly as possible. He mumbles something as I'm leaving, but the jingling bell on the door prevents me from making it out.

Once I get to the office, I take about five minutes to regroup. I leave my computer off, unplug the phone, and kick off my shoes as I recline the office chair back as far as I dare before reaching the tipping point. Cal barges into the room, and I find myself on the floor.

"Are you okay?" he asks, helping me up.

"Yes, I'm fine," I say, slowly standing.

"I didn't mean to scare you."

"It's okay. You probably saved me from missing my class. I was just about to fall asleep."

"The dream?" he asks. I nod. "I'm sorry, sweetheart. I wish there was something I could do to make it all go away."

"I know. The dream is disturbing, but it's the why that keeps me on edge."

"Understandable. Have you thought of paying a visit to one of the psych professors?"

"And let the entire school know I'm nuts? No thanks!"

Cal laughs. "Just a suggestion, and you're not nuts."

"Yeah, well that hasn't been determined officially."

"As Felton would say, I know nuts, and nuts you ain't," Cal says doing a nearly spot on impersonation of his father. I laugh.

"I appreciate the confidence."

"No problem. Okay, I came in for a little bit

of lovin' to get me through the day. You game?"

"What do you have in mind?"

"Heavy kissing, light petting. Although I want much, much more, I'm not going to be greedy."

"How about light kissing and heavy petting? That way my makeup doesn't get smudged," I playfully tease.

"I like the way you think," he says, pulling me in closely for a sweet and gentle kiss. My cell phone rings, and I let out a groan. "Well, that was fun," Cal says with disappointment.

"You know it was bound to happen," I say, reaching for my phone.

"I'm going to class. See you tonight?"

I nod and wave as I answer the phone. "Hello."

"This is Felton. You got a second?"

"Hi, yeah. I have a couple of minutes."

"I'm at the station poring through these files, and I haven't found one picture that indicates that anything you're seeing is accurate. No peacock feathers, no rings, nothing. I was giving your situation some thought, and I'm not sure if you're a religious kind of person, but maybe you should consider paying Father Donnelly a visit. He told me he'd met you, and he's pretty good at helping people figure out their problems."

"I'm really not religious…"

"Just keep in mind that you don't have to be to talk to a priest. All in all, he's just a person."

"I suppose. Do you really think he can help?"

"Couldn't hurt."

"I'll think about it. Thanks for looking through the pictures for me. I was going to go to the library this afternoon, but I guess there's not much point now."

"Yeah, well if you have any more questions, just give me a call."

"Thanks, Felton."

"Anytime, darlin'."

I end the call and quickly gather my things for class. I'm a few minutes late, but the majority of the class is still seated. I'm told by one of the students that Billy refused to stay, so I make a note to talk to him about the fifteen minute policy. Class runs very smoothly, and I'm finally feeling more like myself once the workday is done.

I think about stopping in at the library just for the hell of it, but knowing that Cal is coming for dinner changes my mind. I run to the grocery store to pick up a few things before heading home. I'm disheartened to catch a glimpse of the blue car with dark tinted windows behind me. I immediately search for Brant's number and press dial.

"Major Collins."

"Brant, this is Cheyenne. The blue car's back."

"Where are you?"

"Just leaving Frankie's Supermarket. It's about three cars back, but it's definitely the same car."

"You're not too far from where I'm at. Don't go home. Do you know where Riverview Park is?"

"Yes."

"Head this way, but don't speed or do anything else to let this person know that you're onto him. Just keep it as normal as possible."

"Okay. I'm turning down the street with the post office."

"Good. Keep coming this way."

I glance in the rearview; the car's still there but about five car lengths back now. I relay the information to Brant, and he continues to encourage me in his direction. I'm making the turn into the park, but the car keeps going past the entry gates. Brant throws shells up as he takes off after the vehicle. "I've got it from here, Cheyenne. Go on home, and I'll let you know what I find out."

After ending the call, I do as instructed, even though I really want to follow Brant to see what happens. Cal is in the driveway when I arrive.

"Hey! Get lost?" he asks, opening the car's back door to grab the grocery bags for me.

"No. I was being followed again."

"What? Are you okay? What happened?" he asks, looking up and down the street.

"Brant's on it. I called him as soon as I noticed the car."

"Good because this is getting ridiculous."

"I agree," I say, following him up the stairs then unlocking the door. One glass of wine is down, and supper is almost ready to be served when there is a knock at the door. Cal opens it to find Brant on the other side. The two men introduce themselves quickly before Brant makes his way over to sit at the kitchen counter.

"Here's the deal. I followed him for a while, and then he took off. I kept up with him the entire time, but he double backed then went into a pond. By the time I got there, he'd already jumped from the car and was spotted in the tree line. If he'd still be out there in the woods, we could send some dogs after him, but right on the other side of the tree line is a highway. We lost him. I don't know if someone picked him up, or what, but there was no trace of him."

"Do you know who he is?"

"No. He's a white male who was wearing bulky clothes. That's all I could make out before he got into the tree line."

"What about the car? Can't you run the plates?" Cal asks.

"We did. It's stolen."

I sigh. "Any chance it was just a coincidence? I have no clue why someone in a stolen car would have any interest in me."

"Possibly, I suppose. Stranger things have happened, but I lean more towards the fact that you were being followed. Have you been honest with me about all of your interests?"

"What do you mean?" I ask.

"Anything illegal going on that you might be scared to report to me? Drugs? Anything of the sort."

I rapidly shake my head. "No. Never."

"Well, we really don't have much to go on. You've got a security system; use it. You have my number in case you notice anything off; call. What about the secret admirer? Still getting surprises?"

"They've slacked off a lot, but I do get them occasionally."

"Keep me posted on all of that," Brant says. I nod.

"Thank you for all of your help," I reply.

"Well, it wasn't much help. I was hoping to get this mystery solved."

"I know the feeling. Say, would you like to stay for dinner? I'm just finishing up some shrimp linguine."

"I wouldn't want to impose…"

"No imposition. Please, I insist."

"I'm not one to turn down a home cooked meal. I've been eating out or microwaving dinners since my wife left a few months ago," Brant says.

"Well, we have plenty. Would you like something to drink?" I ask, topping off my wine glass.

He starts to unbutton his shirt. "I'm off duty, so I'll have a glass of whatever you're having, if it's okay."

"Of course," I say, reaching for a wine glass while he removes his vest. He's left in a t-shirt and uniform pants once he takes off his gun belt. I offer to put them in the bedroom, but Brant insists that he can do it. I'm stirring in a bit of freshly chopped parsley into the linguine when he calls from the bedroom.

I look to where he's pointing and notice that gently swaying in a slight breeze is balloon bouquet. "How in the hell did that get on the bedroom balcony? Please don't tell me someone climbed the wall, because I don't even see how a superhero could scale that sucker without a ladder."

"My guess is that it was tossed up. See how one of the balloons is tangled in the rail?"

I sigh. "Do you think this has anything to do with the person who was following me?"

"I think your theory about a love sick student is more in line with this," he says, pulling some of the balloons close for inspecting. "I doubt the guy who crashed into a pond to evade arrest would go out of his way to leave you sappy balloons. Seriously?" He holds up a Mylar that is shaped like an owl. "You're a hoot?"

"Yeah, they've all been equally cheesy," I mention, pulling the bouquet inside so I can pop the balloons and get them into the garbage. Once that's done, we sit at the dinette to enjoy our meal. The conversation is mostly small talk, but towards the end of the evening, after several glasses of wine, the topic shifts to my nightmares. Brant offers to research the case for me, but once I tell him about Felton already doing so he nods.

"That's probably the best person to talk to about it all, especially since he was one of the responding officers." He looks to Cal. "I didn't get to know your dad very well because he retired not long after I entered the department, but I've heard lots of stories."

"Good ones, I hope."

"For the most part. I heard that even though he liked people to think he was a bad ass, he was quite the prankster."

Cal nods. "That's the truth."

"Yeah, they used to be able to get away with a lot more stuff back then. Things weren't so freaking PC. You could cut loose and not give a shit about offending someone else."

"You're right. A lot of that stuff would be frowned upon at the very least. He'd probably be on the receiving end of quite a few law suits now days."

My eyes widen. "What kind of things did your dad do?"

"Nothing that would truly hurt anyone, but many would whine about now—like scaring the crap out of prisoners. Lord knows they probably deserved it, and who knows, maybe it actually scared some of them enough that they didn't commit crimes again.

But criminals have more rights than anyone else these days, so things like that can cost you your job now."

"Ah, I see. It's the same in every profession now. We have to walk on eggshells sometimes with our students because everyone's quick to file a grievance. It's really sad," I say.

Brant raises his wine glass. "To the old days." Cal and I clank our glasses against his before we all drink. The meal wraps with Brant offering to help with the dishes, but Cal and I insist it's unnecessary. I'm showing him out when he mumbles, "What the fu.... you saw that, right?" he asks, pointing to the small red blur dashing through the darkness. We're no longer able to see it, but from the sound of rustling leaves, it's clear that it's near the far corner of the fenced-in yard. The sounds grow fainter until silence once again fills the night.

"That's another issue I've been having ," I mention.

"I looked up the history of this place. That," he says, pointing in direction of the red blur, "combined with that..." He points to the shadow of Agnes in the window above. "Combined with all of the other stuff... I'm surprised you're still living here."

"Everything is great as long as I stay inside," I answer.

"What was it?"

I shrug. "I wish I knew."

"I don't believe in ghosts," Brant states.

"I don't either."

"I'm going home," he says, rubbing his eyes. "Call if you need anything. Wait. Are you playing a joke on me?"

"Sorry to say, no. It's just another one of those unexplained issues that seem to be plaguing me lately. I'll call if I need anything. Thanks again," I say, smiling because I remember being right in his confused frame of mind about the red blur not that long ago. The shock has pretty much worn off for me. I still have no clue what's haunting the courtyard, but at least it doesn't scare me anymore. I wave goodbye to him, but it's lost because he doesn't bother looking back. I join Cal on the sofa, plopping heavily onto the cushion beside him. He puts his hand on my knee.

"Been one hell of a day, huh?" he asks.

"That's an understatement," I answer.

"Ready for bed?" he asks.

"You're staying the night?"

"I thought I might. You okay with it?"

"Are you staying because you want to, or because you feel an overwhelming urge to try to protect me?"

"Both."

"Cal, I'm okay. I can take care of myself."

"I know you can, but it's a guy thing. Tell you what—you let me stay, and I'll give you first whack at any intruder stupid enough to come here."

"Deal," I say with a grin. I dash from the sofa. "I call the shower first."

"First?" he calls after me. "Isn't showering a tandem sport?"

"Not tonight, honey," I tease, practically shutting the door in his face. He bangs on the door. "I hear that ghosts and crazy stalkers like to attack in bathrooms. It's really a matter of safety. The buddy system saves lives, Cheyenne."

I crack the door. "Cute, but not funny. Come

on in here," I say. He smiles broadly once he's in the room.

"Want me to strip for you?" he asks, gyrating his hips as he pulls off his belt.

I laugh. "No! We have an early day tomorrow. Shower. Bed. Sleep."

"You're no fun," he teases, dejectedly tossing his belt onto the floor.

"But you still love me, don't you?" I ask.

"Always." He pulls me near. His tone gets very serious. "Please stay safe. I need you in my life."

"I'm trying. Hopefully, we'll get some answers and these incidents will soon be distant memories."

He kisses me. "Let's hope so."

I'd been asleep for hours when my body seizes from fright while the dream plays out once again. The emotions are more intense because sound is finally incorporated into my dream. A song plays in the background as I make my way through the house, but it's not a full song. It's just a snippet that keeps repeating over and over—like a record player that keeps skipping to the same spot. The piece is classical, and something I can't identify, but an intense feeling of dread comes over me when I hear it. The composition is beautiful, and not really ominous, but it stirs a lot of negative feelings within me.

I'm sweaty and panting when I lurch from the bed. I fight with the bed sheet that's tangled around my legs and upper arm for a bit before carelessly casting it in Cal's direction. Tears fall before I can stop them, and Cal pulls my trembling body into his arms.

"Why won't the dreams stop?" I plead.

"They seem to be getting worse."

"They are. With each one, the scene becomes more vivid. This time I heard music."

"Music? Anything familiar?"

"It's something I've heard before—classical, but I don't know the name or composer." I shake my head in an effort to clear the mental fog enveloping my brain.

"Do you want me to help you try to identify it? We can listen to some classical clips…"

"Not right now. Maybe some other time." I wipe my face with my hands and move to the window. "Oh, freaking great! The girl in red is back." Cal joins me at the window, and we watch as the red dress falls from one of the trees and scampers across the yard. The darkness and shadows make it too difficult to make out any features other than a silhouette. Into the back corner and out of view she goes. "That's it. I'm losing my mind."

"If you're losing your mind, I am, too. I witnessed the same thing you did."

"Maybe my insanity is rubbing off on you."

"I doubt it. I think you're stressed, confused, and afraid. You should talk to someone."

"I don't want to go back to therapy. It would be like going back to high school once you've graduated."

"Uh, I don't think that's an accurate analogy…"

"I feel as though I'd be taking a step backwards."

"I understand that, but sweetheart, you can't keep this up." Cal stands behind me rubbing my shoulders. "What about Father Donnelly?"

I shrug. "Maybe so. He's a priest, not a therapist, but I'm not joining his congregation. If this becomes a sales pitch to convert me, I'm gone."

"Fair enough. Father Donnelly will respect your wishes. He's been a family friend for a long time. I'm sure he'll be able to help you make some sense of these dreams."

"I hope you're right. I'll call him a little later—after the sun comes up," I say sardonically.

"Come on. I'll hold you until you fall asleep."

"That sounds wonderful. I was going to fix a cup of coffee and watch some TV, but I like your idea better."

"Good. If you tell anyone I said this, I'll disown you. Let's get our snuggle on."

I laugh loudly while climbing back into bed. Cal wraps his arms around me in a comforting embrace, and though it doesn't happen quickly, I'm finally able to enjoy a refreshing, dream free slumber.

ELEVEN

Once I arrive at the church, an ancient secretary with drawn-on eyebrows and carrot orange hair ushers me down a hall and shows me a door with a plaque that says *Fr. Seamus Donnelly*.

"You just go on in, dear. He'll be with you shortly." She pulls her jacket edges together and hunches slightly as though she's freezing and trying to get warmed up. I take a seat in the dimly lit office and listen as the puffs of air coming from the secretary's orthopedic shoes grow less pronounced.

Father Donnelly's office smells of pipe smoke and mentholated rub, and much of the furniture appears to be an assortment of turn of the century pieces mixed with a hodgepodge from the sixties or so. For instance, the chair I'm sitting in is covered in rust orange tweed while the one next to me has avocado green vinyl. Rows of dark wooden bookshelves are stuffed with books ranging from Christian education resources to horror. Obviously, Father Donnelly is diverse when it comes to literature.

An old wooden and brass gramophone sits perched atop a varnished stand; a record stands by ready to be played. His desk, also intricately carved dark wood, is covered with stacks of papers, file folders, and a collection of prayer beads. In a crystal bowl are gobs of peppermints. I'm just reaching to take one when Father Donnelly startles me by entering the room.

"Wait," he says, sucking in his girth to make his way behind the desk. "I keep the good stuff in here." He opens the top desk drawer and lays out a vast assortment of candy bars. "Help yourself."

"Thank you," I say, reaching for the peanut butter cups. He pushes the stash in my direction.

"In case you want something else later," he says, reaching for a pen and paper. "Did Delores offer you a drink? Coffee, water, soda?"

"No sir, I'm fine, though. Thank you."

He taps the pen against the paper for while before tossing it aside. "How about we just get right to it? Felton and Cal tell me you're being plagued by nightmares which make no sense to you."

"Basically, but it goes deeper than that. A simple reoccurring dream is no big deal to me. This dream came about after I toured Azalea Downs."

He sucks in a breath. "Yes, terrible tragedy that happened there. Shocked the whole community."

"I imagine it did. Well, ever since I toured the house, I've been getting these visions of the crime scene, but they're not real visions."

"I don't understand," Father Donnelly says, steepling his fingers and planting them against his lips.

"Felton worked the scene."

"Yes, I'm aware."

"The things that I'm seeing in my visions

aren't accurate depictions of what actually happened that night, yet they keep replaying over and over again. Usually, each dream offers a new detail I'd missed in previous ones."

"Hmmm. What are these details that appear to stand out now?"

I pull a few items from my memory. "A gold ring, a rhinestone broach, peacock feathers, a white shawl or cloth of some sort, and most recently, a classical composition. My dreams didn't have sound until recently."

He leans back in his chair with a smirk. "You and Cal have been dating pretty exclusively, right?"

"Yes, sir. I suppose so, but I don't get what…"

"Have you been married before, child?"

"Yes, sir. He's a bad man with whom I have no contact."

"Does the thought of marriage scare you?"

I shrug. "Not really. Well, maybe somewhat. I'm not too sure. What are you getting at, Father?"

"Isn't it obvious? White cloth. Gold ring. Classical music. Rhinestones which could easily be diamonds. Your fear is stemming from marriage anxiety." I silently absorb what he's saying. "Plantation homes are often used as settings for weddings. It's only logical that you'd correlate the two."

"I do. Maybe the tour of Azalea Downs did trigger something in my subconscious? Are these dreams really just my body's way of expressing anxiety over a future with Cal?" I ponder some more, and it makes sense. It really makes sense. "Father, you're a genius! My fear of commitment is taking over my subconscious. Wow! I feel like a weight has been lifted from my shoulders. I can't thank you enough!" I'm almost giddy.

He chuckles. "I'm glad I could help, my child. You know, if you would like to come in with Cal, perhaps we could work on making some of that anxiety subside."

"As much as I appreciate the offer, I think I'll decline for now. Identifying the problem was the hardest part. I think I might have it from here."

"Well, you know where to find me if you need me. You're welcome anytime."

"Thank you, Father." I thumb through my wallet to retrieve some bills. "My donation to your church."

"Not necessary but very much appreciated. I hope to see you again soon, Cheyenne."

"Absolutely. Thanks again," I say, quickly dashing behind his desk and hugging him tightly. Laughter bellows from him, especially after I grab one more candy bar from his desk and shove it into my purse. "One for the road," I say, patting my purse before leaving his office.

I'm so insanely relieved that I can't wait to tell Cal the news. I'm anticipating awkwardness; how could it not be with my upcoming confession that my nightmares stem from commitment phobia and the things in my dream represent marriage. I'm a little upset with myself that I didn't put those clues together for myself. I suppose it's easier for someone away from the situation to see it.

When I get back to my apartment I'm surprised to see Brant on my porch. "Hey you," I say, taking the stairs two at a time. "What are you doing?"

"I'm installing a camera. That damned thing freaked me out. I'm going to figure out what in the hell is going on once and for all. Two birds with one stone."

"George is going to be pissed."

"George doesn't even have to know. See?" He shows me one camera before he nestles it inside of a flower pot."

"Nice! So the ghostly apparition freaked you out?"

"There are no such things as ghosts. Why a child is wandering around your place in the middle of the night is the mystery that needs to be solved ASAP."

"It can't be a child. The thing disappears into thin air sometimes."

"It's not a ghost," Brant asserts.

"Okay. So what's with the two birds, one stone bit?"

"Second bird will be your secret admirer. We can finally catch this person on film, I can scare the crap out of him, and we all move on."

I smile. "You're such a softie."

"Yeah, don't let that get out," Brant grumbles.

"Your secret's safe with me. Are you staying for dinner?"

"I hadn't really thought about it. Oh, who am I kidding! All I've been thinking about is food since I ate here the other night."

"Good. I've got beef stew in the crock pot, and there's plenty."

"Sounds great. Thanks. You seem particularly chipper today." He goes back to setting up the outdoor cameras.

"I feel chipper. I finally have some answers about my dreams thanks to Father Donnelly."

He looks over his shoulder. "Do you now? Anything interesting?"

"I'm a commitment phobe."

"Good for you," Brant jokes.

"Seriously, you have no idea how much these dreams bothered me. I thought I was cracking up. Losing it. Checking out."

"Hey, we all have our issues."

"You seem to have it pretty together," I mention.

"For the most part, but people think I'm an asshole."

"What? Why would they think that?"

"Because I'm an asshole."

I laugh. "You're one of the sweetest assholes I've ever met." I give him a light kiss on the temple before opening the door. "You want something to drink?"

"A soda if you got one."

"Absolutely." As I'm walking out to give Brant his drink, Cal jogs up the stairs.

"Hey, what's going on here?"

"Brant's installing some eyes so we can stake out some perps," I answer. Brant gives me a disapproving look. "What? Cops don't really talk like that?" He shakes his head and rolls his eyes.

"That's great. Thanks for looking out for Cheyenne," Cal says.

"It's more than that. I want answers," he says, adjusting some of the wires.

"Ghost girl?" Cal asks.

"Ghosts aren't real," Brant says. "I'm going to

figure it out."

Cal nods. "How did your meeting with Father Donnelly go?"

"Excellent," I say, grinning from ear to ear. "He figured it out like that." I snap my fingers.

"Really? So…"

"So, I'm scared of marriage, particularly marriage to you."

He looks at me questioningly. "Did I ask? Because I'm not remembering…"

I laugh. "No. Relax. It's just my subconscious putting the cart before the horse. You're off the hook, so you can get rid of that deer in the headlights look."

"What? Scared? Me? No way. If you want to talk marriage, we can talk marriage. I'm all about open and honest…"

"You look like you're about to vomit."

"No way," he says with a large fake smile.

"Let me allay your concerns. No marriage-talk for a while because I'm not anywhere near ready. Okay?"

Relief shows on his face nearly instantaneously. "Only if you're sure."

"I am. Now, onto other things. I asked Brant to stay for dinner again. I hope you don't mind, but with the trouble he's going through hooking up the cameras…"

"I don't mind at all. If you wouldn't have invited him, I would have."

"Great," I say, tip-toeing to kiss him. "I'm going to make a salad. You make yourself comfortable." He sits across from me as I start pulling fresh vegetables from the refrigerator. Brant pops his head in the door.

"Hey, I'm not going to be able to stay after all. In fact, I can't finish with the cameras tonight, but I'll swing by tomorrow to finish up. I got called out. Jumper on the bridge."

"Really? That's terrible," I say with a gasp.

"Drugged up and drunk fool thinks he can fly. They're trying to talk him down now. I gotta get out there."

"I understand. I hope it turns out okay."

"Yeah, me too. It's a pain in the ass doing post-mortem paperwork. Don't do drugs, and don't drink and drive, kids. Okay, that was your public service announcement for the day. Later."

"Well, looks like it's just you and me tonight. I vote we do full nude supper club," Cal says.

"I vote no."

"We need a tie-breaker vote."

"My vote counts twice since it's my place."

"Cheater," Cal says with a smile.

After supper, we turn in early, mostly because I'm so excited to possibly get a full night's sleep now that my issues have been identified. The dream never came, but that is the least of my concerns when I awaken during the night.

It's still dark out when I dash across the room for a potty break. It's not until I'm groggily climbing back into bed that I hear a slow and steady thumping sound against the bedroom window. Fear hits like a sledgehammer until rationality kicks in. One of the limbs from the oak tree is smacking the window. The forecast has called for wind and rain for the morning commute, so the storm more than likely made its way in a little early. I breathe a sigh of relief. When thunder grumbles in the distance I relax even more.

As I pull back the covers, I steal a quick glance at the window while deciding if I should check out the mystery noise just to put my mind at ease. At that precise moment, lightening fills the sky with brilliant white light, and through the closed blinds I'm able to make out the frightening silhouette of a person on my balcony. I can barely speak as I shake Cal awake.

"Someone. Someone. Balcony. Out there."

"Slow down," Cal says, rubbing sleep from his eyes. "What's wrong?"

"Someone's on the balcony," I whisper in a panic.

Cal lurches from the bed and hustles to the kitchen where he wields the largest kitchen knife I own. He slowly makes his way to the French doors. "Stay in the kitchen and call the police," he whispers as he creeps closer to the balcony doors.

"Be careful," I whisper back as I dial the number. The operator asks me to stay on the line with her, and I somewhat follow her command. I don't disconnect the call after giving her the information, but I do toss the phone onto the counter so I can give my undivided attention to Cal.

He is at the doors, his back pressed against the wall, when he uses the blade of the knife to slightly pull the blinds away from the door. Stunned by whatever he sees, Cal stumbles backwards and the knife easily slices into the fabric of the blinds. The whole thing tumbles down as he continues to reel back from the doors, and I'm left a mortified, quivering mess. Lightning illuminates the lifeless body of Odell the janitor while he hangs from a tree limb over the balcony. Beads of water drip from the ends of his long scraggly hair, and his willowy body moves slightly in the swift breeze. His bulged out eyes are pinned open, as is his mouth, like he's trying to emit a scream that just won't come. I handle that part for him.

I'm still shrieking when the officers enter the apartment, guns drawn. I slump down in the corner, covering my ears while tightly closing my eyes in a desperate attempt to remove the image that is now seared into my brain.

"Are you hurt? Are you okay, ma'am," one of the officers asks. Both of them have their guns pointed at Cal. "Hands on your head! Now! Slowly walk backwards towards my voice," one of the officers instructs.

"No," I finally manage to say when I replace the shrieking with rocking back and forth. "No, he's my boyfriend. He didn't hurt anyone."

"I got him, you secure the knife," the other officer says once Cal reaches them.

"No. The knife…. It's not what it looks like."

"We're going to handcuff you for our safety, as well as your own safety," the younger of the two officers says as though he's reading a script.

"But he didn't do anything wrong." I'm still trembling, and don't realize it until the older officer wraps my shoulders with a throw.

Brant assumes command as soon as he enters the scene. "He's good. Uncuff him. What in the hell is going on here, Cheyenne?"

I rush up to Cal, and he holds me tightly. "We wish we knew," Cal answers. "Cheyenne woke me up to tell me someone was outside. I grabbed a knife for protection and went to check it out. That's when we found Odell." Cal lowers his head as he points towards the lifeless body swaying in the wind.

"Any clue why Odell was here in the first place?" Brant asks. Cal and I shake our heads.

"When are they going to get him down?" I ask, working hard to resist the urge to vomit.

"I'm sorry, but it'll probably be a while. The detectives need to come in and gather evidence before the coroner will release the body. However, there's no reason for you to sit here watching it all. Cal, I really need you two to hang here, but you can take Cheyenne up front to the living room."

He nods, giving me a gentle nudge in the right direction. He holds me in his arms once we're on the sofa, and we remain silent and in shock for hours. Disbelief and uncertainty dominate my thoughts.

The sunlight starts to stream in when George makes his way inside the apartment. "I've been trying to get up here, but they wouldn't let me until they finished processing the crime scene. You got something you need to tell me?"

"I... I don't understand. What do you mean?" I ask.

"Well, there was a dead body hanging from my tree, and he was near your window. I don't think he was here to visit me."

"I have no idea what he was doing here, and I certainly don't know anything about his death," I answer.

"I should kick you out."

"But George, I..."

"Hush. I'm not doing it, although I'd understand if you want to leave."

I shake my head. "It's too early for me to decide that. I need some time to figure out everything."

"Well, get with me whenever you decide what you want to do," George says, backing out of the door. "Oh, if anymore dead bodies pop up though, we'll have to renegotiate your lease."

"Understood," I answer fighting the urge to launch a snide comment in his direction. Once George is gone, I work to piece together the pieces of the puzzle. However, I can't for the life of me understand why Odell was here. Why would he be in the tree? Was it an accident? Maybe he tied a rope to stop himself in case he was to fall while peeping in, and the rope slipped… I gasp. "Brant! Do you think he was spying on me and accidentally hanged himself?" I'm grasping at straws to find any answer that makes sense.

Brant looks skeptical. "I don't think so. He might be your admirer, but this was no accident. He was definitely murdered."

Through the opened front door, I spy a wheeled gurney topped with a black body bag rolling down the driveway below. Nausea returns. "I'm going to take a personal day. I need to call the school."

"I will, too," Cal says. "I'm not leaving you alone today."

"Thank you," I say, putting the phone to my ear. Once I'm finished, Brant tells us he'll make sure we're informed of how the investigation is going. He also promises to reach out to Felton and explain to him what's happening as a professional courtesy.

"If only I'd finished setting up those cameras,"

Brant fusses, his voice heavy with disappointment. "I'll be back to finish that up this afternoon. Until then, try to get some rest."

"I will," I say, showing him out. Once he's gone, I turn to Cal. "I'm going to take a shower. Will you please take me to breakfast afterwards?"

"Absolutely," Cal says. "I need lots of caffeine and some food, too."

"It won't take me long," I say, getting some clothes from my closet and carrying them into the bathroom.

The hot water running over my tense body doesn't provide much respite to the tightness of my muscles. Since nearly scalding myself doesn't work, I try another proven stress reliever—crying. Sobs rack my body as I slide down the wall of the shower. Death is something I don't handle well, even if it's someone I don't really know. Odell was murdered outside of my bedroom. Murdered. A killer is on the prowl and was just outside my door. The sobs turn into borderline hyperventilation, and I force myself to push aside the speculations, or else chance a meltdown of epic proportions. The police are working the case, Cal is by my side, and answers are sure to come soon. Until then, I simply need to hang on.

Dressing in very plain and simple attire and my hair done in a damp quick braid, I have zero desire to appear presentable to anyone. It's not until Cal and I are nearly finished with our breakfast that I finally feel the shock wearing off somewhat, and the more time that passes the better I'm able to accept the unfortunate event. Felton gets in contact with Cal to say that Brant's been in touch with him. No new leads or information on the case, but they are continuing to work on it. Evidently, Odell's murder is the top priority in the parish at the moment. Cal thanks Felton for the information.

"Hey."

I look in his direction.

"You were a million miles away."

"I know," I say, shaking it off.

"You want to stay at my place tonight?"

I was set to say no, but I don't think I'll sleep if I go back to my place. I'm mentally and physically exhausted, so after some brief contemplation, I accept his offer. He asks if I want to stop by my apartment to pick up some clothes, but I shake my head. "Not now. It's still too soon. Maybe tomorrow. I'll just pick up something from that shop over there, okay?"

He nods and instead of driving to his place, he pulls the car into the parking lot of a little boutique. I'm only in the store a few minutes before leaving. "Screw it. Take me to the apartment. I need a toothbrush, hair brush, make up… It's just easier to pack a bag."

Cal half smiles as he pulls back into traffic. We're in and out of the apartment quickly, and though I don't feel nearly as uneasy as expected, I'm still nowhere near confident enough to stay. There's one last stop before heading to Cal's, and that is swinging by our offices to check our messages and to pick up paperwork for the next day's lesson.

Sitting atop my desk is a gift wrapped box with a large white bow. I give Cal a perplexed look. "Did you do this?"

He shakes his head. "It wasn't me."

My stomach tightens with nerves. I don't

know of anyone else who might send me a gift. Instead of opening it, I rock in my office chair playing out various scenarios in my head. Normally, I'd just rip into the damn thing, but in light of the recent tumult, I consider simply tossing it unopened. I'm not sure how long I zone out, but it's long enough for Cal to become concerned. "Should I open it for you?"

A knock at the door stops Cal just as he loosens the bow. "Oh, I'm glad you found it," Gillian, the departmental secretary says.

"Do you know who it's from? There's no card," I say.

"No, the guy didn't leave a name, and to be honest, that's why I'm here." She looks at Cal, embarrassment shows on her face. She nods her head to motion that I should join her in the hallway. Cal holds up a hand to stop us before mentioning his need to run by his office, thereby leaving us to talk in private.

"What's with the secrecy?" I ask once he's in the hall.

Gillian looks hesitant at first, but finally opens up. "People talk and rumors fly around this campus at lightning speed. If the rumors are true, you and Professor Gage would be…"

"A couple?" I finish her sentence, while offering her a seat. This conversation is already taking longer than I expected. Once I'm seated behind my desk, I continue. "It's hardly a secret, but it's not something we necessarily want to flaunt, either."

"I think it's great. I mean, if that's what you want…"

"What am I missing, Gillian?" I give a look

meant to encourage the conversation along.

"The man who left the gift. He's SO good looking, handsome, and charming... well..."

"Did he say who he was?" I ask, my curiosity thoroughly piqued.

"No. He came in wearing this huge grin, and he had the box hidden behind his back. He stopped at my desk to ask if you were in, and when I told him you were out for the day, he said it was for the best because he wanted to surprise you. He'd simply intended to leave the package behind whether you were in or out of the office. He asked me to give you the box, but not before giving me a simultaneous smile and a wink that was so—hot. There's just no other way to describe it." She's lost in her memory of the encounter before drawing her hand to her lips. "I'm sorry. I don't know if you're romantically involved with him, and here I am going on like a lustful bimbo."

"Wait," I say, waving my hand to stop her. "Relax. The only person I'm romantically involved with is Cal, so if the mystery guy interests you, then you have my full permission to pursue him. However, I'm curious as to who he is and why he felt compelled to leave me a gift." I'm almost scared to hear her reply because it suddenly occurs to me that the only person I can think of is Richie from the furniture store. Is he really her idea of gorgeous? To each her own, I suppose. "Was there anything else that stood out? What did he look like?" I anticipate she'll say thick mustache, slicked back hair, dressed in a jewel toned mostly unbuttoned shirt, dress slacks, and patent leather loafers.

She sighs dreamily. "He's tall, broad

shouldered, brown hair, dark green eyes, and is loaded with tattoos. Oh, he spoke with a country accent. So unbelievably sexy!"

I want to cry. Trying to keep my voice steady, but failing miserably, I ask, "Do you remember what any of the tattoos looked like?"

She flushes. "Well, the reason I thought you might be involved with him is because he has 'Cheyenne' written across his forearm."

My breath catches and panic consumes me. I viciously struggle against the overwhelming urge to run away. Closing my eyes, I shake my head. "No. No. No," I quietly repeat over and over.

"Uh… are you okay? Should I get someone?" Gillian asks with an uncertain tone.

"It can't be. He can't be here."

Giving me an awkward stare, Gillian slowly rises from her chair. "I'm gonna go get Cal." She's off like a rocket as soon as she hits the door. Rightfully so, I suppose, being that I'm ranting gibberish. Cal enters the office and softly rubs my forearm once he squats beside my office chair.

"What's wrong, sweetheart? Talk to me."

"No. No. It can't be him," I mumble. Trying to overhear the conversation, Gillian is very slow to shut the door behind her, and once I hear the click, I look to Cal with panic. "It's Luke. He's found me."

"Luke? As in your ex-husband Luke? Isn't he supposed to be in prison?"

I nod my head, and a sob flies out. "He's not supposed to be out. He tried to kill an officer. They don't just let people out for crimes like that. He had to have escaped, and now he's after me."

"Are you sure it's him? Wouldn't you know if he escaped?" Cal asks.

"Gillian described him to me. It's him. No doubt. I was supposed to be informed of any changes in his status, but obviously that didn't happen. It was him. He left this."

"So what's in the box?" Cal asks, eyeing it suspiciously.

"I don't know because I still haven't opened it. Maybe I shouldn't. I don't think I want to know what's in it."

"I'm calling Brant," Cal says, pulling his phone out. "I don't want you to be scared, sweetheart. We're going to take care of you, and you're going to be fine."

I shake my head as tears begin to fall. "You don't know Luke, Cal. He's going to pay me back for leaving him. He didn't want the divorce, but I didn't give him a say in it. I did it anyway. He was so mad about it."

"It's okay. Come here." Cal pulls me into his arms while he fills in Brant on some of the specifics. Brant instructs us to stay put and promises to arrive on campus shortly. He also requests that we leave the package unopened, which is fine by me.

It seems like an eternity passes before he enters my office. Obviously on duty because of his attire, he speaks some sort of code into the microphone on his lapel before taking a seat across from me. Cal moves to join him in the other chair beside him then they both stare at me expectantly. When I remain silent, Brant speaks up.

"Luke Nelson White, thirty-nine years old, was recently released from prison due to overcrowding and good behavior despite an attempted murder charge."

I shake my head. "No. I was told that he'd never get out because he tried to kill a police officer. It was supposed to be life in prison automatically—end of story."

"Well, I don't really know how or why he did it, but the officer Luke shot showed up at his parole hearing and petitioned for his release."

"What?" I ask. "That makes no sense."

"Regardless, he's going back to prison, and I don't think he'll be getting out this time. He broke parole because he hasn't gotten in touch with his parole officer like he was ordered. If we catch him, he's done," Brant states.

"But how did he find me?" I ask.

"It's not very hard to find anyone in this day and age. A simple search of your name surely pulled up the college's page where you're listed as faculty. Do you think it was him leaving the roses and such?"

I shake my head. "That's not his style at all. He's very aggressive and rough. Demanding and callous. He believed that his being with me was present enough."

"Arrogant punk, isn't he?" Brant asks.

I nod. "Very. However, now that I think about it, he may have been the guy in the car—the one following me. That's more in-line with his style. He was probably trying to find out where I live, but I noticed him before he could get that information."

"I was just thinking the same thing," Brant agrees. "You're going to have to be extra careful, Cheyenne. That means not going anywhere alone, being very aware of your surroundings, and calling in immediately if you notice anything off or suspicious…"

I put my head in my palms. "I thought I was done with this. Cal, I'm so sorry, and Brant, I'm sorry for dragging you into this, too. What is it with the dark cloud that seems to be following me lately?"

"Stop it right now. You didn't ask for this, and you certainly don't deserve it," Cal says. "She can stay with me as long as she needs, and I'm sure my dad would love to help out when I can't be there," Cal offers.

"Good. I'll give Felton a call and give him the new information. We've put it off long enough. I think it's time to see what's in the box," Brant suggests.

"You can open it. I want nothing to do with the package." I gesture with my hand to show my contempt.

Brant gives the box a gentle shake once he raises it close to his ear. Baffled, he sets it back on the desk and gently unwraps the layers of paper and ribbon. Once the top is pulled off, he stares into the box for almost a full minute before clicking his tongue and shaking his head.

"What is it?" I ask, my head in my hands. Actually, I'm actually afraid to know, but it's going to happen regardless. Might as well get it over with quickly.

"I think I know who murdered Odell," Brant answers.

"What! What's in the box?" I yelp, moving to get a peek inside. The name tag from Odell's janitor's uniform lays nestled amongst a wad of tissue paper. Beside it is a note. *Caught this no good perv at your place. Don't worry, I'm taking out the competition one dumbass at a time. Professor man is next, and after that, you'll be all MINE!*

I plop back in the chair and put my head on the desk. "Cal, you're in danger," I manage to eke out between the throat spasms I'm having because I'm fighting back tears.

He's behind me, softly rubbing my back. "I can take care of myself, and I'm not scared. If Luke wants to do something, let him bring it. I promise I'll be the one who finishes it."

"No, Cal. He's not the type of person you want to get into a pissing match with. I'm sorry, but I can't stay with you. It only puts you in more danger."

"Well, you're not staying by yourself," Cal fusses.

"Why don't you both stay with your dad?" Brant suggests. "Or rent a room somewhere? There are other options out there, you know?"

Cal looks at me, and I nod. "I'll call my dad," Cal says, excusing himself just before leaving the room. Brant takes one look at my heartbroken, confused, and frightened face and his posture becomes less uptight.

"You know this is only temporary, right? I'm on the case, so you know our department will be closing this one really soon. We don't take too kindly to fugitives hiding out and starting trouble in our neck of the woods. Consider Luke as good as caught," Brant assures.

"Thank you for everything. You've been so kind and have gone out of your way so many times to help me. It means a lot to me."

He shrugs. "Part of the job."

"I'm serious though, Brant. Luke is a bad man."

"So are ninety percent of the people I come in contact with. I'm kind of used to it."

Cal comes back into the room and tells us that his father insisted we stay with him. I nod, rise from behind the desk, and pile the things I need into my arms. "Brant, you can do whatever you want with that package," I say once I reach the door.

"I'll need to process it as evidence."

"That's fine. I just want it gone. I'm going to tell Gillian to cancel my classes for this week due to a family emergency. If this situation continues past a week, I'll readdress the issue."

"I think that's a great idea, Cheyenne," Cal says. "While you do that, I'll keep my routine as normal as possible. Maybe he'll start following me instead of you, thereby making it easier for Brant and the others to catch him?"

"No way," I argue. "Cal, you can't do that. It's not your job, plus we've been through this—Luke is a very dangerous and ruthless man who shouldn't be taunted."

"He needs to be caught, sweetheart."

Brant interrupts. "So, Cheyenne will stay at Felton's, and Cal, you're going to stay at your apartment?"

"Yes," Cal says at the same time I say no.

Brant changes his tone to one that alludes to his understanding my apprehension. "Cheyenne, I know where you're coming from, but in my opinion, Cal's plan has merit. I think it's for the best. We'll keep eyes on him. It truly is the best way of luring out Luke, aside from using you as bait."

"Then use me," I speak up.

"No," Cal and Brant say simultaneously.

"Here's what we'll do: I'll bring you to the station with me, Cheyenne, and we'll arrange for Felton to pick you up from there. He can park in the private garage so if Luke is watching, he won't be able to see you leaving in his car. Cal, we're going to do the opposite with you. You're going to stay here until I can get one of my undercover guys on campus. You'll leave like it's a normal day, go to your apartment, get something to eat, whatever keeps you visible—but you'll be tailed.

"I hate that you all have to go through so much trouble, and Cal, I wish you'd reconsider," I plea.

He pulls me close. "Stop. I'm doing this. Go talk to Gillian, and I'll arrange for my dad to pick you up at the station. Remember to get your bag from the car before you go." Cal pulls me close. "Everything is going to be fine. You'll see."

"I'm going to be a nervous wreck—well even more of a nervous wreck," I say, correcting myself. I give him a feeble smile before departing to finalize my leave with Gillian. I tell her that I have to fly back to Oklahoma because of a dying uncle, and she buys the story with no questions asked. She promises to submit the paperwork and get my classes covered right away.

Cal and Brant meet me in the hall where I offer Cal a quick wave before leaving with Brant. My stomach is in knots, and my anxiety is nearly out of control. Every corner we turn, I expect to run into Luke, and I eventually get to where I'm walking behind Brant instead of beside him. Fear is the devil, and I know I shouldn't falter, but each step finds me closer and closer to completely giving up.

TWELVE

It's so awkward being confined to Felton's residence. I get along with the man, but he's an old, cantankerous bachelor who is very much set in his ways. He tells me to make myself at home, but it's somewhat hard to do so in a glorified hunting camp with only one bedroom. Cal once told me the second bedroom was converted into a hobby room/office a long time ago because Felton's pastime collections began to spill from the workshop to the carport, and finally, to the living room. Now most of the eclectic assortment is jammed in this cramped space. Various gun parts are scattered across a desk that has a large lighted magnifying glass mounted to it. A table in the corner holds an antiquated train set, and the floor is covered with box upon box of magazines, file folders, and books. Walking through the musty room is very much like navigating a labyrinth.

Because the living room sofa is essentially my bedroom at Felton's and because he spends the majority of his time camped out in said room parked in his tattered recliner watching westerns, I opt to sit on the back porch and read. At least the view is nice—lots of trees, the water, a small boat house. I'm completely entranced with my book as I gently sway in the hammock until Felton steps outside. I barely notice that the sun has set until he clicks on the porch light.

"You'll go blind trying to read with the spillover from inside the house. If you need a light, turn the damned thing on," Felton grumbles.

"Thank you, I will. I just got caught up in the story and didn't even realize how late it's gotten."

"It's time for me to turn in. Knock if you need anything."

"I will. I appreciate that you're letting me stay here."

"Gotta keep my boy's girl safe. He's pretty smitten."

"Yeah? Me, too." Adjusting my tone to something more somber, I say, "Felton, I'm really sorry about all of this. I'm worried about Cal."

"Don't you worry about my boy. I taught him how to take care of himself long ago. He's smart, tough, and he's not going to let anything happen to himself or to you. I raised him right."

"Yes, you did. He's by far the most amazing man I've ever met."

Felton stands a little taller. "Thank you for that. Sleep well, Cheyenne."

"You, too. Goodnight."

I shimmy out of the hammock and somewhat hesitantly traipse into the house. Felton has converted the sofa into a comfy looking bed with sheets, a fluffy pillow, and soft blanket. After a quick shower, I don my favorite pajamas and curl into the shockingly comfortable makeshift bed. I drift off to thoughts of the characters in the book I'm reading, but sometime during the night, the dreaded evil dream resurfaces with a vengeance.

I'm screaming hysterically when Felton runs into the living room with a semi-opened plaid bathrobe, rubber boots, and a .44 magnum. When he realizes my shouts aren't related to an intruder, he lowers the weapon and cinches the belt on his agape robe. I'm still trying to catch my breath when he begins to grumble.

"You scared the shit out of me, woman. What in the hell are you screaming at?"

I pull my knees to my chest and wrap the blanket around me tightly. "I'm sorry," I say with a pant. "It was the dream again."

He rolls his eyes and tosses his weapon onto a nearby TV tray. "Why are you still having this dream? I thought it was all over and done with."

"So did I. I haven't had one since talking to Father Donnelly."

"Well maybe you should go see him again. These early morning wake up calls aren't good for my ticker."

I start to feel sorry for myself. "Like I don't have enough going on with Luke's reappearance, but now the dream is back with even more scary images."

"More?" Felton asks. "What now?"

"There were two ghosts this time. I finally made it out of the house because a gray ghost pulled me from the closet and brought me outside to meet a black ghost. It was so dark and terrifying. The gasping lady, the faceless man, the blaring music."

"Music?" he asks.

"Yes, the last couple of times that I've had the dream, it was like a theme song was being played as I walked through the house."

"Interesting. What song?"

"I don't know. It's something classical, but I'm not familiar enough with classical music to name it."

Felton smiles. "See, another point that discredits the dream. There was no way music could have been playing after the murders because the piano player was shot."

"That's right," I say, feeling a tad better.

"I really think you're putting too much into figuring out this dream. Nothing relevant has come from it. You can't control whether or not you're going to have it, but you can control how you react to it when you do. You need to learn to shake it off."

I sigh with relief. "You're right. Father Donnelly seems to think the dream is related to Cal. Maybe I'm having it again tonight because I'm worried about him."

"I'm willing to bet on it." He glances at the wall clock. "It's almost five. I'm going to go meet the group for some coffee. You're welcome to come if you wish."

I shake my head. "I think I'll try to get some more sleep." The thought of joining a slew of cantankerous elders who complain while slurping coffee doesn't sound very appealing to me.

"Suit yourself. Should I bring something back?"

"If you don't mind, I'd love some biscuits and gravy, please."

He smiles. "Breakfast of champions. Don't answer the door for anyone unless you know for sure who it is. I'll keep this here," he says, pointing to the massive gun on the TV tray. "Aim and squeeze. Shoot until it's empty."

"Uh, I don't think I…"

"Trust me. If your life is in danger, you'll be able to do it. Just make sure it's a bad guy you're aiming at before pulling the trigger." Wide eyed, I glance between him and the gun. "Call me if you need anything."

I simply nod before slinking back down onto the sofa. I click off the small lamp on the end table, and take slow deep breaths until I begin to fall asleep. Felton leaves the house, and the last conscious thought I have is when his car backs out of the driveway. It's me hoping to have the amount of courage he thinks I'll have if I'm put into a life or death situation.

The smell of freshly brewed coffee wakes me, and I smile knowing the dream didn't reoccur. Felton hands me a Styrofoam tray that is piled with biscuits and gravy.

"There's no way I'll eat all of this," I say, diving in with a plastic fork.

"Eh, it's how it came. Nelly says to tell you hi."

"That's very nice of her. The food is absolutely delicious. Thank you for bringing it back."

"No biggie," he says, flipping on the TV and plopping into his chair. Awkward silence fills the room as I eat and Felton watches his western. Once I finish eating, I hop in the shower just to have something to do. The water runs cold faster than I'd have liked, so I dress and go off exploring Felton's property. Pecan trees dot the land, and I try to skip the brown shells of the fallen ones across the water like stones. Even though I fail miserably, it's still more fun than watching Felton watch a movie.

By four in the afternoon, I can't stand it anymore. I'm bored out of my mind, so I give Father Donnelly a call and ask if I can meet with him. I can't imagine anyone getting upset over me wanting to visit with a priest, even though I really prefer to go window shopping or something else equally mind numbing. He is happy to do so which makes my next hurdle getting Felton to agree to let me go. He doesn't put up as much of a fight as I thought he would, in fact, he's very encouraging of the outing. Maybe he finds me just as boring as I find him? Felton tosses me the keys to his beast of a car, and before long, I'm outside Father Donnelly's office door.

"Nice to see you again, Cheyenne. How have you been?" he says, rising from his desk chair.

"I've been better," I answer honestly. He gestures for me to sit, and I choose the avocado green chair this time.

"Another rough patch, my child?"

"Yes, sir. You could say that."

"I heard about the murder outside of your apartment. Tragic and quite shocking to say the least."

"Yes, incredibly. Father, I don't understand why all of this is happening. Odell was somewhat strange, but ultimately, harmless. Luke should've known better than to feel intimidated by him. I don't know why he had to kill him."

"Luke?"

"My ex-husband who is supposed to be spending life in prison."

"Oh, yes. I forgot that you were married before."

"He is a vile man—very abusive, mean-spirited, and arrogant. He was imprisoned for nearly killing a police officer, but despite that, we learned he was recently paroled."

"And you believe he killed Odell? How did this conclusion come about?"

"That's what the police believe. Luke came to my office and left a package that contained Odell's name patch from one of his uniforms and a note warning us that Cal would be next. He wants me to be his and only his."

"Why do you suppose he feels this way? Have you maintained contact with him since the incarceration?"

"No. I divorced him immediately after his sentencing, and I haven't spoken to him since."

"But has he tried to contact you?"

"Yes, a few times, but I thought it was over and done with once I moved." Father Donnelly nods. My phone rings, and I excuse myself to answer it. "It's Major Collins with the department," I explain. He waves me off, and I go into the hall to take the call.

"Brant, is Cal okay?" I ask without as much as a "hello."

"He's fine, but listen— I've got some new information about Luke. He's not in violation by being in Louisiana. I finally got in touch with his parole officer and was able to clear up a few things. Luke's cleared to be here because he was offered a job offshore. Now, there are stipulations: he can only come two days before his hitch starts, and he has to be back in Oklahoma two days after he gets back. According to the PO's records, Luke is supposed to be on a rig out in the middle of the Gulf. We're trying to track down the exact rig number and such and verify with the hiring company that he is indeed out there. It'll make it a whole lot easier to pick him up if he is. He pretty much sealed his coffin with this janitor mess. Surely he had to know he'd end up back in prison by pulling that stunt. Guess he's one of the dumb ones. He'll probably say he strung him up in self defense or some other equally idiotic defense. It's happened before."

"But Brant, if he's on the rig, then Cal and I aren't in immediate danger, right?"

"True, but don't get antsy on me. Let me make sure before you start to let your guard down."

"I understand. Thanks so much, Brant. I appreciate everything." The church bells begin to chime in the background.

"Cheyenne, where are you?"

"I'm visiting with Father Donnelly. I had the dream again last night, and it nearly scared Felton to death. Gray and black ghosts appeared this time. I have no clue how that ties in to the whole scared of commitment theory, so I figured Father Donnelly could offer some insight."

Brant is livid. "I told Felton that you aren't to leave his house without an escort. Damn it! It's not that complicated."

"Don't be hard on him. I'm totally disrupting his life, and we needed a break from one another."

"Still," he growls into the phone. "I could've

sent an officer to escort you. The old man is slipping. Cal and I discussed that not too long ago—Felton's poor decision making and slipping memory."

"Look, I'm absolutely fine. I promise to call you once I'm on my way back to Felton's place, and I'll call you again when I get there so you'll know I'm okay. Is that a fair deal?"

"Do it, and don't forget," he orders.

"I will, and I won't. Bye, Brant."

"Bye, Cheyenne."

I close the door behind me once I'm back in Father Donnelly's office. "I'm sorry about that. It seems as though danger might not be as imminent as previously feared. Luke might be on an offshore rig."

"Well, wouldn't that be helpful."

"That's pretty much what Brant said. Father, the reason I'm here is because I had the dream again last night, and I'm really stumped by the new additions this time."

"Why's that?" He kicks back in his chair and crosses his hands across his rotund belly.

"This time there were two ghosts, for lack of a better term. They were transparent blobs, but I could tell they were supposed to be men. One was gray, and one was black."

"Interesting. I think I have an answer for you. In keeping with the general theme of your dream, perhaps the black ghost is representative of Luke, and the gray, or lighter ghost, representative of Cal."

I shrug. "I suppose that might be it. Father, while your theory absolutely makes sense, part of me thinks that maybe there is something more to it. Like the story is fitting, but it's not quite right. I should feel relieved, but I feel unsettled instead."

"That's the bad thing with dream interpretations, the possibilities could be endless."

"It's just so real when I see it—so vivid in my mind."

Father Donnelly begins to rock back and forth in his chair. "I understand your apprehension. However, didn't you tell me the events you've witnessed in your dreams are inaccurate according to the actual police reports?"

"Yes, but…"

His tone changes to one similar to the one reserved for the ill—soft with a pinch of sympathy. "Listen, sweet child. You're under a lot of stress. You've been through so much lately, and the extra stress you're putting on yourself because of this dream isn't helping things at all. Perhaps this move wasn't in your best interest. The experts say that death, divorce, and moving are some of the most stressful events a person can go through. You've dealt with them all in a relatively short period of time."

"Are you suggesting that I move back to Oklahoma?" I ask, slightly flabbergasted by his comments.

"Maybe it would be for the best."

"But Cal's here. The problem stems from my ex-husband. If I can get him back in the prison where he's supposed to be then I see no reason why I need to move. I love Cal, and he loves me. I'm not about to ask him to leave Louisiana."

"But the reoccurring dreams…"

"I guess I should make an appointment with a licensed therapist," I snap. "I've run from my problems once; I'm not inclined to do it again. I'm tired of running. I want to establish roots. Real roots with the man I love, and if I have to spend months on a shrink's sofa to make that happen, so be it."

"I never proclaimed to have all the answers, Cheyenne. But, I do think you should leave. If you do it quickly, I'm sure it will cause the least amount of hurt."

"You're kidding, right? Have you not heard what I just said? I tell you I want to make this work, and you're telling me to steal away into the night. Not even tell Cal where I'm going or why? What is wrong with you? That would tear him apart, not to mention how much it would kill me."

Father Donnelly shakes his head. "I'm sorry to have upset you. Forgive me. It was just a suggestion. I don't know much about romantic relationships, and it shows. I was simply trying to offer other options."

"I think I should go," I say, nearly making it to the door before Father Donnelly stops me.

"Please be careful, Cheyenne. You're a good girl, and I'm fearful you'll be caught up in a web of darkness."

"Relax, Father. Luke didn't win the first time, and I'm not going to let him win this time, either."

He outstretches his arm and makes the sign of the cross with his hand. "May God's light shine upon you, keeping you safe and comforted."

"Thank you," I say, shutting the door behind me. Once I get to the end of the darkened hallway, I drop to my knees. It's happening again. I can't move. I can't talk. I can't see anything but darkness, but I can hear. Panic fills my gut, and I tremble with anxiety. Recapturing my breath, I'm finally able to stand, and with wobbly legs, I bounce off of the walls while making my way back to Father Donnelly's office. I'm ashen when I throw open his door. "That song. That music…"

He quickly pulls the needle off the record on his gramophone. "It's Vivaldi. I play it to relax. Dear God, are you okay?"

Bright flashes of light occlude my vision as I stumble back down the dark hallway. I need to get some air. My brain is desperately trying to conjure up images, but something is blocking them. The result is a rapid array of pictures that last barely a nanosecond. I can't even begin to process them.

"Cheyenne!" Father Donnelly calls after me.

"I have to go," I say, hugging the wall. "I have to get out of here."

"Please. Stay. At least have a glass of water before you leave," he calls after me.

I don't even acknowledge his last request. Finally making it outside into the crisp, cool night helps to alleviate some of the symptoms. The visual disturbances cease, and even though I'm still incredibly shaky, I start Felton's car and zoom off to his place. There is something I'm supposed to be doing, but the brain fog has me utterly discombobulated. Then I remember Brant.

I stop the car on the side of the road to dial his number, and he answers right away. "Hey," I say, stopping him before he can say anything to me. "Something happened at the church. I'm shaky, but I'm okay. The song I've been hearing in my dream—Father Donnelly played it in his office. It's Vivaldi. Anyway, hearing it caused some weird things to happen, and I just want to…"

"Cheyenne, stop and listen to me. Get to

Felton's right away, and call me when you get there. Luke's job is a fake, and someone went to great lengths to make it look legit. The company doesn't exist. He flew into New Orleans from Oklahoma, but that's all we know right now. I'm getting a warrant to pull the videos from the airport to see what happened once he arrived. He's out there somewhere, so please be careful."

"I will. Thanks again, Brant. How's Cal?"

"He's fine. You'll be seeing each other again soon. I promise."

"Okay. I'm holding you to that. Maybe I should call him?"

"No, you need to get to a place that's safe and secure. Don't forget to call once you get to Felton's, and be sure to catch some big ones tomorrow."

"I won't, Brant. I'm on my way as soon as we disconnect. Wait. *Big ones* what?" Too late, he'd already ended the call.

RHONDA R. DENNIS

THIRTEEN

The beams of the headlight illuminate Felton's stout body as I park beneath the carport. The chilly air has him trying to keep warm with an oversized red and black plaid jacket, while his balding head is covered with a knit cap. He's messing around with his boat across the yard, and he waves when he notices me getting out of the car.

"What are you doing?" I call as I make my way to him. "It's too cold and dark to be going out in the boat."

"I'm just getting it ready for tomorrow. I got big plans to go out and join the guys. You're gonna have to stay sequestered though, sweetheart."

I wait to finish the discussion until I get close enough to no longer warrant shouting. Pulling my coat tightly against my body, I'm desperate to ward off the icy wind cutting through to my bones. Stomping my feet to increase the blood flow, I ask Felton if he's spoken to Brant.

"I did. He's worried about you because that

Luke guy came down under false pretenses. Not to worry, if they don't catch him by morning, you'll just have to go fishing with me."

"I'm not much on fishing, Felton. You might just have to leave me behind. Can't I stay sequestered in your house and not your boat?"

"That would be very dangerous and callous on my part," Felton argues. "Besides, I already told Brant that we'd probably be out of communication until tomorrow evening since we're planning to go out to the Gulf."

"I'm really uncomfortable with being out in a boat all day long, especially after the incident at the church…"

Felton pulls his half chewed cigar from his mouth and gives me his undivided attention. "What happened? Are you okay?"

"I finally know the song that was playing in my dreams. Father Donnelly played it on his gramophone as I left his office and hearing it did some very strange things to me. It was almost as if I blacked out, but I was still conscious." I shake my head. "None of it makes sense, I know, but I think something is trying to surface from my subconscious, and it's being blocked. The last thing I need is to be in a boat in the middle of nowhere and have it happen again."

"Did Father Donnelly say anything to you before you left?" Felton tosses his cigar into the water before joining me on the dock.

"I pretty much ran away before he could. He tried, but I had to get out of there. It felt like I was suffocating."

"You must've been very scared," Felton says,

reaching for me and pulling me in for a paternal embrace.

"I was. I still am. I don't know what's wrong with me."

"I'm sure you'll find out soon enough," he whispers, patting me softly on the back. Before I can react, his embrace tightens to the point that I can no longer breathe. It feels as though my ribs will crush under the vice-like grip he has on me, and the pain is so intense that even though my mouth is agape, I can't pull in enough air to make a sound. "Shhhh," he whispers into my ear. "Don't fight it. Just go to sleep, and everything will be okay. Promise."

With desperate eyes I hope will put an end to the torture, I try to look toward Felton, but he continues the ruthless assault to my upper body. Tighter and tighter he squeezes like an anaconda until finally the dark spots I'm seeing turn into complete blackness.

My mouth is so dry that I can barely swallow. That's the first thing I notice when I begin to regain consciousness. The second thing I'm aware of is I'm freezing everywhere except for my back. I pull my eyes open to find myself in a heavily wooded area. The slightly fishy smell in the air lets me know that wherever I am, it's near the water. Reaching deep to find the strength to move, I try to sit up. Pain and soreness worse than anything I've ever experienced before halts me.

Instinct says to guard my ribs, but when I try to do so, I realize I can't because my hands are tied behind my back. Utterly disheartened, I start to tear up.

"Cheyenne?" A voice calls. I stop my pity party.

"Luke?" I ask, pushing through the pain to finally roll over. His face is swollen and bruised, but with one partially open eye, he looks in my direction.

He's bound very much the same way I am, hands behind his back, harnessed around his chest, and tethered to a run set up between two trees, much like how one would secure a dog. He scoots on his rear to get closer to me. "Cheyenne, what is going on here? Who's doing this? Why?"

"I'm pretty sure it has something to do with you, Luke. Why are you stalking me? I divorced you because of the things you've done. I want nothing to do with you anymore, Luke. You had to know that coming after me wouldn't end well, especially when they found out you didn't really have an offshore job. I must say, that's a pretty elaborate ruse even for you."

"Wait, there are some things you should know. Before we talk about how I got down here, I need you to know that I never stopped loving you, Cheyenne. I wanted to be the man you expected me to be, and I worked hard to become that guy in prison. I'm not the same thug. I've changed."

"Changed? You couldn't have changed too much since you recently murdered a man at my place!"

"Murder? I didn't murder anyone. Cheyenne, I don't even know where you live. You mean to tell me you aren't in Oklahoma anymore?"

"It's kind of pointless to play dumb at this point, Luke. We know all about how you faked a job to get down here, presumably to get closer to me."

"Cheyenne, I came down here to work offshore and hopefully make enough money to try to support you the way I never could before. I was recruited, and I swear, I had no idea you were living here. How did we end up tied up together out here? Who did this?" Suddenly, the events that lead me to the wooded clearing come back to me. "Son of a bitch. Felton did this. He hurt me—squeezed me until I lost consciousness. Why?"

"Who's Felton?" Luke asks.

"My boyfriend's father. This definitely makes no sense." I try shaking off the cobwebs to connect the dots as to what happened and what's going on, but I keep hitting dead ends.

"What did you do to piss him off, and what does it have to do with me?" Luke asks.

"I'm trying to figure that out, Luke. Along with how in the hell we're going to get out of this mess. How did you get here?"

"When I was granted parole, one of the stipulations was that I get a job. This recruiter for an offshore company that hires people like me said he could get me on a rig right away. They paid for my ticket and had some guy pick me up at the airport. He was supposed to bring me to the company's headquarters to do some paperwork, get a physical, drug test, all that stuff. Instead, I wound up getting my ass whooped and stuck on this island."

"We're on the island?"

"I don't know about 'the' island, but we're on an island of some sort."

"Cal pointed out this place to me before. He used to play here when he was a kid. It's not far from his dad's place, and obviously, we don't want to signal that way for help. However, I remember seeing the island from a restaurant I ate at once." I sigh. "The bad thing is, Felton is connected everywhere. Even if we get someone's attention, it might not do us any good. They'll cover for him. Brant!" I search my pockets in hopes that he left my phone behind when he dumped me off. No such luck.

"Okay, who's Cal and who's Brant?"

"Cal is my boyfriend, and Brant is a police officer I became friends with after moving here."

"So if this Cal guy used to hang out here, how do you know he isn't in on all of this with his dad? Maybe he put his dad up to the kidnapping?"

My head begins to throb contemplating it.

"And you said something about a dead guy at your place? Maybe it was them who did it, 'cause it sure wasn't me."

"Odell was the janitor at the college where I teach, and he was found hanging from a tree outside my apartment." I go silent for a while afterwards because I'm not sure what to think anymore. Could Cal be involved in all of this?

Luke loudly clears his throat. "What in the hell have you gotten yourself into, Cheyenne?"

I shake my head and fight back the tears. "I don't know. Luke, I'm so scared I'm losing my mind. On top of all this, I've been having weird dreams and visions, and this little girl in a red dress is haunting my courtyard, and this fortune teller cautioned me about most of it, but I ignored her because her warning made no sense…"

"Hold up. Talk about not making any sense. Cheyenne, you need to snap out of it and focus on the here and now. We are hurt, tied up, and in the middle of nowhere on some deserted island in the Louisiana waterways. Gators, wild hogs, and snakes live in places like this, and here we are trapped like bait. I don't know about you, girl, but I'm thinking it's time for less talk and more escaping. Can you wiggle out of your hand restraints?"

"What do you think I've been doing since I woke up, Luke? I wasn't just sitting here gabbing because I had nothing better to do. You always thought I was stupid and couldn't take care of myself. That's why you marched around with your rotten macho attitude. 'Oh, look at my dumb ass wife who can't figure anything out on her own. I gotta take care of my stupid broad because she can't handle living life on her own,'" I say mockingly.

"I never once said that, Cheyenne, and I definitely never thought you were stupid. If anything, I was intimidated by your smarts. You said you're teaching now? At a college? Dumb is something you never were, and I damned well knew it even back then."

"Then why did you treat me that way?"

"Because I was jealous, okay? I was young, ignorant, and even though I knew better, I couldn't seem to help myself. Having fourteen hours a day to reflect because you're confined to a prison cell tends to give a person some insight into his faults." He grimaces as he struggles against his bindings.

"I appreciate that you admitted it," I say, fighting to pull my hands free, as well. He stops what he's doing so he can look at me with his good eye.

"Going to prison made me a man, but losing you made me want to be a better one."

His words slam my heart like a ton of bricks, and I stop fidgeting. "Whatever the reason, I'm glad you're on the right path," I say softly.

"Did you know I got out for good behavior? That cop I shot, I spent a few minutes every day writing him a letter telling him how sorry I was for doing that to him and also telling him a new lesson I learned that particular day. At first, I thought he wasn't getting them 'cause I got no response, but like a year later, I got a letter back. The back and forth kept up all the years I was incarcerated. He'd come by to visit me, to counsel me, to guide me in the ways of the Lord." I stop writhing once again to give him a shocked look. "Yes, Cheyenne. I'm born again. I go to church when I can, and I minister to the needy. My life is now about serving others."

"Luke, I... I really don't know what to say. That's a wonderful thing."

"It took me longer to figure it out than you 'cause your parents raised you right. My parents... well, you know."

"My faith has teetered since the day my parents died." Exhausted from fighting with my restraints and sore from the beating my body's taken, I slouch my back against the base of the closest tree.

"Cheyenne, I didn't know. What happened?"

"A house fire. The coroner said they didn't suffer. The smoke killed them before the flames reached them. They just drifted off to sleep and never woke up he says. I guess I'll be seeing them again soon," I say, emotions getting the best of me.

"Not if I can help it," Luke assures, scooting beside me. He leans his body against mine since he can't put his arm around me. "Would you like for me to say a prayer?" Sniffling, I nod. Luke begins to pray. "Dear Lord, Jesus in Heaven, please look after me and Cheyenne as we fight our way out of this mess. We don't know what caused this, but we have faith that you will reveal all when the time is right. Please give us strength, courage, and the ability to escape this terrible situation. If we don't make it through, please know our souls are ready to be called home if it be your will. This we ask through your name. Amen."

"Amen," I nearly whisper. "You really have changed, haven't you?"

"I have, Cheyenne. I really have."

Loud methodical applause draws Luke and me from the moment. The bright moonlight that beams through the tree branches serves like a spotlight announcing Felton's arrival. "So sorry to break up this touchy feely moment, but it's time to get a move on, folks. I need a couple of things from you before I can wrap this plan. Miss Douglas, I'll start with you."

He pulls a folded up piece of paper from his pocket and flicks it hard so that it snaps open. He produces a pen, which he tucks in his mouth before pulling a pocket knife from his pants pocket. He saws at the rope binding my wrists, and I can barely bring my arms to the front once I'm free. My appendages feel as though they're made of lead, and though I manage to get them beside me, I'm still unable to lift them.

"I'm gonna need you to write a little note for me," Felton says. "No funny business or this knife will slit that pretty throat of yours. Understand?"

"I couldn't even if I wanted to because my arms won't work," I answer honestly.

Felton sighs loudly. "I'm working on a timeline here!" he fusses. "You. You do exactly what I say or she gets it. You understand me?" He pulls his .44 magnum from his coat and pushes the freezing cold barrel against my temple. Luke nods emphatically.

"I'll do whatever you want," he agrees.

"Good. Behind me is a shovel. I'm going to cut you loose and then you're going to start digging me a hole, nice and wide. You're a strapping guy. Shouldn't take you too long."

Felton holsters his weapon to remove the bindings from Luke's wrist. Before Luke has a chance to recover, Felton pulls me upright and stands behind me. I yelp from the pain and find the hard steel barrel of the gun pressed against my head once again.

"Please don't hurt her," Luke implores as he slowly bends for the shovel. "I'm doing what you asked." He stabs the blade into the thick black dirt, quickly turning shovelful after shovelful of clay aside.

"You. Those fingers working yet?" He quickly releases me, spins me around, and makes like he's going to backhand me. Instinctively, I throw my hands up to cover my face. "Yep, working just fine. Here, write exactly what I say on this." He shoves the pen and paper at me, and I squat so I can transcribe his message. Shivering from the mix of cold and fear, I can barely hold the pen steady.

"Felton, why are you doing this?"

"Shut up and write," he growls. "Cal. I'm sorry to do this to you, but I have to go away. Luke found me, and now I realize leaving him was wrong. He's a fugitive, but I love him, so we're going to disappear somewhere far away so we can be together. I'm sorry for hurting you. Please move on quickly. Cheyenne."

I'm scribbling out the last of the note when it suddenly becomes very apparent what Felton's end game is. Luke is digging our graves. What I can't figure out is why. Thousands of questions rapidly flash through my mind. *What does he have to gain by getting rid of me and Luke? Maybe it has nothing to do with Luke, and he's just a necessary part of the puzzle to explain my disappearance. But why such an elaborate ruse? Is Felton jealous of Cal's relationships with women?* Regardless of the reason, there's no way in hell that I'm going to just lie down and become a homicide victim. If Felton wants me dead, he's going to have to work for it.

I grip the pen as tightly as I can in my hand when I slowly stand to give Felton the note. Just as his fingertips are about to touch it, I release it, and the wind sends it flittering about.

"Son of a bitch," he says, forgetting about me as he makes a mad grab for the letter. Right as he's about to get a hold of it, I leap onto his back and ram the pen as far as I can into the soft tissue on the side of his neck. He flails his arms madly while his pain-filled shouts resonate through the night sky. I hit the ground with a solid thud, and despite the pain, I'm able crabwalk away from his reach. Felton spins around, his mad eyes wide from the shock, as the wound forms a sluice of dark blood down the length of his body. Teeth exposed in an agony and rage induced grimace, he raises his gun and aims it right at my head. Quickly searching with desperate eyes, I realize there is nowhere to go, so I curl into a ball, tightly close my eyes, and brace for the shot. It doesn't come, so I crack an eye to see what's happening.

Luke lurches from the hole and makes a mad dash for Felton, his shovel raised high in the air and ready to attack. Completely expressionless, Felton pulls the gun away from my head, and points it in Luke's direction instead. A thunderous explosion rumbles through the air, but it doesn't dominate for long because my shrill screams soon replace the echoes of the thunderous *crack*. Clutching his chest, Luke stumbles backwards a few steps and falls into the hole he'd been digging.

"NO!" I cry out, my vision blurring from the tears welled in my eyes. The recently warmed steel barrel presses against my head once again, and knowing how great the odds are stacked against me, I begin to hyperventilate. Felton can barely keep the gun steady, but I don't doubt for one second that he's able to pull the trigger even though he appears to be losing strength quickly. Again, I brace for the inevitable when another *crack* breaks the silence. *Crack, crack, crack.*

Felton's body snaps backwards then lurches forward with each new sound. Four hits to the chest finally make him lose control of his weapon, and he barely has time to grab at the pen in his neck as his limp body buckles to the ground. Not even caring how it happened or who did it, I run full out to the hole where Luke collapsed, and without a second thought, I jump in with him.

His eyes stare ahead, and I'm convinced he's gone until he blinks. "Luke, hold on. Help is coming. Felton is gone. Hold on." His eyes shift to look in mine.

"I'm not scared. I want to be with Him. Please don't be sad for me, Cheyenne. I'm going to be just fine." He musters up enough energy to brush the tears from my cheek with his dirty and bloody hand. "It's important that I tell you how sorry I am for failing you as a husband. You're the love of my life. Do you accept my apology?"

"Of course, but listen. You need to hang on Luke. We can talk about this more later, once you're feeling better…"

He feebly shakes his head. "You always did talk too much," he says, with a slight smile. "Just listen, okay?" I nod. "There's something I want."

"Anything."

"Live a happy life.

"I'll do my best," I say, sniffling.

"Will you kiss me goodbye, Cheyenne? In prison, I'd get through many tough days by dreaming of the day you'd kiss me again."

I wipe my face with my sleeve before lowering my head to softly press my lips against his. With a gentle touch, he reaches to embrace me as best he can in such an awkward predicament. I can feel his life's energy slipping away.

"Pray with me, Cheyenne?" Luke asks. I nod, lest he hear the heartbreak in my voice. "Our Father…" I lie in his arms, cold dirt surrounding us, with my head propped on his shoulder. The warmth of his blood seeps through my clothes, and I fight the urge to scream out into the night.

"Our Father…" I begin. By the time I reach the final line, Luke is gone. His body goes limp, and I sit up so I can see his face. "No, no, no, Luke," I say, gently running my fingers over his handsome face. Once I close his eyes by running my fingertips across his lids, I lightly kiss his forehead. I slump my head against the damp, dark soil in the hole. It's then that reality comes crashing back. *I'm not alone. Someone shot Felton. He is dead, isn't he?* I can't even think straight.

I reach up to grasp the edges of the hole to pull myself out of the makeshift grave when a strong hand helps me onto solid ground. "Brant!" I say, lurching myself into his arms.

"There's blood everywhere," Brant says, pulling me away from his body to shine a bright flashlight up and down the length of my body. "How much of it is yours? Help is on the way."

I shake my head. "None that I know of. Oh, my God, Brant! What just happened? Do you know why Felton did this? He was going to kill me. He killed Luke! He set him up and was going to make it look like we left town, and I can't figure out any of this ..." I glance over to see that Cal is standing over his father's body. "Cal! Cal, do you know what this was about?"

He looks up, shock and disbelief show on his face. He simply shakes his head then goes back to staring at his father's lifeless corpse.

"We don't have to figure it all out right here and now. You're safe now, Cheyenne." Brant turns away from me briefly to say into the portable mic on his shoulder, "All clear. Come on in, guys."

I take advantage of Brant's diverted attention to move closer to Cal. I place my hand on his shoulder, and he pulls away like my appendage was a scalding hot piece of iron. "Cal, this isn't my fault."

"I need some time. I'm not angry or upset with you, but I need to be away from you right now. I have to come to terms with the fact that you shoved an ink pen in my father's neck."

"Are you kidding me?" I demand. "Do you know what I just went through?"

"Yeah, I believe I do since you happen to be drenched in my father's blood."

I feel as though he's slapped me. "So, you'd feel better about the situation if I'd let him shoot me in the head instead of trying to protect myself. I see. The majority of this is the blood of my ex-husband who was MURDERED by your father, while trying to protect ME! Your father wanted me dead, Cal. DEAD! If you need time to come to terms with my method of self defense, maybe you were in on it, too? Do you want me dead, Cal?"

"I can't believe you'd ask that," he says. The wounded look in his eyes proves my words strike like daggers to his heart. Cal runs his hands through his hair. "Why would my dad do this?" he asks, his eyes pleading for the answers.

"That's what I'd like to know, too. Cal, he made me write a note to you saying that Luke and I took off together then he planned to kill us and bury us there—in that hole he made Luke dig. The only thought I could come up with is that he wanted to keep you single. But would he really go through such an elaborate scheme and plan to kill two people to make it happen?"

"Three," Brant offers. "That we know of."

"Three?" Cal asks with disbelief.

"Odell. It wasn't Luke who killed him. He was on a flight to Louisiana at the time. DNA came back with a match for Felton from some of the fingernail scrapings taken at Odell's autopsy."

"What?" Cal questions.

"Wait, you haven't heard the half of it yet. Airport footage shows your dad picking up Luke and driving off with him in a white van with a false company logo on the side—probably one of those magnetic signs you can get off the internet. It seems as though he's the one who made contact with Luke and drew him down here with the promise of a fake job."

"But how did he know Luke was paroled or that he even existed for that matter? Maybe it was me? Maybe I mentioned to him about Cheyenne being married before. Shit, I can't even comprehend what's going on right now, much less remember the past," Cal asserts.

"That's how I've felt since touring Azalea Downs," I explain.

"It's a terrible feeling. I'm so sorry, Cheyenne. I should have been there for you more— more protective. More attentive…"

Cal is interrupted by Brant. "No use dwelling on it now. Your dad still had lots of contacts within the department. I'm sure he reached out to get the information he needed to put this plan together. Plus, he's obviously good at what he does. I've heard some rumors about past cover ups, but largely ignored them because they weren't relevant to me."

"But what if Luke hadn't been paroled? I ask.

Brant shrugs. "I guess he'd have come up with a different plan. Oh, and speaking of plans, Luke wasn't the guy who left the box at your office, either. We pulled film from the school and though the guy looks a lot like him, it's not. Guess it was Felton's way of throwing you off your game. You know? Making you frazzled so you didn't think straight."

"He did a good job of that." I shiver violently, so I stomp my feet to force blood to my extremities.

"Look, can I count on you to get her home and make sure she's okay? I know you've been through a lot too, man, but it would be better for you to be there for each other while we sort through this mess," Brant suggests to Cal.

"Of course I will. I'm sorry I was harsh earlier. I guess it was the shock of it all. I do love you, Cheyenne, and I can never apologize enough for my father putting you through this."

"It's not your place to apologize, Cal. You didn't do this; he did. You're a victim, too." I turn to Brant. "Are we free to go? I need to get cleaned up. The blood…"

He nods before calling over a uniformed officer and instructing her to get us home. She's also instructed to confiscate and bag our clothes as evidence before she leaves. She affirms the request and leads us to one of the boats waiting near the shore of the island. Cal carries me in his arms and gently places me in the boat to spare me the added discomfort of wading in the frigid dark water. More boats with more officers arrive, passing us as we head towards Frenchman's Cove. As much as I want to forget the night's events, I can't seem to turn my eyes away from the island. I pull the wool blanket the female officer hands me tightly across my body. So much information to process, so much sadness to get over, so much hope dashed, so many questions unanswered— how will life ever get back to normal?

RHONDA R. DENNIS

FOURTEEN

Cal and I are in our night clothes while drinking coffee in the kitchen, each with a throw over our shoulders to stave off the chill that still remains in our cores. Brant knocks at the door, and Cal gets off his stool long enough to open the door before hopping back up to finish his coffee.

Though freshly showered, it's evident from the dark circles under his eyes that Brant hadn't rested very well. I don't even ask; I simply reach over to pull a mug off of the rack and fill it to the brim with piping hot dark roast. He doesn't add anything to my offering, and simply downs it black.

Once he's had a few gulps, he pulls a thick file folder out and starts to thumb through it after slapping it onto the counter. "Ready to try to get some of this figured out?" he asks, taking a pen from his pocket and clicking to ready it for notes.

"I have a question. How did you know where to find us last night?" I ask. "And Cal, how did you get there, too?"

Brant looks to Cal, and once Cal nods, Brant begins. "Right after you called me from the church, I got the footage from the airport. Once I realized it was Felton, I reached out to Cal immediately. Something was definitely wrong with that situation, and we were going out to Felton's to confront him about it. On the way over, I realized you hadn't called me back to say you made it to his house. We did a quick run through of the place, and when Cal noticed the car there but no one home, he went straight for the boat shed. The boat was missing, and he knew where to go from there."

"I think if there are any answers to be found, they're going to be at Dad's house. The first place I'd look is the Just in Case box," Cal suggests.

"I agree," Brant says. "I'm actually waiting for the warrant to be signed."

"Don't worry about a warrant. I'll consent to a search," Cal says.

Brant nods. "That'll help to get this done faster. Thanks."

"What's the Just in Case box?" I ask.

"It's a lock box that Dad kept just in case something happened to him. There's a key, but I have to go through an act of Congress to get to it. The stipulation is that it can only be opened if something happened to him."

"Then that's where we'll start," Brant says. "If it's okay, I'll help myself to another cup of coffee while you two get dressed?"

"Help yourself to anything: food, coffee, TV," I offer, finishing up my mug and placing it in the sink.

"Hey," Brant says, stopping me in my tracks. "You look pretty good for nearly getting murdered last night."

"Let's just say my near death experience gave

me new enthusiasm for living," I utter with a slight smile.

"I can relate. See you in a few," Brant says, propping his feet on my coffee table while aiming the remote at the television. As soon as Cal and I are ready, Brant chauffeurs us to Felton's in his work car.

It's incredibly eerie, and uneasiness and dread consume me as we enter Felton's house. Everything is just as it was when I was last there, down to the sheets and blanket remaining on the sofa. Hard to believe that as I slept there, Felton was secretly plotting my demise. A shudder tears through my body.

Cal and Brant temporarily disappear into the office/hobby room, and Cal returns holding a small, portable lock box. "Well, this isn't going to be much fun," he says, setting it on the kitchen table.

"Because?" Brant questions.

"Because he wanted to make it as difficult as possible for me to get into it so I wouldn't be tempted to open it prematurely. The first thing I'm supposed to do is go outside to his tool shed and look for the blue coffee can on the third shelf. Inside is a map of where to dig for the next clue," Cal says.

"Did you ever go searching for it before today?" I wonder out loud.

"Nah. Dad would know what I was up to if I started digging up the yard. It wasn't worth it. Guess I'll head outside," Cal says with hesitation.

"Or we can try these," Brant says, jingling a key ring brimming with an assortment of various shapes and sizes.

"Or we can try that," Cal agrees. "Dad always kept the original key on his person."

"I thought we might need it, so I took it from evidence."

Cal nods, taking the key ring from Brant's outstretched hand. He fumbles through the collection until he finds one he believes will open the box. The tumbler turns easily, and the latch clicks as it releases. With bated breath, we anxiously watch as Cal opens the lid. Inside is a stack of cash, some documents, and perched on the very top is a handwritten note.

The priest knows my guilt, and he shares the blame. If I'm gone, find him.

Make him explain.

"Father Donnelly?" I ask. Cal nods.

"Has to be. The two of them go way back."

"I'll send a unit to pick him up. We'll keep searching through this stuff until they get him to the station, if that's okay with you, Cal?" Brant asks.

"Of course. Yes. Whatever you need," Cal answers.

"Good." Brant calls into the station and asks the dispatcher to send a police car to the church to pick up Father Donnelly for questioning. Once he's finished with his instructions, he moves towards the office. "Something in there caught my eye. Do you mind?" he asks Cal.

"Not at all," Cal says, following him into the cluttered room. I opt to stand in the doorway for two reasons: one, because it's incredibly cramped in there; and two, because the room gives me the chills, but I'm not brave enough to hang out by myself in the other part of the house.

After the dust settles from his yanking open the rust colored curtains, Brant goes straight for the desk chair and sits. He pulls a huge file folder from one of the boxes and plops it on the desk. "We haven't used these file folders in ages. I have a feeling I know exactly what this is." He turns it around so he can see the front. Marked plain as day on the tab, as well as across the midsection of the folder itself is *Nuit Rouge*.

Brant pulls a photo from a massive stack of 8x10s and studies it carefully. He lowers it to look my way.

"No," I say, my heart suddenly thudding in my chest. He places the picture flat on the desk and pushes it in my direction. I'm nearly trembling when I take the few shaky steps to pick up the photo. Gasping, I throw my hand to my mouth. "He lied," I say with disbelief.

"What are you talking about?" Cal asks, positioning himself to see what I'm seeing.

"The crime scene I saw in my mind. This is it. This woman and this man were in the parlor in my vision, but look, the white dress is exactly the same, but the broach is gone. Her hair is the same style, the wounds are in the same place, her makeup... Cal, I saw this!"

Brant continues to flip through photos, laying each new one that further corroborates my visions in front of me. "This is the parlor. No bodies, but look! Peacock feathers in a vase." Part of me is excited because I feel validated, but the larger part of me is desperately trying to hold it together because I'm freaked the hell out.

Brant withholds some of the more gory photos from me, but as I recall to him what I saw in the dreams, he nods whenever he finds a picture that matches my descriptions.

"The only thing you don't have is the broach, the gold band, and the white shawl," I comment. No longer caring about the clutter, I plop right onto a dilapidated folding chair before losing my ability to stand on my own two feet. Brant squints like he's in deep thought before turning a final picture in my direction. It's not a white fringed shawl; it's a bloody white blanket.

Brant digs through the box the file folder came out of to retrieve a brown manila envelope. He opens it and pours the contents onto the top of the pictures. The rhinestone broach and the gold ring tumble out with a few shell casings. He shakes his head. "Looks like someone was definitely on the take."

A stone faced Cal stares at the trinkets. "I swear I knew nothing about any of this."

Brant's phone buzzes loudly, and he answers before anything more can be said. "Got him?" he asks into the microphone without any of the customary formalities associated with phone decorum. "On our way."

"Son of a bitch," he says, collecting the assortment scattered across the desk and tossing it into the cardboard box they originally came out of before taking the entire thing with us. "Let's see if we can get some answers."

"We don't normally allow things like this to happen during an investigation, but since Father Donnelly refuses to speak to anyone unless you two are present, we're going to make an exception," Brant says as he walks me and Cal down a long cinderblock corridor.

"Anything we need to know before going in there?" I ask.

"Just try to stay as quiet as possible. If he directs any questions to you, look at me. If I nod, answer. If I don't, let it go," Brant instructs.

I'm expecting to see a tiny room with a metal table bolted to the floor, a couple of chairs and a huge two way mirror. Instead, we're ushered into a very nice meeting room with rolling orthopedic chairs and a coffee bar. Father Donnelly's portly body is wedged into one of the chairs, and a jolly grin is upon his face. If it weren't for the unorthodox circumstances, you'd swear he was just there for a friendly visit.

"Kids," he says when Cal and I walk into the room.

"Father," we say simultaneously.

Everything is quiet for a few seconds, and finally, Father Donnelly speaks up. "I'm sorry to hear about Felton, Cal, and your ex-husband, Cheyenne."

We nod.

Brant starts a recorder then begins the questioning. "We're not going to beat around the bush here, Father. Felton Gage left a note behind stating that you know the answers to one of the area's biggest mysteries." He consults a piece of paper in front of him. "His exact words are: *the priest knows my guilt, and he shares the blame. If I'm gone, find him. Make him explain.*"

"Well, obviously I have no clue what he's talking about," Father Donnelly says stuttering through most of the sentence.

Brant gives him a stone cold look. "I'm just doing this as a courtesy—a favor, if you will. You see, Felton left very detailed records for us to go through. I have them sitting on my desk right there in the other room. Will it be tedious to read through all of the mess? Yes, but necessary. See, if you just spill the beans about what you know, you'll save me and my people a lot of grunt work. The DA and I love when we're spared grunt work. So much so that perhaps we could reward the person who makes our jobs less—what's the word?--difficult, I suppose you'd say? Yes, a nice reward could be in that person's future."

Father Donnelly is bright red as he ponders what Brant has told him. Cal and I know this is a huge bluff and that there really are no secret files. Even though I'm knee deep in this case, I'm in awe of Brant's interrogation techniques. He's a damned good cop.

"Felton says you share his guilt. Is it because he confided his secrets to you and you held them in even though the law obligates you to divulge them?" Brant asks.

Father Donnelly presses his forehead into his hands. "I only wish it were so simple." When he raises his head to face us, tears run freely down his rounded cheeks. "I bear guilt and shame that has weighed heavily upon my conscience for over three decades. I've committed so many sins that I spend hours a day begging our Savior for forgiveness."

Stone faced, Brant prompts him to continue.

"I can hardly think of a proper place to start," Father Donnelly says with a shaky voice.

"Tell us how you became involved with Felton," Brant offers as a suggested starting point.

"Before I begin, please know that my heart is heavy because I have to lay all of this on you. I won't even begin to ask for your forgiveness, but please know that my intentions were always good, even when I partook in things I knew were wrong. What I divulge will affect all of you."

"Let's get on with it, Father," Brant prods.

"You don't understand, Major. Once the secret is revealed, there is no going back." A very somber Father Donnelly faces me and Cal.

Cal looks around nervously. "What do you mean, Father? I don't understand."

Father Donnelly, ignoring the rest of us, shifts his chair closer to Cal so he can look him directly in the eye. "Yes, I'm a man of the cloth, but all in all, I'm just a man—a mortal who makes mistakes, a person who often struggles with unfulfilled needs and wants. These needs and wants are easier to live without the older I get, but I joined the priesthood at a very young age. I was fresh out of seminary when I was called to serve at a little church down the bayou. One of the parishioners was a very lovely young woman by the name of Gretchen Belanger." His gaze drifts from Cal to some random spot in the room. "She was the most beautiful woman I ever laid eyes on. She was always smiling, eager to serve the church, and smart as a whip. She was perfect in every way." Father Donnelly returns his gaze to Cal. "I developed feelings for her—feelings unlike anything I'd ever felt before, and when she confided that she loved me as well, my heart nearly burst with joy. But, I had my obligation to the church that I had to fulfill."

"What does any of this have to do with my dad?" Cal interrupts.

Father Donnelly nods. "I'm getting there. My flesh was weak, and with reckless abandon, we made love." He hangs his head in disgrace. "I broke my celibacy vow, but worse than that, I made her with child. I struggled for a long time about what I should do about it—two years to be exact. Her family abandoned her, but she loved that baby so much that she had no problem raising it on her own. She followed me to my new church, where every Sunday she'd attend with the little one, thereby presenting me with the gift of seeing that beautiful child who was half mine. I was going to leave the church for her. In fact, I was on my way to tell her when I was called by Felton to give last rites to an individual he found dying in an alley. It broke my heart when I found out it was Gretchen. Beside her, watching as she drew her last breath, was our frightened little one."

Hearing the story Father Donnelly tells is heartbreaking. I reach for a tissue to wipe at my eyes.

"Here I was, a young priest with no other skills, no way to care for a young child, watching the love of my life wilt away from stab wounds left by a robber who murdered her for seventeen dollars. Felton didn't call in the case. You see, he left me alone for a while with Gretchen, and eventually, he came back with the suspect. When he emptied out the man's pockets, he found the money and her watch. He put the suspect in the back of his squad car, and then found me a sobbing mess while holding the child. He was a smart guy, and he knew right away that something was up. I confessed everything to him, because frankly, at that point in time, I didn't care if I lived or if I died."

"What happened next?" Brant asks after a few moments of silence.

"Felton suggested something to me.

Normally, kids such as those were sent to foster homes or orphanages. Many were abused, tortured, and never given a fair shake in life. He said that as long as the child was young enough, and there was no family looking for it, there was no reason why we couldn't place the child ourselves in the homes of good Christian families."

"My dad helped you give the kid away?" Cal demands.

"Some, but not this one."

Cal looks sick. "What are you saying?"

"Felton raised you as his own. It was the only way I could stay involved in your life, yet remain in the priesthood."

"No, I'm sorry, but it can't be. I've got records. I've got pictures of my mother. I've got…"

"They're all fakes. You were the first one— the one he experimented with to see if we could get away with it."

Cal slams his fists against the table. "And you let him! You let him use me as a guinea pig! Your own flesh and blood!"

"He took good care of you, and you know it. You never wanted for anything, Cal. Felton was a good father to you," Father Donnelly asserts.

"He was a baby thief! You just admitted it! Just exactly how did this child peddling ring of yours work?" Cal demands.

Father Donnelly nervously twiddles his thumbs. "Aren't you even the least bit happy to know that I'm your father?"

"Are you kidding me? You robbed me of the life I was supposed to have."

"I saved you from a life of hell," he shoots

back.

"No, you saved yourself from hell on Earth, but it's clear you've bought yourself a one way ticket to eternal damnation. Everything about my life is a lie. All of those children you and Felton stole to put into other homes, their lives are lies. You disgust me."

"I understand your reaction, but son, it really was for the best. All children placed went to much better homes than they would have if they'd been left as wards of the state. The children were young enough to have their memories manipulated, so they didn't even remember the bad things that happened to them. They had no one, and we gave them hope, love, and security. But then something unexpected happened."

"What was that?" Brant asks.

"Cheyenne came to town and started having those dreams," Father Donnelly answers.

"How did my dreams affect your side business?" I ask.

"Felton figured it out when you started reciting details about the case. Only two people knew that two of the bodies started out in the parlor. Felton and the little girl who hid from the gunfire only to come down and catch him moving the bodies." The scene slams back into my memory, and any mental blocks that I had before are now gone. I begin to tremble as the tragedy unfolds before my eyes. My speech gets progressively faster and faster as I recall the events of that night.

"Oh, my God. I was there—in the upstairs playroom. My mother wanted me with her because I was getting over an illness. I wore a long white nightgown and carried a soft yarn blanket—it was white with fringes…," I say with disbelief. "The shawl. It was my blanket. I'm remembering. I heard the shots, but I thought they were fireworks. I didn't want to miss them, so I sneaked onto the balcony. The shots continued to sound, but the sky never lit up. Disappointed, I walked back inside. Everything was over by then. The guys had already finished the massacre and taken off. Blood—it was everywhere. I slid in it when I went to the ballroom. I kept crying for my mother while searching through the bodies for my parents.

"Something crashed down in the parlor, startling me. It was my mother! She'd heard my cries but couldn't come to me, so she knocked something over so I could find her. My father was on top of her…" I shake my head. "I still can't make out his face, but hers. Oh, she was so beautiful. I have her eyes. She kept telling me to go upstairs. To hide. To run away, but I didn't want to leave her behind. I heard someone coming in the front door, so I did what she told me. I ran up the back staircase and hid in one of the bedroom closets. Everything is kind of sketchy after that." My eyes dart rapidly as though I'm chasing the memory as it shoots around the room. "Gray ghost! Gray ghost took me from the closet. It was Felton wearing a gray uniform."

"That would have been the right color for that time period," Brant affirms.

"The black ghost…" I look accusingly at Father Donnelly. "You and I were in a car—a big black sedan with no seatbelts—an older model car. You were playing that music. Oh, my God," I whisper. "How can I have those memories locked inside, yet have memories of the same time period with the people who raised me? Explain it to me!" I demand.

Father Donnelly's tone is much more timid than it was previously. "Like mentioned before, there were many criteria that had to be met. The children had to be of a certain age, one that the new parents could easily override the previous memories with false ones. All of the children we placed went to good homes. I thoroughly researched them myself. They paid for the documents, the doctored photos, and a fee for placement. It wasn't to be greedy, you see, it was to make sure they were willing to go to any lengths to make sure the child was well provided for. I don't know what Felton did with his portion, but every cent of my share went to the church."

"So these people just lined up to buy children? How can you say they were good candidates, no matter how much money they spent?"

"Cheyenne, your parents wanted nothing more than to be parents. They tried, but your poor mother miscarried multiple times, two of which resulted in still born babies. Can you imagine that heartache? When I say I thoroughly researched the candidates, I mean it. I remember all of their stories."

I begin to cry as I shake my head. "It wasn't right."

"Were you treated well?"

"That's beside the point," I argue.

"Did you love your parents?" he asks.

"I don't remember because you stole them from me. The people who raised me aren't my parents. My parents died at Azalea Downs."

"No, the murderers stole your parents,

Cheyenne. I made sure you went to a good home because there was no one left to raise you."

I shake my head. "My mother was alive when Felton brought me to you. She was reaching out for me."

"No, there were very strict rules about the children. They had to be orphaned."

"Brant, may I see the picture of the crime scene? The one that shows where my mother was positioned."

He rummages through some things and produces the photograph. I point to it. "My mother and father were shot in the parlor. My mother had one gunshot wound to her abdomen when I saw her. She has two in this picture. One to her abdomen and one to her chest—center mass. Your baby finder was making kids orphans when they actually weren't."

"No," Father Donnelly says.

"She was in the parlor with one wound! How did she end up in the heap with the others with an additional wound? Nothing else makes sense. Felton murdered my mother so he could peddle me off like some piece of junk."

"No, it was never like that," Father Donnelly insists.

"The spare casings we found with the jewelry corroborate this," Brant says.

"And what about our families? You can't tell me that we didn't have other family members willing to look after us," I demand.

"I can answer why no one came looking for you, Cheyenne," Brant says, tossing down case notes and a couple of photos. He begins to read from the file. "The youngest victim, four year old Cynthia

Badeaux, is presumed to be deceased. A bloodied blanket was found in the backseat of the getaway vehicle the assailants were driving, but no trace of the child has been found. This is an update from two years later: *Missing child from Nuit Rouge murders now officially listed as deceased.* Case closed. Signed by none other than Detective Felton Gage."

"I don't remember the news articles or anything else I researched mentioning a missing child," I say.

"That's because Felton did his best to keep that detail to a minimum. He knew how to work the reporters, playing up the fact that the tragedy was horrific enough, much less to sensationalize the possible murder of a child. It was important for people to put the event behind them and to move on. The whole area was basically a ghost town for a month afterwards because people were scared to leave their homes."

I shake my head. "Wow. You truly think you're a savior—a beacon of all things great?"

"I never proclaimed to be."

"Where am I from? Where do I get information about my real family?" I demand.

Father Donnelly hangs his head. "The Badeauxs are from New Orleans."

"And my family?" Cal asks.

"I'm your family."

"It's too early for that stuff, Padre. I'm asking about my mother's family."

"The Belangers used to live in Cypress Grove."

"I want a DNA test before this father thing goes any further," Cal demands.

"Anything you wish, but without a doubt, you are my son."

Brant interrupts, "Getting back to the here and now, your official statement is that Felton Gage figured out that Cheyenne Douglas was one of the children he sold on the black market after her parents were murdered the evening of the Nuit Rouge murders. He concocted a scheme to make it appear as though she had died to keep family members from looking for her and to justify her disappearance. Upon her returning to town as an adult, he felt threatened because of her recollections, so he decided to get rid of her. He opted to make it appear as though Cheyenne left town with her ex-husband, all the while intending to murder them and hide their bodies."

"Yes," Father Donnelly affirms.

I run my hands over my eyes. "This is crazy. It can't be real."

"I feel the same way," Cal says, just as wearily as me.

"Cal…," Father Donnelly calls.

"Is that even my name?" he demands.

"It is. Your mother allowed me to pick your name. I have her picture. It's quite worn from all the years of my handling it, but this is your mom." He reaches into the top pocket of his jacket and pulls out a pouch. Inside are a rosary, a small vial of holy water, and the tattered picture. He passes it to Cal. I can tell he's holding back his emotions from the size of the lump in his throat.

"She's so beautiful," he manages to say.

"Indeed. Didn't I tell you that she was the most beautiful woman I've ever laid eyes on? I was smitten the moment I saw her."

"I wish I could have known her," Cal says, lightly tracing her face with his finger.

"I wish you could've too, son."

"What happened to her killer?" Cal inquires.

"Justice was served," Father Donnelly says.

Brant shifts in his seat. "I'm sure it was, Felton-style if I were to guess from your tone." Father Donnelly nods. "So, over the years, how many children did you two makeshift social workers place?"

"Ten."

"I'm going to need all the information you can give me on those children. They have a right to know their histories," Brant says.

"But they were all placed in better homes," Father Donnelly says defensively.

"Better than her birth mother?" he remarks, raising his voice and sitting straighter in his chair. "You know, the one Felton put a bullet in so he could make a few extra dollars. How many more of those ten children have the same story, Father?"

"I don't know anything about that part. I just searched out the prospective families and transported the children to them. Felton handled everything else."

"And now he's gone, so it's all on you," Brant barks.

Father Donnelly stoically raises his head and sits straight in his chair. "I've been waiting for this since the day Felton Gage and I crossed paths. I've made my peace with God, my son, and one of the children we placed. I'm ready for whatever awaits me."

"Yeah, you're at peace, but these two just got thrust into hell. You know what's awaiting you?

Prison. Come on. Let me finish getting you processed. You can bond out after your arraignment, unless the judge denies it."

"However it must be is how it shall be." He stands and turns his outstretched wrists to Brant.

"No need for all that, Father. Come on. Follow me to the booking desk."

Father Donnelly stops just as he's about to cross the threshold. "Cal, I do hope you'll forgive me one day, and that you'll keep in touch. Seeing you grow up has been one of the highlights of my life. I'm proud of the man you've become."

"I wouldn't hold my breath, but you never know what a day holds," Cal offers.

Father Donnelly nods. "You'll be in my prayers, son. I love you. I'll always love you," he says as he shuffles down the hall thanks to Brant's nudging.

Cal grabs my hand under the table and squeezes it hard. I see that he's fighting back tears, but I'm not afraid to let mine flow. He pulls me to him, and once we're locked in a deep embrace, we stay that way for a while. In a matter of minutes we became strangers to ourselves. Our lives are nothing more than elaborate ruses, and we are simply puppets used in a sick game of greed and God-playing. We've been through so much, and I know we'll overcome this eventually. The question is where do we go from here?

RHONDA R. DENNIS

FIFTEEN

Cal and I spend the rest of the evening at my apartment. We're together, but we barely speak, opting to spend the time in silent deliberation. We even go to bed at different times, but both awaken with a start thanks to Brant. I quickly throw on a pair of jeans and a sweater then open the front door to find him hard at work on the camera system.

"What are you doing, and why are you doing it so early? Don't you ever sleep?" I question.

"I sleep when the mysteries are solved. There's one that's still bugging me."

"The secret admirer?"

"No, I solved that last night. I didn't want to call you because you had enough to process after Father Donnelly's confession." He points to a small screwdriver on the wrought iron table and signals for me to hand it over. "I paid a visit to your favorite student Billy, and I got all the information I needed."

"What? Why would you visit Billy?" I ask, giving him the screwdriver.

"Frankly, the kid has no reason to have beef with you, so I wanted to find out the real story. His parents weren't very happy to have a uniformed officer ask to speak to their son, so Billy was very quick to speak up once mom and dad got involved."

"And…"

"Billy's pissed because he wanted this place. He and some of his friends have this club that searches for ghosts and paranormal stuff. You know, like the stuff on TV?" I nod. "Well, because of the history with the place, he and his friends planned to rent the apartment for about a month to do their hoodoo voodoo stuff and then split. George was onto them though, and wasn't happy about renting to such young kids. That's when you came along and stole young Billy's thunder."

"He hates me because I ruined his plan to hunt for a ghost?"

"Pretty much. It doesn't take much to piss off a hormonal teen. Anyway, I could tell there was something he was holding back, and after some nudging I got him to come clean. He and one of his buddies were hiding in the bushes near the English building hoping to scare Odell. Evidently, it's a game they play on a regular basis."

"Lovely children, aren't they?" I say sarcastically.

"Yeah. Real winners. Anyway, they hesitated to jump out of the bushes because Odell wasn't alone that night."

"Really?" I ask. "Who was he with?"

"I'll give you one guess," Brant says, tossing down the screwdriver.

"I'm guessing Father Donnelly or Felton."

"That's two guesses. Boy, you're bad at this." I smile. "Felton. I showed Billy a picture, and he identified him right away. He overheard part of their conversation, too."

I decide it's probably best to sit down. Not caring that the metal chair is ice cold, I slide back into it anyway. "What were they talking about?"

"When Felton showed, he must have used his old credentials because Billy said he flashed a badge and carried a side arm. I'm guessing it was for the intimidation factor. Odell started to freak, confessing right away that he'd been the one leaving the stuff here at your place. He'd been threatened with arrest for stalking before. Sorry to say, you weren't his first crush."

I playfully roll my eyes. "I'm so jealous," I say monotone. "Get back to the story."

"This is what struck Billy as odd. He said Felton asked Odell about the Nuit Rouge murders and wanted to know why he would tell you to search them out in the library. Billy said that's when Odell really freaked because he couldn't figure out how Felton knew he'd suggested that to you. He started going on about government conspiracies and wire tapping and all kinds of other nonsense, but Felton finally calmed him down. He told him it would be best for him to not have any contact with you again. Odell refused—said he was too in love with you."

I put my head in my hands. "This is so unbelievably strange."

"Felton said he understood and encouraged him to leave a final gift for you at your apartment. He must've waited for the right time to slip a noose around his neck, sling it over the branch, and leave him bobbing like a piñata in front of your bedroom window."

"You're so crass," I scold even though I'm really not offended. Being around Brant has made me more appreciative of gallows humor. "So you think Felton murdered Odell because he didn't want me researching the Nuit Rouge case?"

"That's exactly what my thoughts are. He needed to pin the crime on someone, and who better than a jealous ex-husband?"

"And that's how Luke became involved." I sigh. "Felton had every bit of it planned out, and it would've worked, too. Wouldn't it?"

"Sorry to say, but I think it would've. He certainly covered all his bases. Some say the best cops make the best criminals. There's obviously some truth to that."

The shock of it all starts to wear off, so I stand. "Want some coffee?"

"I'd love some. It's freaking cold out here," Brant says quickly rubbing his hands together.

"You can come inside to get warm."

"Nah, I want to finish this up, but thanks."

I pause for a moment. "What mystery are you trying to solve, Brant?" I question.

"The little girl in the red dress. That's the only thing we haven't been able to figure out yet, and damn it, I'm going to do it."

I laugh. "Hey, as long as she stays outside and doesn't end up in my apartment, she doesn't bother me anymore. Her little spirit can play all it wants to out in the courtyard."

"There are no such things as ghosts."

"Suit yourself, but you might want to keep an open mind. Actual children don't float around in trees, glide across pavers, or vanish into thin air."

"Hence the camera." He points at it, and I shake my head.

"I'll be right back with your coffee."

Cal has coffee brewed, and it's not until I feel the sting of the warm heated air that I realize exactly how cold it truly is outside. I give him a quick rundown of what Brant said, and I also explain why Brant is outside hooking up a camera system.

"Is that considered detective work or paranormal research?" Cal chides.

"According to Brant, detective work. He's very adamant that there are no such things as ghosts."

"And what do you think?" Cal asks.

"I honestly don't know what to think. If you'd have asked me the question last week, I'd have easily answered no. But now…"

"Yeah, I'm feeling the same way. Have you made up your mind yet as to whether you're going to search for your real family?"

"Not really. Curiosity is pulling me in that direction, but then again, these people withstood and overcame a terrible tragedy. Suddenly popping into their lives after all of these years might be devastating for them. Maybe it's best that Cynthia Badeaux stay dead and forgotten."

"That's a valid concern, but trying to put myself in their shoes, I think I'd want to know. Even if they decide they want nothing to do with you, or if it upsets them, at least they will have the knowledge. Maybe Cynthia was never forgotten. Only one way to know for sure."

I mull it over. "Maybe I can find them and do one of those things like pretend I'm selling magazines or something just so I can get a sneak peek at them?"

Cal shrugs. "I don't see why not. I'll go with you."

"Thanks. What did you decide?"

"My family is a little more complicated than yours. My family disowned me and my mother once she became pregnant out of wedlock. They cast us aside when she was alive, and obviously, they didn't come looking for me once she died. It's pretty obvious they want nothing to do with me."

"That's just your mother's side. Does Father Donnelly have living relatives?"

"I guess that since the secret is out, he might divulge that information to me. I'm not ready to see him yet, though. It's hard not to be bitter knowing my father chose the church over his own flesh and blood."

I place my hand on his shoulder. "You were in the dark about his true ties to you, but he did make a point to always be a part of your life."

Cal considers what I said. "Felton was a good father to me, but I'm secretly relieved that he isn't my real dad. Learning that his character wasn't actually what he presented to the public, knowing that he's actually a cold blooded murderer, and also knowing how many lives he's ruined, it all makes me grateful that my real father is a mild-mannered priest. Don't get me wrong—I know he did some heinous things by helping Felton, but he's not a murderer, and my gut is telling me that he truly believed he was doing what he thought was in the best interest of those children. He was a good man doing bad deeds, whereas Felton was a bad man doing bad deeds."

I sigh heavily. "Cal, so much has changed, and we have so much to think about..."

"I know one thing that hasn't changed—I still

love you very much. I'm sorry this is happening, but I'm glad we can get through it together."

"So, you'll help me track down my family?"

"Of course. What do you think? Should we work for the electric company? Be religious disciples spreading the good word? Hot couple looking into settling in the neighborhood? I can be whoever you want me to be."

I arch my brows. "Ah, good looking couple interested in settling in the neighborhood might get us invited in for coffee."

"I like the way you think. I'll search out the Badeaux family and make sure they're still in New Orleans."

I place my hand on his forearm, and he sits back down. "Search for the Belangers, too. Just see if they're in Cypress Grove. You don't have to tell them who you are, but at least check them out."

He gives a tight lipped smile. "I'll think about it." He gently taps my hand before jumping on the computer. Brant comes inside, washes out his mug, and makes to leave without saying a word.

"Hey, you all done out there?" I ask.

"Yep. I've got it set up to where I can monitor it from my place. I'll let you know what I find out."

"Brant."

"Yeah."

"Get some rest."

"I'll rest when I'm dead."

I playfully shake my head. "Goodbye. Be safe."

"You know it," he says, giving a quick salute as he walks out of the door.

I'm a nervous wreck when we park in front of the beautiful Garden District home that belongs to Nathan and Selena Badeaux. Cal's research shows that they are the parents of my father, Nathan Badeaux, Jr. I rub my sweaty palms against the cool fabric of my pant suit and immediately start fanning myself with a pamphlet we picked up from a local real estate office.

"Sweetheart, it's forty-two degrees outside."

"But it feels like a hundred and ten in here," I nervously snap.

Cal turns in his seat. "You are Dr. Cheyenne Douglas, and you and your dashing fiancé, Dr. Cal Gage, are in the market for a lovely Garden District home."

"Boy, you sure are getting into the role playing thing," I say, finally releasing a pent up breath and looking toward the large white two story as I gather the courage to open the car door.

"You're the only real thing in my life, you know that, right?" I turn to him and smile.

"I love you," I say. "Thank you for being here with me."

He begins to forage around in one of the pockets of his sports jacket. "This has been on my mind for a long time. Names don't matter. Cheyenne or Cynthia, Cal Gage or Cal Donnelly, or even Cal Belanger. Who knows who we're supposed to be? But I know who I WANT to be. The only thing that matters to me is spending the rest of my life with you. You are my world, and together, we can overcome anything. We're proving that right now. Cheyenne, I want to be your husband. Will you marry me?"

With fingers as shaky as mine, he props open the lid of a black velvet ring box. Nested inside is a very simple, yet elegant diamond ring. "You decided that this was the best time to propose?" I ask, choking back tears and laughter at the same time.

"I probably could've waited until tonight, but I figured the ring would be a good prop for this afternoon."

"I love it. It's absolutely gorgeous," I say, pulling the ring from the box and sliding it onto my finger. I'm awestruck as I see it sparkling in the sunlight.

"Cheyenne?"

"Hmmm?" I ask, admiring my ring.

"You never answered the question, sweetheart."

I gasp. "Oh! Of course I'll marry you. I'm going to save all the mushy stuff until tonight, because I'll start crying if I do it now."

"Hey, I got my answer," he says, proud as a peacock when he exits the car. He opens my door for me, and once I've finished straightening my outfit and smoothing my hair, we walk hand in hand up the steps to the magnificently decorated front porch. Hay bales, pumpkins, scarecrows, and gourds are all perfectly arranged to welcome future Thanksgiving guests. A glistening lead glass door stands between us and the people inside. Cal gently raps on it, and I fight the overwhelming urge to run away.

After a series of clicks, a gentle looking elderly woman with silver hair tucked high in a bun opens the door. She smiles genially at first, but she quickly loses the smile as her face goes ashen and slack. "Nate!" she yells into the house. "Nate, I need you."

"Wait," I say, rapidly because I'm thoroughly ashamed that we scared the poor woman. "I'm sorry to have startled you, but my fiancé and I simply had a couple of questions about the neighborhood. We are thinking of buying the house…"

"Nate!" she yells again. A dark complexioned man with a face full of wrinkles slowly shuffles towards us with the help of a cane.

"What's wrong, Selena? Are we being robbed?" his asks with a feeble voice.

"No. You need to see this," she says, pulling the door open more widely once he joins her.

"We should be going," I say, shifting on the balls of my feet for a quick getaway. "We've clearly upset you, and I'm very sorry."

"Wait!" the elderly couple calls simultaneously. "Please. Stay there for just one moment," Selena says as Nate's eyes stay fixed upon mine. I can see a storm brewing behind his thick glasses, and I grow more anxious with every passing second. He wants to speak, I can see it, but he resists the urge.

Selena returns with an old metal picture frame tucked in her arms. "I've had my heart broken many times before because I believed, but I was always wrong. How many Cynthias have I passed on the street, begging and praying for it to be OUR Cynthia? I'm not wrong this time. I feel it in my heart. You've come home to us. You're finally home." Her eyes are brimmed with huge tears that begin to slide down her cheek when she turns the picture to face me.

I can barely breathe. In the frame are my parents, and me! My father finally has a face, and that face is almost identical to mine. I shake my head in disbelief. Selena looks at me expectantly, and I do what feels most natural to me at the time—I pull her in for a tight embrace.

"It's me. I'm home," I say between gasps. She squeezes me tightly, and for the longest time, we stand in the doorway sobbing.

"Nate," she says, breaking the hug to reach for his hand. "Cynthia found her way back to us. It's her. Our grandbaby. Our beautiful, beautiful grandbaby." She takes my cheeks in her hands and dots my face with kisses. Normally, I'd likely be repulsed, but the act is so unbelievably comforting that I hate for her to stop. "Look at her, Nate. Isn't she gorgeous?" She spins me so that I'm facing the older man. His eyes question whether it's real or not, but I see that deep down, he's begging for it to be so.

"I'm sorry, I don't remember what I used to call you," I say, truly perplexed. *Are they Nate and Selena? Grammy and Grampy? Grandmother and Grandfather?*

Selena answers, "You used to call me Sugar and you called him…"

I interrupt her because it rushes back to me, "Cookie because cookies are my favorite." I nervously laugh between tears. "I guess it was a bad idea to let me pick my own names for you."

He drops his cane and snatches me into his large arms. "It really is you. Oh, my sweet girl. We prayed so hard for this." His smell is familiar, warm, and welcoming, and for someone who was so terrified to visit their home, it's funny that I now have an overwhelming desire to stay forever.

We're dashing away at the tears with a box of

tissues that Selena pulled from the entryway table when I joke that maybe I should come up with new names for them.

"No way," Nate argues. "Are cookies still your favorite?"

I give a guilty grin. "They truly are."

"Then Cookie I will remain."

I feel emotionally drained, yet unbelievable refreshed and relaxed knowing that I'm right where I'm supposed to be. "Oh goodness, Cal! Cookie, Sugar, this is my fiancé, Dr. Cal Gage."

"Doctor? Impressive," Sugar mentions.

"Not really. History, not MD," Cal says, shaking each of their hands.

"Do you teach?" Sugar asks.

"I do. At Shadow Oaks with Cheyenne."

"Cheyenne? Is that what your name is now? And you teach?" Sugar asks.

"I suppose I should explain it all."

"Before you do, have you been by Viv and Sam's? Obviously not because surely they would've called," Sugar states.

"Viv and Sam?" I ask.

"Vivian and Sam Miller—your mother's parents."

I'm taken aback. "We searched for them, but found nothing. You're still in contact with them?"

"Of course. They live about two blocks away. I'll give them a call and invite them over for coffee. We'll save the big surprise for when they show," Sugar says picking up the phone.

My eyes once again brim with tears. "Two sets of grandparents. My cup runneth over," I whisper to myself.

"Darling, you don't even know the half of it. Wait until you meet the rest of the family," Sugar says with a huge smile. "I think Thanksgiving is as good a time as any. What do you say? Will you join us?"

I'm truly overwhelmed. "Uh…" I look to Cal, and he nods. "Okay. We'll be here."

"Excellent," she says with a huge grin while dialing the phone. "Viv, this is Selena. Are you and Sam free for coffee? Good. No, right now is perfect. Come on over." Once the receiver is back in its cradle she asks us to join her in the kitchen. It's large, with huge glass windows that let the afternoon sunshine stream in. We get situated around the table as Selena handles the coffee, and we'd no sooner settled in when a spry looking elderly couple comes up the back porch steps and marches right into the kitchen.

The woman has freshly dyed black hair tightly curled and stiff as a board which makes me believe she spends a lot of time in the beauty parlor. Behind her, wearing a matching zebra print wind suit is an elderly man with thick gold rings on every finger, a large gold chain around his neck, and wayfarer sunglasses. The memories begin to flood back. The only thing that has changed other than he's much more aged, is that his wardrobe choice used to be a leisure suit instead of a track suit. Grandpa must always be a decade or two behind the fashion trends. Nearly everything else is the same. He even has the same cowlick poking up in the very back of his head. I remember a game he used to play with me where I'd smooth the cowlick then he'd shove his thumb against his lips and blow. I'd burst into peals of laughter each time it sprang back into place. How could I have forgotten all of that, and why is it coming back to me so easily now?

"You didn't say you were having company over, Sel. I'da brought a cake or something," Viv says, pulling the dark wraparound sunglasses from her eyes. "Hi there, young 'uns. I'm Viv, and this is Sam. We're the Millers from around the block." She steadily talks as she pours two cups of coffee. Frankly, I'm surprised she's even noticed us sitting at the table since she hasn't even glanced in our direction.

"Viv, I think you and Sam should sit down," Sugar suggests.

"Hold your horses, Sel. I'm making my way over," she says, picking up the mugs and sighing heavily when she reaches the table. "I thought you already had yours. You didn't tell me you hadn't started yet. These people must think we're so rude. I apologize for…" She looks to Cal, and then to me, and then she freezes. "It's not," she says, looking to Selena. Selena nods. "Oh, dear Lord! Sam! Sam!"

"What?" he asks, searching the room.

"Take the glasses off Sam," she fusses. He gives her a nasty look before sliding them from his face.

"They're off. What am I looking at? Huh?" he says, casually perusing the room. He does a double take when his eyes land on me. I can see his breathing become erratic as he reaches for a chair.

"Maybe we should've warned 'em before they came over. You okay, Sam? The ticker still ticking?" Nate asks. Sam points in my direction.

"Is it? It has to be. She's the spitting image of Nate, Jr. Oh, and those eyes. I haven't seen those eyes in almost thirty years. How? Where? When?"

he asks, finally taking a seat. He stares at me with disbelief.

"She just showed up. We didn't want her to have to tell the story over and over, so I called you over. Cheyenne—that's the name she goes by now—Cheyenne, do you remember Viv and Sam?" Sugar asks.

"Vaguely. Pop and Gran, right?" I ask. They nod. "Pop, I remember playing a game with you. I'd smooth down your cowlick, and you'd pretend to blow it back up."

His face softens. "It really is you. Where have you been, sweetheart? What happened to you?"

"I wish it were a fast and easy story to tell, but I'm afraid it will take a while. In short, I spent the majority of my life in Oklahoma where I was raised by a couple who made me believe I was their birth child. I was so young and traumatized when everything happened, that I guess it was easier to wipe out that part of my life and start fresh. My mom, the woman who raised me, she had pictures that were supposedly of me all the way through my life. She even told me stories about my birth, and my firsts. It's only recently that I discovered it was all lies."

"Did they hurt you?" Viv asks defensively.

"No. They never hurt me, and they loved me very much. They may have been a little on the strict side, but they always encouraged me to excel. With their help, I became Dr. Cheyenne Douglas, and I'm currently the department head of the English department at Shadow Oaks University." They all look around at each other. "What?" I ask.

"Your mother, my daughter, was a high school English teacher," Viv offers.

"There's so much information I need to get from you. What about my dad?" I question.

"He was an engineer for a chemical company. Very smart man…," Nate says.

I smile. "Wow. I can't even begin to tell you how much this means to me. My heart is bursting right now. I want to know it all. Everything. Their likes. Their dislikes. Were they fun parents? Strict parents? Did they have hobbies?"

"We'll get to all of that. We have plenty of photos, old videos, and documents for you to go through, don't we, Sel?" Viv asks.

"We sure do. First, we want to finish hearing about you."

"Of course," I say. "But, I have to know… what made you believe I was still alive? The police ruled it a murder, but you told me you searched strangers' faces with the hopes you'd find mine. Why?"

"We're family. Connected by blood. Sometimes you just know things in your heart even though you can't explain them," Selena says with a smile only a loving grandmother can give. "Now, how'd you wind up in Oklahoma?"

I spend the rest of the afternoon and a good portion of the night informing, answering questions, and basking in the love that fills the house. Cal and I agree to see them again soon, in one week, at Thanksgiving dinner to be exact. I don't stop smiling the entire ride home. I'm a different person. I feel lighter, happier, complete. I want Cal to experience it, too. I hope his family is as receptive as mine. I'll find out soon enough when I sneak over to Cypress Grove in the morning. Cal's not going to do it, and I have anonymity on my side. It doesn't hurt to look, right?

RHONDA R. DENNIS

SIXTEEN

Cypress Grove is a tiny little bayou community much like ones Cal and I pass through on our way to New Orleans. I wouldn't have known I was in Cypress Grove if it hadn't been for the rickety wooden sign stating as much. I veer off the main road following the smug and confident voice that calls from my GPS device. I'm convinced the voice is wrong when I find myself parked in front of a car repair shop.

I'm just about to drive away when a very loud whistle has me pushing the brake. "Hey, yo! I'm over here if you need something," an older muscular guy calls as he peeks from behind the raised hood of one of the cars in the garage bay. Unsure what to do, I finally decide to get out mainly because I'd driven all this way, and frankly, I was sick of being in the car.

"Yeah, you got something wrong with your car there, darlin'?" he asks, wiping his greasy hands on a red cloth as he makes his way towards me.

"Actually, I was hoping you might be able to help me find the Belanger family," I say, desperately wishing my voice sounded more confident. He sets his jaw and points upwards. Drawing my eyes to where he is pointing, I feel foolish when I notice the sign that says *MJ Belanger and Sons*. "Are you MJ or a son?" I ask, trying to break the ice.

"What's it to you? You a lawyer or something?"

"No, no. Not a lawyer at all."

"So why are you here inquiring about my family?" he repositions the backwards ball cap he's wearing before crossing his arms over his chest. He gives me the *I'm waiting for an answer* look.

"I'm sorry. You're obviously busy. I was looking for someone related to Gretchen Belanger, but I can see it's not a good time, so I'm just going to go now," I say, hastily making my way to my car.

"Wait!" he says. He'd just as well held a gun to my back and yelled *freeze* with the posture I assume—hands up, unmoving, barely breathing. "What about Gretchen? She's been dead for years now." I slowly turn around.

"I know, and I'm sorry for your family's loss. I heard she was a beautiful and kind woman."

"Who's been talking to you about Gretchen?" he demands.

"Look. Mr. Belanger…"

"Antoine," he interrupts.

"Mr. Antoine."

He rapidly shakes his head. "Just Antoine."

"Okay. Antoine, it's a very long and complicated story. Are you familiar with Father Seamus Donnelly?"

"Naw, can't say that I am. Oh, but wait. Now that you mention it, I think he was the priest down here when I was a kid or something. Yeah, I'm pretty sure he was now that I think about it. What's he got to do with anything?"

"For me to tell you, I really need to know what your relation is to Gretchen."

"She was my older sister," he almost shouts. "Look, can we stop with the guessing game and just tell me what in the hell you're doing here?"

"Gretchen's son is my fiancé," I blurt. He gives me a baffled look then smiles.

"You're confused, sweetheart. Gretchen didn't have no kids. She went off to some island to do humanitarian work or something, and she was murdered." I close my eyes. More secrets. More lies. I begin to wonder if people ever truly know who they are.

"I don't think you were told the truth." I thrust my palms in the air to ward off the immanent verbal attack. "Please, hear me out."

He considers it for a moment before conceding. "Let's talk in the office. It's cold out here." I follow him into a room that holds a rolling desk chair, two metal folding chairs, and a recliner. He points to the desk chair as he sits in the recliner.

"I'm sure this is going to be difficult to hear, but trust me, all of it is true. If you don't believe me, a simple DNA test should prove that what I'm saying is accurate."

"I'm listening," he says, once again wiping away at the grease on his hands with the rag.

"Gretchen and Father Donnelly were in love. She became pregnant, and when your family found out, she was forced to live on her own. When her son Cal was two, she was murdered in a dark alley. He was with her when it happened, but he remembers none of this. Being that the family wanted nothing to do with her, much less the baby, Father Donnelly gave the child to a police officer named Felton Gage to raise as his own. We've only just found out that Felton had a hand in many other illegal child adoptions, one of them being mine."

"Don't you think I'd know if my sister was pregnant? She would have come to someone for help. I was too young, but maybe Frank? He was older than her."

"I heard all of this from Father Donnelly himself. She followed him to his new congregation, and though they weren't together romantically after that, he tried to support her and the baby as much as he could, which was very little considering his profession She needed to fill in the gaps with supplemental income she earned by cleaning office buildings at night. It was one of the only jobs she could find where she could bring the baby with her. She was walking home from work one night when she was murdered."

He shakes his head. "I always knew my dad was a mean son of a bitch, but I never knew he disowned his own daughter and grandchild." Anger etches deep lines across his face and a tempest brews in his eyes. Family life must not have been very good for the Belangers. "Frankly, I don't know what to say."

"Is your father still around? Maybe he could explain…"

"Nah, old man's been dead. Buried next to Ma and poor Gretchen at the cemetery down the road a ways. If only we'd known. Now the poor woman's forced to spend eternity next to the old bastard." He shakes his head with disgust. "So, what's the kid up to? He's not looking for money or something, is he?"

"No, nothing like that. He's the head of the history department at one of the local colleges."

"Don't sound like he's done so bad. So why ya here?"

"Because he never got to know his real family. All he's seen is a tattered picture of his mother. He has no clue who he's related to or where he comes from," I explain.

"Yeah, well some things are better left unknown. He has an uncle who runs a garage. The end."

"It's more than that. It's about having a connection."

"Look, I ain't into all the touchy feely crap, and if he is, then better he not know anything about me or this family. In fact, I think that's for the best. Don't even mention anything about this. Leave him be. He seems to be doing real good on his own."

"But I know he'll want to…"

"I said leave it be."

Feeling dejected, I slowly nod. "I'll do as you wish, but if you ever change your mind, this is my number." He quickly tosses the slip of paper into the trash can. Swallowing hard, I manage to thank him for his time before leaving the office.

"Hey!" Antoine calls after me. "You wouldn't happen to have a picture of him, would you?" I smile while scrolling through my phone. I turn the screen for Antoine to see. He nods. "He looks a lot like Frank. I see Gretchen, too, because them two always favored each other. I was told most of my life I wasn't my dad's because I looked so different from the rest of the family. Maybe it was true, and that's why the old man went off on Gretchen. Guess it's a secret that'll never be found out. It's good the kid didn't get none of my looks; he might not have landed himself such a pretty lady." He winks before closing my car door for me.

I wave as I'm leaving the garage. Disappointed that it didn't go smoother, at least I finally have an answer—even if it isn't the one I was hoping for.

The long ride home offers plenty of time for reflection. I missed out on so much with my real family, but it looks as though Cal was spared by being yanked from his. After pondering nearly every aspect of the issue, I conclude that there is no point in trying to figure out what life would have been like. What's done is done. As much as I'd love to rewind the hands of time for a do over, it's never going to happen. I'm determined to make the best of what I have. As for Cal, I'm going to remain quiet unless he happens to want information. It's obvious that the love my family is willing to give is more than enough for the both of us, and I'm happy to share.

Sleep comes easy that night, and it's more restful than anything I've experienced since the move. No nightmares, no horrid thoughts, no uncertainty—just purely appreciated rejuvenation. At least it is until Brant calls at four in the morning.

"What's wrong?" I groggily ask while rubbing sleep from my eyes.

"Do not come outside. No matter what you hear, stay put," he whispers into the phone.

"Brant, you're scaring me. Where are you?

What's going on?"

Cal sits upright upon hearing this part of the conversation to give me a questioning look. I shrug.

"I can't talk now. I'll explain soon. Just stay insi...." The call ends suddenly, and I lurch from bed throwing on the first clothes I find. Cal does the same.

"What's happening?" he asks.

"I don't know. It was Brant. He said to stay inside no matter what and then the phone went dead mid-sentence."

"He said stay inside. He didn't say anything about not looking outside," Cal says, clicking off the bedside lamp I'd turned on. The room is pitch-black when he slowly peels back the curtains to peep outside. I'm on the opposite side doing the same.

Nothing looks out of the ordinary at first, but after our eyes adjust to the very dim glow of the moonlight, it becomes clear that we're being visited by the little girl in red again. She's barely visible, as usual, and the figure looks more like a red dress floating through mid-air than anything else. Across the courtyard she bounces almost as though she's weightless, and then out of nowhere, she launches from the ground and into the tree. Brant stumbles out of the shadows, and like an athlete completing an obstacle course, he makes a leap for one of the lower branches and swings his legs up to lock the hold. If the man wouldn't be wearing a light colored shirt, it would look like a windstorm was raging around the massive oak. Branches bob and sway, leaves scatter to the ground, and Brant jumps limb to limb just as quickly as the red dress floats through them.

We lose sight of them, but we know the chase

is still on because of the shimmying tree limbs. Finally, an ear piercing shriek echoes through the night just as Brant takes a tumble from the tree onto the cold hard ground. I gasp loudly while fighting the urge to rush to him. I know he must be conscious because his hands clutch the red dress, but whatever is in it keeps trying to get away from him.

The force of the fall leaves him stunned, and seemingly out of nowhere, a uniformed individual emerges from the vicinity of the driveway. The loud shrieks continue to spill into the night, so shrill, so loud, so familiar? Where have I heard that sound before? The commotion sends George outside, and soon as he flips on the overhead lights, Cal and I burst into laughter. Brant is on the ground rolling around with a chimpanzee wearing a little girl's red dress. The shrieks I'd heard were similar to those at the zoo! As hard as I try, I can't for the life of me figure out why a red-dress-wearing chimpanzee would be frequenting our courtyard, but seeing Brant wrestling with it is funny as hell.

The other uniformed officer is animal control, who is trying his best to help Brant secure the beast. The chimpanzee clocks Brant one good time in the face, and he loses his grip on the primate. Up the tree it runs, stopping to curl up like a scared little child. It stares down at Brant with a look that says, *how could you do this to me?* My heart melts, and be damned what Brant warned, I decide to go outside. Once I've got on my boots and coat, I crack the door and the new sounds filling the air are Brant's swear words.

"Son of a bitch! Stop! I'm going to kill you, you no good mother..."

When I realize why Brant is cursing so much, I

nearly double over from laughter. He ducks and weaves like a boxer waiting for the impending punch.

"If you launch one more shit bomb at me, I'm going to skin you…" The pile lands dead center of Brant's chest, and he tumbles to the ground where he dry heaves violently. The other person comes forward with a tranquilizer gun, and within minutes, the chimp is caught as it falls from the tree. The animal control officer wraps the sleeping mammal in a warm blanket before caging it. I rush down to check on Brant.

He's still flat on his back, staring straight ahead, and huffing angrily. "Brant?" I ask, squatting beside him.

"Twenty-five years on the force, and I've been roughed up, shot at, spit on, puked on, bled on, and once, I'm pretty sure a drunk pissed on my boots. Never. Never have I ever been taken out by a chimpanzee shit bomb."

I want to laugh so badly, but that would mean removing my finger from under my nose and the threat of getting another hit of that vile aroma has me releasing more of a snigger than the full belly laugh I'm containing. "But are you okay," I ask in between giggles.

He slowly rolls to his side, and with Cal's assistance, he's able to stand. George, who has been surprisingly quiet through the entire escapade, waves his arm in an exasperated shooing motion before shuffling inside. In about a minute or so, he shuffles back outside and tosses a shirt in Brant's direction. "Here. You stink," he grumbles before going back inside and flipping off the light. We're once again forced to adjust our vision to the dim light of the moon.

Brant shucks off the monkey poop shirt and tosses it into the large rolling can near the garage. He's a shivering mess in no time, so I send him upstairs to shower before he leaves. Brant shakes hands with the animal control guy then takes the steps two at a time to get up to my apartment. Cal makes sure he has a warm coffee waiting when he gets out.

"I can't thank you enough for the shower. I'd have puked the entire ride home if I had to stay smelling like that," Brant says when he joins us in the kitchen.

"No problem," I answer. "Why was there a chimpanzee at large? Wait, let me add to that. Why was a red-dress-wearing chimpanzee at large in the bayou region of South Louisiana?"

"Hell if I know. It freaked me the hell out when the dress appeared out of nowhere. The damn thing's hair was so dark that it blended in with the shadows. That's why we only saw the dress floating around. I was watching it move around on my phone, my mind reeling because I couldn't figure it out. Then, I swear to you it was like something from a horror movie. It launched from the tree and landed in front of one of the cameras. It went from floating dress to snarling incisors in seconds flat."

"Did you pee your pants?" Cal teases.

"I came close, dude. I'm not even going to lie. Anyway, it backed away from the camera enough for me to finally make out what it was, so I dispatched animal control. I didn't want you outside because I wasn't sure how the animal would react."

"So, all mysteries are now solved, right?" I ask.

"All the ones related to this case. I can finally

rest. Good night, and see you two Thursday." He starts to walk away, but stops once his hand is on the door knob. "Are you sure about this Thanksgiving thing? Shouldn't it be time spent with just you and your new family?"

"My Sugar said I was to invite anyone I wanted, and Brant, in case you haven't figured it out yet—you are my new family. Blood ties simply mean you're related; being there for each other is what makes you a real family."

He nods briefly and smiles before opening the door. "See you Thursday at Sugar and Cookie's." He chuckles. "I still get a kick out of that. The old man lets you call him Cookie." With that parting thought, Brant disappears into the night.

RHONDA R. DENNIS

SEVENTEEN

Christmas is a couple of weeks away when the semester ends, and we find ourselves amidst a much needed break. It's refreshing to have life slowly become normal—more normal than it's ever been for me or Cal for that matter. The chimpanzee mystery was solved when Brant discovered the owner was scared to report it missing, but after the reports were released in the paper, she finally came forward and fessed up. Poor thing had been missing for months and was surviving by foraging in the neighbors' yards.

We've been spending lots of time in New Orleans with the family. Some days we explore the past, but more often, we leave it behind to create new memories. We were there to help take down the fall decorations and replace them with Christmas ones. Gran Viv and Pop Sam insist on equal time, so we start at one place and finish our New Orleans visits at another. Sometimes it's much nicer when everyone just meets at one spot, but those days often run into nighttime visits, as well. Though it's not incredibly far away, Cal and I find ourselves spending most of our time on the road or in the city, so after much debate, we decide to make the move to New Orleans sometime after the holidays.

In the meantime, Cal has let go of some of his anger and has been making regular visits to see his father. After lots of soul searching, he's decided to drop Gage as his last name and has legally assumed Donnelly. Felton raised him, but discovering how tarnished the Gage name truly is, and being that he has no true ties to it, the decision was actually pretty easy. The hard part for him is getting used to being Cal Donnelly after being Cal Gage all these years.

We decide to make the best of our first and last Christmas at the quaint apartment, so Cal chops, hauls, and sets up a beautiful tree for us to decorate. We're snuggled together on the sofa, our attention shifting between the twinkling lights on the tree and the Christmas movie on the TV when there is a knock at the door. Cal moves to answer it, but I stop him by resting my hand on his chest.

"I'll get it," I say with a smile. Fully expecting to see George or Brant on the other side of the door, I'm shocked to find a bundled up Antoine looking down at his boots. He shuffles nervously once I open the door.

"Hey, look. Sorry to barge in on you like this, but I figure turnabout's fair play, right? Like you didn't give me no warning before you looked me up and showed up at my shop…"

I nod. Hearing the conversation, Cal is by my side in an instant. "Who's this?" he asks.

"I'm not here to start no mess or anything. I just been thinking about what your girl here was saying when she came down to visit me at the garage, and I started to see her point. I'm Antoine Belanger, and I suppose that technically makes me your uncle.

Sorry I ain't got much to offer."

Cal looks stunned. "No, please. Come in. It's nice to meet you." He turns to me as Antoine sets down the box he's carrying to remove his coat. "You searched him out?"

Not sure if I should be apologetic or proud, I take the middle ground and simply say, "Yes." I offer Antoine a cup of coffee, which he accepts. I head to the kitchen to get it brewing while he and Cal take a seat on the sofa.

"Before anything gets all out of control and such, I want you to know that I asked your lady there to forget she visited. I ain't smart, don't have much money, and our family name ain't the best. The old man was a mean, rotten bastard who beat the crap out of us on a regular basis just because he felt it would make us grow up strong. I run a garage, I work hard, and I do okay."

"Will you tell me about my mom?" Cal asks.

"She was quite a bit older than me. Look, I brought you this box of stuff. We aren't the most sentimental family, so sorry to say there's not much in there, but you might find some of it interesting."

Cal opens the box and pulls out a stack of pictures. Antoine starts narrating the story behind each one, and before long, the men are deep in meaningful conversation. The coffee finished brewing long ago, but hearing them connect, especially when Antoine insisted there would be no common ground leaves me a bit weepy. Everything has come full circle. We both have our pasts, our presents, and our futures mapped out. Life can't get any better.... but then it does.

One thing I have to say about my grandparents is that they fully believe in making up for lost time. The five of us sit in the bride's chamber awaiting our cue to prepare for the processional. It was such a difficult task to choose which grandfather to ask to walk me down the aisle that I consulted with my grandmothers. Much to my chagrin, I was accused of being sexist because women can escort brides down the aisle just as well as men can. So, because my grandparents seem to be perpetually fixated in the generation of protests and demonstrations, I have FOUR people escorting me down the aisle to meet up with my future husband.

Cookie landed the St. Louis Cathedral for the wedding, a tremendously larger venue than their home, where I'd originally planned on having the service. So as the grandparents work to figure out their final placements before the wedding, I sneak one final look in the mirror. Everything is simple and elegant from my dress to my veil. My Sugar told the seamstress that she should think of Grace Kelly when she made the gown, and she did just that. I feel like a princess, and though some might have been upset that they didn't have much input into their wedding, I relished having bossy family members eager to make my day as special as they could. Family is something that many take for granted, but not me. I'm blessed, and I know it.

The volume escalates as the geriatric quartet argues over who will be first, so on and so forth. Finally, I stop them. "Sugar and Cookie, why don't you wait midway up the aisle ahead of us. Gran and Pop, you walk me up halfway then I go with Cookie and Sugar the rest of the way with you right behind us. From there, we all spread out with one couple on each side of me until the Father asks about giving me away, blah, blah, blah...." They stare each other down before eventually conceding.

We're told it's time for the wedding to begin, and I take a slow calming breath before meeting up with Gran and Pop. Arms interlocked we make our way down the aisle until it's time for Sugar and Cookie to join in. Seeing Cal melts my heart, and I'm so brimming with happiness that I completely ignore the fact that Best Man Brant is winking and waving at the cousin I introduced him to after we met during Thanksgiving dinner.

"I don't deserve you," Cal tells me when I meet him at the altar.

"Damn straight," Pop grumbles, "but you make her happy, so you'll do."

I playfully roll my eyes while mouthing, *sorry*. The service goes incredibly smoothly, and being that he's on bond pending trial, Cal's father is able to attend the service—something that meant a lot to both of the Donnelly men. The cathedral rumbles with applause after we share our first kiss as husband and wife, and as soon as we're announced as Dr. and Dr. Callahan Donnelly, Cal whisks me from the church.

Once we're at the base of the steps, he hugs me tightly, twirling me around and around. "I'm the luckiest man alive right now!" he screams to the growing crowd. My giggles are smothered by his kisses, and I don't even care that random tourists are snapping our picture. The congregation makes their way outside, we're sent off with loud applause, cat calls, and whistles. "See ya'll in a few!" Cal hollers, taking my hand and running towards the horse-drawn buggy waiting to bring us to the reception hall.

A hard yank stops me in my tracks, and I realize someone has a tight grip on my wrist. Cal stops to see what's happening, and I want to scream when I realize it's the same fortune teller from my first trip to New Orleans. "No. I don't want to hear anything you have to say. My life is only just calming down from the last time you stopped me."

She smiles broadly, her colorful scarves shifting in the breeze. "You'll want to hear this."

I vehemently shake my head. "You said that the last time. No. I don't want to hear it."

"It's my gift to you. A wedding present."

"Will you please let go of me?" I say trying to break free from her grip.

She closes her eyes and inhales deeply. "Blue. Pink. Blue. Then time just for two. Marriage is great. Love is grand. Together forever, Cal is your man."

"Wait. How did you know his name?" I ask, stunned. "Cal, how does she know your name?"

Wide-eyed he shrugs. "I haven't gotten past the blue, pink, blue. Does that mean kids?"

The mystical woman's bright red lips curl in a devious smile. "Carlyssa knows all." With a wave and a laugh that echoes loudly through the Quarter, she lifts her long flowing skirt to sashay towards Pirate's Alley. Her laughter is still heard even once she's disappeared from sight.

Still stunned, Cal helps me into the horse-drawn carriage. "Did you get her to do that?" he asks.

"No! I was going to ask you the same thing. How did she know your name?"

"Maybe there really IS something to all of this

stuff? She was pretty accurate with her first prediction."

"Yeah, she was," I concur.

"So three kids? Ready to get started?" Cal asks before kissing me passionately. The passersby on the street cheer madly, some yelling obscenities, and the carriage driver clicks the reigns so the horse will get to our destination quickly. The carriage lurches forward, and we're off to officially begin married life. I can't imagine being happier than being Dr. Cheyenne Donnelly, but it happened the day I welcomed my first son into the world, and I became Mom.

In Oklahoma, I was lost, sad, and uncertain. Truth be known, I was a hair away from ending it all before that recruitment email came to me. Not only did I find eventual solace from going on this journey, I literally found myself—my REAL self. Whatever or whoever it was that brought me here—be it fate, God, ghosts of the past, or anything else-- I'm incredibly grateful. Red dirt is my past, but black dirt means I'm home.

The End.

Romantic Suspense by Rhonda R. Dennis

<u>The Green Bayou Series</u>

Going Home: A Green Bayou Novel Book One

Awakenings: A Green Bayou Novel Book Two

Déjà Vu: A Green Bayou Novel Book Three

Unforeseen: A Green Bayou Novel Book Four

Between Four and Five: A Green Bayou Extra (Short Story)

Deceived: A Green Bayou Novel Book Five

Green Bayou After Five: Connie's Wild Night (Short Story)

Between Five and Six: A Green Bayou Extra (Short Story)

Vengeance: A Green Bayou Novel Book Six

Romantic Comedy by Rhonda R. Dennis

Magnolia Blossoms

Contemporary Romance by Rhonda R. Dennis

Yours Always

ABOUT THE AUTHOR

Rhonda Dennis lives in South Louisiana with her husband, Doyle, and her son, Sean. She would love to hear from you. Visit her website for more information. www.rhondadennis.net.

Or write to her at:

Rhonda Dennis
P.O. Box 2148
Patterson, LA 70392

To like me, follow me, or leave a review:

Facebook: The Green Bayou Novels
Twitter: @RhondaRDennis
Goodreads Author
Amazon Author